THE GRIFFIN
A PATH OF MAJESTY

THE GRIFFIN SERIES

The Griffin Series

Ashes of Honor
The Dreams of Men and Pandas
The Dragon's Price
A Path of Majesty

THE GRIFFIN
A PATH OF MAJESTY

PHILIP WILLIAMS
CAT WILLIAMS

THE GRIFFIN SERIES

ISBN 978-0-9888257-5-8

COVER DESIGN
PHILIP WILLIAMS
WWW.THEGRIFFINSERIES.COM

COVER ART
JUNG PARK
WWW.JUNGPARKART.COM

COVER ILLUSTRATION
ELISABETH ALBA
WWW.ELISA-ALBA.COM

INTERIOR DESIGN
TYPEFLOW
WWW.TYPEFLOWNYC.COM

To Amy

Home is where one starts from.
—T.S. Eliot

Contents

IV

A Path of Majesty

Dragon's feast, soldier's chore
The Path moves on forevermore

— Sid Panda

1

Nralda

BEYOND THE LONG, LOOPING ORBIT OF THE THIRTEENTH planet in the Skarasgard System, only a few million kilometers from one bulbous edge of the trade volume known as the Wyxian Proctorialship, six ships met in silent vacuum. The Skarasgard primary was a mere fleck of brilliance in a sky that offered a million such frosted kernels, yet even in the featureless darkness four of the ships stood out as markedly different. Their long, angular slabs of cerasteel armor were rusted yellow with corrosion from hundreds of descents into moist planetary atmospheres. Charcoal-colored scars rippled from one end of their gnarled, walking-stick-shaped hulls to the other. The forward quarter of each Jave O'War was pitted with gouges—

small, finely-shaped ruts from minute interstellar debris that slipped through poorly-modulated shields, and deep, rough-edged gashes from less natural phenomena: plasma and blast cannon.

In contrast, the two remaining vessels that floated above them were tapering giants, with skins as slick as icicles. The finely hewed, rounded armor plates that so precisely matched the contour of the underlying hull were glossy eggshells, each minor pit filled and polished, their appearances perfectly maintained. The Nralda House Gunrunners were long and narrow, like great, slightly asymmetrical serpents. They looked more like the smooth, alabaster sculptures of their designer, Reilan Foest, than the ripped and jagged Imperial designs. There was a decided artistic bent to Gunrunners. Not in terms of artifice or excessive ornamentation—for they were sublimely minimalist—but in terms of pure aesthetic refinement. Great thought, great pains, and great resources had gone into their conception.

Carrelle Darstin waited impatiently in the frigid Gunrunner airlock waiting for the locks to cycle. He was underdressed, clothed in paper-thin trestins with only a heavy cloak to protect him from his ship's perpetual chill. A heavy bass tone warned him before the outer door slid silently aside revealing the rust and sulphur-colored Gamborian airlock. He was tempted to reach out and touch the aged surface—it looked more like the steel hull of a maritime vessel than an interstellar war craft—but he knew that his hand would fuse instantly to the icy surface. The Jave O'War's outer lock split open and trundled aside with a servo moan. A wave of heat hit him in the face.

He licked his lips and blinked rapidly. The change in temperature was temporarily debilitating; he stepped sluggishly into the Jave O'War. The outer door whined close and the inner opened. More heat and thick, nitrous oxygen, impossibly laden with humidity filled his lungs. Rivulets of moisture ran down all the interior walls, pooling on the floor. He discarded his fur-lined cloak and let it drop into the puddles.

Darstin walked quickly down the corridor, boots ringing on the steel grates welded into place a few centimeters over the collected humidity. The hall was lit with inadequate orange lanterns that further added to the perception that he was walking down a sewage drainpipe. His delicate garments were drenched by the time he entered the next chamber.

He stood just inside the room and waited; he could hear legs rubbing as the Gambor moved about in the darkness. With thumb and forefinger, he pulled his sweaty shift away from his gaunt frame and fanned his chest several times without relief. Four of the beetle giants emerged from the gloom, their hardened body segments glossy with moisture—this is what they preferred, enough heat and moisture to keep their shells from growing brittle.

The beetles wore the mark of the Vaelus burrow, a yellow-fringed bandolier that crossed their chests and was tied just beneath their conical, tri-horned heads. Darstin recognized the slightly rounder shell of Ka'vaelus and noted that its familiar, scarred surface was adorned with new ruts. The fresh wounds were stuffed with moss and fecal material, but the cracked edges still festered with puss. The badge of his rank—the red galen root—swung from his belt along with his satchel of seedlings.

Ka'vaelus stood with his Tginsahi guard and studied the human. Flaxen hair clung to the creature's small skull and sweat dripped off his long nose. The man's thin, unnourished appearance seemed even more insubstantial in the glorious warmth, like a flower that had long since wilted. The human stood erect only by the grace of an internal skeleton that was determined not to let the skin fall completely off. Ka'vaelus always felt an urge to feed the human a big gourd of nice sticky caterpillars, fatten him up with some leeches, try and brace his waning strength with a broth of protein-rich creis'han. It was a wonder the species had gotten so far along with such weak and fragile physical husks.

And yet there were the creature's eyes, those brilliant, intruding orbs that burned with vigor and intelligence. He could see anger and urgency buried in those eyes, emotions the human was trying hard to mask from the rest of his face. Ka'vaelus could see the Director wanted to speak badly, but to his credit he respected the host tradition.

"Welcome to the *Cri't Cha'griei*," the Gambor said with the requisite propriety. "Director Darstin, you do us honor with your visit. I apologize for the state of our facilities, and any discomfort it may bring you."

"Apology accepted, Cha'halen. And unnecessary," the human replied with genuine warmth.

"Of course," Ka'vaelus said, finishing the convention. "You know Oer, Larta and Pi'vaelus from the burrow."

Darstin nodded to the three giants. Ka'vaelus ushered him into the heart of the chamber. Orange glow globes were ignited for the man's benefit, their pale forms reflecting in the puddles. At the center of the chamber, black columns rose out of the floor to varying height. More Gambor were at work here, studying dim sartographic displays that hovered above the columns.

Ka'vaelus reached into a hollow in one of the columns and pulled out an oilskin, uncorking it with a pincer. With careful deliberation he filled his personal gourd with thick, green alcohol and handed it to the human.

Darstin drank it silently, eyes never leaving the Gambor.

"We regret the outcome of our latest venture, Director," Ka'vaelus said solemnly. "But it was not due to a lack of courage."

"Tell me," Darstin said softly.

"With the information from the stolen relay codes, we were able to track down the Imperial task force as they closed in on the Tchelakov shipment. However, we were unable to reach *Destiny's Needle* before the Imperials. Our opportunity to board her first was lost when the ship inexplicably attacked the Imperial fleet and attached itself to the belly of a supply frigate."

Darstin frowned. "*Destiny's Needle* attacked the Imperials?"

"Yes, Director."

"They approached the Imperials, not the other way around?"

"Of this we are certain. Soon after we initiated our attack, *Destiny's Needle* moved into an attack position and headed for the rear guard, a supply frigate trailing the main task force."

Darstin laughed softly. "Never ceases to amaze…" he grumbled with admiration. "*Destiny's Needle* must have been sabotaged somehow, else he would have made a run for it—his ship is faster."

"Than Coryl-Tuluyt Pickets?" Ka'vaelus asked doubtfully. "That might be something of a race."

"Nevertheless, Captain Médeville would never have taken such a risk, boarding the Imperial frigate, unless there was something aboard that he absolutely had to have."

Ka'vaelus trilled his agreement. "And my attack provided the diversion he needed."

"Yes, quite enterprising of him." The Director wiped sweat from the corner of his eye. "You think it was a reckless move, or bold?"

"Neither term is accurate," Ka'vaelus said. "It was simply the act of a warrior who had no other choice."

"He could have picked one side or the other and negotiated for his cargo."

"Out of the question. I have seen the human's eyes — wild and alive like a Breyer sloth's. Thinking eyes, like yours."

"Mmm. So, from that point on you were in an inferior tactical position. Tell me how it unfolded."

"We split forces between attack and recovery. Oer'vaelus led a brilliant disruptive thrust into the Imperial formations and while performing the Reil flanking maneuver, managed to disable one picket."

Darstin singled out Oer and tightened his fist with jaw-clenching pleasure. "Well done!"

"While battling the second, my force was able to successfully board the frigate, anterior to the ship's position. We fought our way hand to hand through the ship, again splitting forces between trying to commandeer the ship's bridge and trying to reach *Destiny's Needle*."

"Why the subsequent division of purpose?"

"At that point we were unsure where the Tchelakov creatures were. We could not risk simply taking the Imperial frigate if the creatures were still aboard *Destiny's Needle*, and likewise we could not take *Destiny's Needle* and risk the creatures already being aboard the frigate."

"A difficult dilemma."

"Unfortunately, we were unsuccessful in accomplishing either maneuver. During the ensuing battle we almost had one of the pandas, but the other you hired, the human, Médeville, did his job too well and they escaped. He is formidable, this human. In trying to cover all angles, you paired off adversaries of equal strength. The outcome, then, became uncertain."

Darstin wiped the sweat from his temple and sighed, "He seems less the man I hired and more Helen's enlisted accomplice—a counterpart in her treachery."

"Somehow, I doubt that. He is a warrior."

"So?"

"He will find her actions repugnant. A betrayer has no use to a warrior. Those who earn their way through blood must be able to trust those at their sides at all costs."

"What then drives this man?" Darstin probed. "Honor?"

"Perhaps," Ka'vaelus murmured, aware that the Director was leading him with his questions. He respected the human's intelligence, and appreciated his gentle, unpatronizing approach. "Or perhaps he recognizes the creatures' value, their inherent importance."

"Perhaps," Darstin took a careful sip of the thick liquor.

Ka'vaelus tried to follow the line of reasoning. "Perhaps he doesn't wish for the Imperials to retain control of the creatures having seen first hand what they are capable of."

"Too broad."

His mandibles ground together as he thought. "Too broad, he hasn't seen what they can do?"

"No, too broad who he doesn't want to have them."

"Not all Imperials, just… Lord Barrett."

"Yes, very specific Imperials."

"The ones who have given him so much trouble."

"The ones he has seen first hand for the last twelve years, the ones he's seen expand from system to system like the plague."

"He is worried what will happen," Ka'vaelus said with quiet pride.

"Oh, yes," Darstin rumbled. "This is a man acutely aware, almost compulsively aware, of the consequences of his actions."

"Or lack of action," he said, thinking of the man's history.

"Very good, Cha'halen. You see it then."

"Médeville must wrest control of the pandas away from Lord Barrett because to do otherwise would lead to the ruin of many more planets. Just like Galzeki," he trailed off, thinking of the smoldering ruin his planet had become under the Imperial occupation.

"Yes, just like Galzeki."

Ka'vaelus paused with concern. "This is a man we have tried to kill aboard the Imperial frigate. You want us to destroy this human?" he rasped uncertainly.

"Not any longer," Darstin sighed. "Priorities change as events unfold. The objective remains the same, but the means to achieving it have changed radically. Too much of the plan has failed."

"You hired Médeville thinking that you would only need his services for a brief time."

"Yes, I hired him for his abilities, for his intimate knowledge of the Empire, so that he would keep the creatures safe from the Imperials until you could step in and take them."

"But that didn't work."

"No, it did not."

"And now?"

"Now it is reported that thirty-five of the creatures disembarked on Wyx—in full view of all who cared to watch. Which either means that two perished during the battle, or two are still with Médeville."

"And what are your orders now?"

"You must protect Médeville at all costs," Darstin stated plainly.

Ka'vaelus rose slightly, the ridged spines of his exoskeleton popping. The three Gambor chittered eagerly beside him, their elytra crinkling upward slightly.

"Yes, protect him," the Director sighed. "He has two pandas, which in itself is enough reason to want to keep him from harm's way—two are better than none. But, with control of two *precognizant* beings he might just have the tools necessary to recover the other thirty-five. We must see to it that he is able to enact whatever plan he has come up with."

"But how can we possibly find out what he is up to, what his plan is, or even where he is? The Imperials no longer chase him—we can no longer simply intercept their transmissions and follow them."

"Correct, Médeville must now chase down the Imperials."

"How, then, can we protect him?"

"By following Barrett's moves once more. The Vice Proctor is keenly aware of the danger of facing an adversary armed with foreknowledge of his possible actions."

"But Lord Barrett has creatures of his own."

"Uncooperative creatures," Darstin pointed out. "It will be some time before he can coax or force the future out of them. Until then, he is in a vulnerable position. He must act to head off Médeville's riposte."

"And you are sure that this man has the motivation to act?"

"You saw his eyes," Darstin murmured. "You and your brethren fought him at close quarters."

"Yes," Ka'vaelus trilled.

Darstin waited a beat. "And he survived." The Director looked up into the bulk work and the long shadows cast from the hovering glow globes. "What," he asked quietly, "does it take for a single warrior to succeed against numerically and physically superior adversaries?"

Ka'vaelus could see what the human's question was alluding to. He considered the ongoing struggle on his home world to oust the vile Imperial presence. He recalled the overwhelming odds his burrow faced and touched the satchel tied to his bandolier. It was heavy, filled as it was the saplings of fallen kin, saplings that he was now bound by honor to carry and one-day plant. "It takes," he said slowly, "a passion that supersedes logic. A will to fight even when all seems hopeless."

"And do you think that Médeville will disappear with his two pandas, find a safe planet somewhere and hide?"

Ka'vaelus understood now. "No, I do not."

"Nor do I. That is why we are here at the edge of the Skarasgard System. I have a closely placed agent who has kept me apprised of Barrett's activities, a doctor placed so long ago in the Imperial ranks that the vice proctor could not possibly ferret him out. The doctor has finally surfaced with information. He confirmed the creature's transport to Wyx, and now informs us that Barrett and his principal players are en route to New Haivello, fifth planet in this system."

"You believe Médeville is there?"

"Or coming soon," Darstin said. "We must protect him as best we can."

"Why does he not go to Wyx? Is he not aware that the creatures are being held there?"

"Maybe not. However, he has two precognizant pandas. I would venture that he has a specific plan in mind, and for whatever reason, there is something he *needs* on New Haivello."

Ka'vaelus shifted his inner wings with discomfort. "It is not possible for you to take Nralda Gunrunners into Imperial space."

"No," Darstin replied. "Highly unadvisable."

"However, four Jave O'Wars are much less noticeable."

"Yes, that would be the only way." Darstin paused. "Médeville has a long history with the Collistas Dynasty and the honorable motivation to try to recover the lost creatures. You, however," he looked carefully at each warrior, "may not. You have done me great service already, and lost many in turn. You may not wish to continue a fight so far from home."

All the Gambor in the chamber stopped what they were doing and looked up. Ka'vaelus turned slowly away and reached down for the oilskin. "Director, there were those among my crew who shared doubts about this mission." He took out four more gourds and began pouring a measure into each. "There are also those who doubted whether we would receive the payment of arms we so desperately needed for our fight on Galzeki, having not secured the creatures as we were commissioned to." He offered a gourd to each of the three honor guard and refilled Darstin's empty gourd. "However, the arms arrived on Galzeki as promised. Thanks to your integrity and this honorable mission, our burrows are safer by a degree."

The Director bowed his head, accepting the compliment.

"As a race, we have four hundred years of historical motivation." Ka'vaelus lifted his protective elytra and stretched out his one beautiful wing, and one darkened stub. "And I as an individual have the *personal* motivation to see this mission through. I have seen this man, Médeville, have seen his eyes. If a simple warrior such as he sees just cause to fight for these creatures, then so must we."

Darstin stepped boldly before the four Gambor. "You please me, Ka'vaelus of the Vaelus burrow. You are the finest warriors in the Shell. I would trust this mission to no other," he said, sealing the agreement.

The Gambor lifted their gourds well over the human's head. Darstin raised a toast: "To Médeville's health."

The three Gambor clicked roughly, and Ka'vaelus agreed in Strahlinvek: "So it shall be."

2

BAIT

VAILETTA STOOD ON THE *CABOT'S* BRIDGE, HAND PRESSED against the cold surface of a gyropod, and watched her breath fog against the glazing. She stared at the ensign that floated within. Yarvek's eyes were closed and his arms and legs were drawn in to his chest, like a fetus. A tangle of tubes trailed away from his head, lost in the murky gel.

The guards at the blast door snapped to attention. "Commander on the bridge!" they called as Arnas swept in, his assistant Finsen in tow. Arnas looked sharp and well-rested, shoulders and spine as stiff as the creases in his freshly pressed uniform. He took a perfunctory glance at the stasis boards, noted their progress toward New Haivello and made his way to the line of elliptical pods that circled the observation bubble.

Vailetta peered back into the gelatinous pod, wondering what part of the datacore Yarvek was traversing. She felt as withdrawn as the *poddie*—her lip still curled at the distasteful word—detached from her wellspring of strength, sent off on a fool's errand. What had the general called her? Bait?

She could feel Arnas staring at her, could see his distorted image in the curve of the pod. She turned to face him, noting the unspoken presence of command in his eyes. He was in charge once more, and looked every bit of it. His eyes glanced down to the pistol tucked in her belt and then met her gaze.

"I trust your quarters are acceptable, Captain."

"Haven't seen them."

"I'm sure you'll find them to your liking. You have diplomatic envoy status on this run—you should find the perks are a pleasant change to what we're accustomed to."

"Is that so?" she stared past him at the sartographs which turned gently in the hollow at the center of the bridge.

"Once the briefing is complete, I'll have one of my men show you to them."

She skipped back to his eyes. Was the purpose of this pleasantry a compensation for their reversal of roles? Polite banter to stem an awkward silence? Or something else? "That won't be necessary."

Finsen's hand shot up to his temple and he winced, fingers scrabbling to reduce the gain on his clipscan visor. "He's here."

"Very good." Arnas turned to the blast door and straightened his green jacket.

"Who's here?" Vailetta asked.

The door scrolled open and Barrett walked onto the bridge.

"Welcome, my Lord," Arnas greeted him.

The sight of the vice proctor startled her. "You're accompanying me, too?"

Barrett stepped up onto the raised platform. "You flatter yourself, Captain Strom."

Her mind scrambled for answers. "What has happened?" she demanded.

Barrett chuckled at his pupil's apt and swift reappraisal. "The good Dr. Crevlin has set my mind at ease. He discovered the failsafe: neural parasites left in the pandas by the quisling, Helen Tchelakov."

"How?" Vailetta asked, still shaken by the vice proctor's sudden appearance.

"They began showing up in the neural scans last night. They were detected moving inside the cerebrum of a cub."

A sickened disbelief soured her expression. She had still harbored doubts that the woman would actually leave deadly failsafes within the creatures. "*Moving?*"

"They came out of dormancy last night and are now moving. And feeding."

Vailetta cringed further. "How could you leave them at this time of need?"

"Dr. Crevlin is deliciously close to unraveling the parasites' genetic coding. He may have a viable antidote within the hour. A prototype batch will be administered to a test subject tomorrow morning."

"Which still begs the question — why are you here?" She hoped the nervous anxiety in her throat and chest did not trickle out with her words.

Barrett called to the pod, "Yarvek, show them."

The tech ensign floated silently in his pod. A light flashed overhead and a new sartograph sparkled into existence in the hollow. The holo showed the *Cabot's* position and projected course away from Wyx and toward New Haivello. The view quickly expanded to include the surrounding systems. A quartered icon showed four ships moving slowly toward New Haivello from a separate direction.

"TacOps picked up four Gamborian Jave O'Wars moving through the Skarasgard System. sartographic triangulation puts them on a course for New Haivello—two hours behind us."

"Probability?" Arnas interrupted.

"Ninety-one percent," Finsen said. "Near certainty."

"But why—" Vailetta started, trying to make sense of it.

"It simply bolsters our projections, my dear," Barrett intoned. "Master Torg asserted that the good Captain Médeville would not give up. I asserted that you are the weak link—the suddenly *merciful* link. Thus was borne the supposition that Médeville must seek you out. The sartographs are currently holding the supposition at forty-seven—up six points since the Gambor sighting. That's forty-seven percent likelihood that Médeville will track you down—five times greater than any other alternative."

"But why New Haivello? How could he know?"

"I listed your name on this ship as part of the diplomatic party. Médeville has managed to find a way to track you—as remarkable as that may sound."

"Well he does have two pandas," Arnas observed.

"And the Gambor?" Vailetta asked shakily.

"Seems to point toward New Haivello being the next focal point of our little drama," Barrett said.

Vailetta took an incredulous tone: "You let it be known that I would be going there?"

"Conflict is inevitable, better it be somewhere within our control—while we still have some control in the matter. It was

important to get you off Wyx—we couldn't have all this trans-
piring so close to the pandas."

"So you're here to negotiate with Tchelakov for the antidote?"

Barrett whetted his lips. "Yes, though that may become unnecessary. Crevlin might have solved the problem by the time
we land tomorrow."

"You leave your *cherished creatures* at a time when they need
a display of your benevolence most?" Vailetta asked acidly.

"I am not a *doctor*," Barrett said, patience with his pupil
wearing thin. "I am, however a tremendous *negotiator*. I go
where my abilities are best put to use, and trust the doctors to
perform their magic."

"But you could win the tribe's trust at this critical juncture—
you standing at their side while the terrible parasites are rendered harmless. They may tell you all you desire after such a
show of benevolence."

The Vice Proctor's face cracked into a thin smile, the hint
of his perceived patience and wisdom sliding along his lips like
a trickle of mercury. "Oh, but that won't be necessary. Didn't
I tell you? The tribe's Elders have already agreed to help me.
They are in the bubble room as we speak," his eyes flicked to
Arnas, "examining the preliminary stages of my Unifying Campaign."

Vailetta looked crestfallen. The Vice Proctor had already
lured the pandas to his side, without having to raise his hand.
The habitat, his selective use of honesty, and promises of safety
that ensured that the tribe could not resist. She thought of
General Shecut departing for the long journey home. It was
already too late.

"Do not look so disappointed," Barrett said, misreading her
expression. "The play has not yet run its course and there is
still much more for you to do."

Vailetta tried to summon up a look of renewed interest. "There is?"

"There is still a negotiation to attend to, and we must prepare for the forthcoming visit of our friends, the Gambor. Not to mention the small matter of the now prescient Garrand Médeville and his cargo of pandas."

"What of my mission?" Vailetta asked.

"That will go on as planned. You will perform the Simonean dance for the Luminaars as scheduled in the Greuk Center For Performing Arts on the planet's like-named capital, New Haivello. It is your cover for being there and will hopefully lure Médeville in quietly."

"And what of the presence of two platoons of Shock Troops?"

"Ostensibly there to protect me," Barrett replied, "though one will be with you to ensure that you are safe." The Vice Proctor looked at Arnas. "What's the status on the surface, Commander?"

"Finsen?"

"Ah, still nothing broadcast. Word of your visit is being kept secret for now, my Lord. The top tier of bureaucrats know, but the local populace has not been informed. Their treating it as a unpublicized visit by a ruling proctor—no state banquets or the like."

"Good. What story did Intel come up with?"

"Officially, you are here to attend the Simonean dance and assess progress in the ongoing negotiations with the Luminaars."

"Perfect. This deep inside the Proctorialship we should have little trouble with the locals—the Luminaars aside. Inform the garrison commander, Colonel..." Barrett snapped his fingers.

"Colonel Sokalis," Arnas supplied.

"Yes, inform Sokalis of our plans and tell him to suspend all passes for the next two days. Have him raise his state of readiness and forward the ship's last known registries to the Port Authority. I want to be informed the moment she makes planetfall."

"As you will, my Lord."

Barrett took Vailetta by the shoulder and led her out of the bridge. "Come, you need your rest, my dear. You have quite a day ahead of you." Vailetta allowed herself to be ushered away. "You shouldn't be so surprised that I am here—I wouldn't miss this for all the stars. Thanks to you and Arnas we should have this wrapped up in two days. The pandas will be ours, uncontested and free from defect. And the last rogue variables will be dead."

❖ ❖ ❖

GARRAND FINISHED REVIEWING THE FINAL CLIPSCANNER AND pushed it wearily aside. He ran his fingers through his hair and leaned back in his chair, taking stock of the uneven clutter of the mess. A quick glance around the chamber confirmed that, on the surface, all was as it should be. Yet there were subtle differences. He frowned and rubbed his lower lip with a finger, eyes darting around the room, looking for visual cues. Something was different, but he wasn't quite sure what.

As he had initially glanced around the room, something had not registered with the visual image he had of the room in his memory. There was a discrepancy with what he subconsciously remembered the room being like—in fact there were several subtle differences. But as he gazed hard around the mess, his eyes found nothing out of the ordinary—nothing missing, no radical changes.

The nagging feeling of change would not fade away though. Something was amiss. The lights in the room seemed brighter, or sharper. The details of the bulkhead (which he had designed!) seemed almost foreign — not at all like something he had gazed indifferently at for years. Was he just now noticing the tiny scrollwork and filigree patterns left in the cerasteel by the Diluvian craftsmen?

He got up and walked over to the main navigational console — hooked directly into the bridge command pod. The layout of the screens was marvelous, subtly angled to provide easy lines of sight for the user, yet discreetly tucked into the grey steel panels — almost invisible. Bailey suggested that, he reminded himself. What's so different about all this?

He closed his eyes and took a deep breath, not wanting to let frustration get the better of him. Sid was right — he needed to relax. He centered his thoughts and began to regulate his breathing, consciously slowing his heart rate. He let pieces of the problem fall away from his conscious thought, discarding the minor details which clouded his conscious perception of the true issue. He turned inward and watched the questions fall into place.

With a flash of self-realization he opened his eyes. Of course; it was obvious. Nothing in the mess had changed in the slightest. It was he that had changed.

So much had been happening lately that he had not even been consciously aware of how much he had learned and grown. His perceptions had altered, his eye for detail enhanced. What he had taken for granted for so long seemed new and fresh to him once again. His ship seemed different, infused with a vibrance and beauty.

He ran his hand down the cool bulkhead and smiled. Maybe Sid was right. There were, perhaps, a few depths left unplumbed, some untapped substance beneath the surface. Maybe he did have a few tricks still left up his sleeve—but would they be enough to conquer the demons?

Garrand patted his ship and walked out of the mess, headed for the bridge. From the shadows of the opposite hall, Sid stirred, licking his upper lip contemplatively. The human was learning.

"WE'RE READY TO make planetfall," Bailey said from the navi pod. New Haivello turned slowly beneath the crystal glazings, enormous and bluish white.

Feet up on the command board and body slumped back in the couch, Garrand tapped the edge of display with a finger. "Clearance?" he murmured.

"Not yet."

Garrand continued to rap his finger with manic persistence. "What registry did you use?" he asked absently.

"*Flogos Turn*—the one we bought off Ziegler six months ago on Letugia. Remember?"

"Mmm."

Helen sat in the weapons pod, and had it spinning around the circumference of the bridge in great lazy loops. Garrand watched it pass over his head; she was sitting cross-legged on the couch playing with something on her lap.

"You're making me dizzy," he called to her as she made another orbit.

Helen smirked without looking up—she'd wondered how many loops it'd take before his annoyance overcame his patience. Eight seemed to be the magic number. She allowed the pod to finish one more turn and then let it settle at the nadir where she could stare at the clouds that wrapped the planet below in a feathery cloak.

"*Destiny*, you got anything for me yet?"

"Minor projections only, Captain," the ship replied. "I've picked up nothing of substance from the surface pertaining to a diplomatic visit from Wyx."

"What's the biggest hit so far?"

"Performance at the Greuk Center For Performing Arts in the Capital tonight with diplomatic party representing the Luminaars in attendance. 'Special Guest Performance' reported on several media relays."

"Performance of what?"

"Simonean dance," *Destiny* said.

"What's that have to do with an envoy from Wyx?" Garrand asked with irritation.

"You asked for the sartograph's biggest possibility thus far, Captain, not all the factors compounding the projection. There's nothing directly linking an exhibition of the Simonean cultural arts with a secret visit from a diplomatic envoy from the proctorialship's ruling planet, however, all military leaves for the city's garrison have been canceled indefinitely. Security is being tightened across the city, and in particular around the Greuk Center. A scheduled lecture to be given by Praetor Hoyle at the Poli Technical Académe has been canceled, and a box reserved in his name at the Greuk. Tickets for the performance are no longer available to the public and the—"

"—All right, all right," Garrand sighed. "I get the picture."

"You should be more precise with your requests. If you wanted to know why the dance was currently getting the highest sartographic ratings, you should have said so."

"I said I was sorry. What's the likelihood?"

"Currently stable at seventeen percent."

"What's second choice?"

"Convention of the Ancient and Revered Order of the Loper at Capetown in the southern arctic."

Garrand smiled. "That's not it."

"Sounds interesting," Helen mumbled from below. She twisted the tiny holocube that lay in her lap, the image it projected sparkling as it hit her legs. Data scrolled slowly beside it as she studied the reports she'd culled from the Archive.

"*Destiny*, if we make the presumption that the preparations for the dance do indeed herald the arrival of an envoy from Wyx, what are the chances that Strom is the performer?"

"Working from that supposition, the probability is 67.2."

Helen's head perked up. "Not bad."

Garrand had another thought. "*Destiny*, pull up a plan of the city. Is there any ornamental tower near the Greuk Center? Public clock, religious edifice, anything that might hold big bells?"

Sid stirred from his spot on an empty acceleration couch. He'd been studying the clouds that passed beneath the world-ship and had almost fallen asleep.

"Treichler Tower stands in the plaza opposite the Performing Arts Center. It contains a large clock."

"That's it."

"What's it?" Helen asked.

"Bailey, get down to the armory and get a full kit worked up for me — inner city, full countermeasures, the works."

The artificial spun the navi pod immediately to the gangway. "Weapons package?"

"Heavy."

The art nodded and disappeared from sight.

"I don't understand," Helen complained. "What do bells have to do with it?"

"Her fate now in the Griffin's hand / Like his before in hers as well / Safely plucked from a warrior's stand / Before the silence of the final bell."

"Ahh…"

Alexander added another stanza: "Before the bell / And death's disgrace / She'll take his hand / And accept her place."

"Clearances received," the ship reported. "Credit approved, landing vectors assigned."

Garrand dropped his legs off the board and shifted forward. He cut the reactors and dropped the ship immediately out of orbit. The planet pivoted beyond the glazing, brilliant white clouds now filling the view.

Destiny's Needle roared across New Haivello's late afternoon sky, rocketing by the crystalline spires and rust-red towers which thrust skyward. New Haivello sparkled with energy and life, brilliant colors reflecting off the garish architectural floodlights and the clouds of smog that hung like a thick paste over the city. Fiery city lights mingled with the winking collision lanterns on the hundreds of airborne craft crisscrossing in the traffic patterns.

Garrand located the proper landing beacon on the navi, a flashing purple dot in the southern corner of the sartographic display, and banked *Destiny's Needle* south away from the towering central city structures. The midtown docks serviced mostly private starships and smaller inner-system craft, leaving the large commercial business for the immense Tamarae yards on the flood plains east of the city proper. The ship was just small enough for a large landing berth at midtown; it would keep them a fair distance from Imperial warships at Tamarae and deeper in the less conspicuous private sector. Hopefully the doctored ship registry would hold up.

The landing beacon coded specifically for the '*Flogos Turn*' was activated along with a compressed microburst of landing vectors and import-custom regulations. The data scrolled down the side of the display.

Helen fingered her holocube as the city slipped beneath her and stared at the dark-haired woman it projected. She well knew the 'Thief of Ships' that Garrand and Sid had sought from the Archives. The Captain of Barrett's Imperial Guard had made quite an impression on her. She'd made her own inquiry on Archiva and she now knew everything she could about the woman who had forced her to strip aboard the Imperial frigate, who had ruined everything for her above Eemon Nores.

She had pressed the Archives a bit harder than Garrand had. The captain, in his eagerness to get off-planet, had stopped too soon in his excitement of discovery. Under her direction, the holo ghost had dug into Strom's past, uncovering some intriguing discrepancies. With the Archive's enormous resources, it had not taken Helen long to unravel the mystery. She twisted the shimmering image as the ship landed, recalling bitterly the naked confrontation, the woman's steadfast refusal to heed her warnings that the pandas would die without her. It was all Strom's fault, refusing to take her along with the pandas. Now they were all in danger. She stared at the image of *Princess* Strom.

Barrett could not discard her so easily. She had one more trump to play.

3

NEW HAIVELLO

THERE WERE FOUR OF THEM IN THE PRAETOR'S SECURITY room, high up a tower overlooking the Greuk Center plaza on New Haivello. Yarvek-EZ slumped in a chair looking ill at ease, electrical feeds trailing away from the back of his skull to a Sartok. A soldier stood close behind him, ready to catch him by the handholds on his robe should he fall; tech ensigns didn't have the musculature to sit upright for very long. Arnas and Finsen stood by the sartographic projection board speaking in low voices. It was clear from Arnas' expression that he did not like what Finsen was telling him. A chime tinged security clearance and Barrett strode in. Arnas turned to him angrily.

"This is impossible, you've left her too vulnerable—" he stopped short as he saw that Barrett was flanked by two administrators from New Haivello.

"Commander, at ease," Barrett dismissed him casually. "I'd like to present the governor of New Haivello, Provost Preston, and his chief magistrate, Praetor Hoyle."

The two men bowed to Arnas, who stiffened and nodded, "Provost, Praetor. Pardon my outburst.

"Commander Arnas leads the 41st Marine Battalion," Barrett explained. "He's under quite a bit of pressure at the moment."

"Shock Troops," Provost Preston nodded with approval. "Quite impressive. I feel safer already."

"Arnas, we've just received word that Gamborian Jave O'Wars have been given clearance to land. We're awaiting confirmation." The Vice Proctor glanced at the tech ensign. "Yarvek?"

"On line with Port Authority—no response as yet." Barrett appraised the poddie's drooping limbs and almost translucent skin. He wasn't swayed by the boy's frail form, this one had the makings—Captain Strom was right. The ensign sat straight as he could, willing himself to stay upright. If anyone could be brought out of the pods, this one could. And he was a wonder with the cores—he had the Sartok's pulse, the data pulsing through his mind like blood. He was the perfect candidate to work with the pandas.

"My Lord," Arnas persisted with calm determination. "I still feel she is too much in the open. It is hard enough to guard the Center from one man, but if the Gambor—"

"Captain Strom will be fine," Barrett broke in. "She has you to protect her. The Gambor are not yet here. It's just Médeville for now."

Arnas did not look convinced, but remained silent.

Barrett walked to the balcony overlooking the busy plaza. A light mist softened the details of the hurka-boys and flyers that flashed past. Crowds of busy citizens filled the plaza below. A near constant stream of traffic traveled over their heads, slowing to dip down to flyer pads and roto platforms that jutted out from surrounding buildings. The ornate face of the clock in Treichler Tower read half past eleven.

"The Dance commences at a quarter till. That gives us time to catch up. Finsen, why don't you bring us up to speed on the local situation."

The assistant, half blinded by his clipscan visor, bumped into the edge of the projection board. "Sorry, sir," he mumbled to it and patted the surface absentmindedly. "What we have here is a territorial dispute between the original settlers of this area, the Dengbaz and the subterranean creatures who call themselves the Luminaars, the Warlords of Light. For the last twenty years, they've produced energy for the entire territory in exchange for absolute control of mining operations."

"Some deal," Barrett murmured. "Dryexcellon?"

Preston stepped forward. "Jewels, mostly. The energy flux has allowed them to go deeper than before and excavate under the city itself."

"Under tunneled," Yarvek observed, "like Galzeki."

"Yes—except there *we* are the burrowers," Arnas muttered.

"It's good of you to come personally, Lord Barrett," Praetor Hoyle effused. "It was a minor problem at first, the attacks. But they've grown increasingly—"

"Tiresome," Preston finished. "We worried that the conflict might grow to an unacceptable level."

"There's a diplomatic solution to everything," Barrett said absent-mindedly. "That's the purpose of this dance performance. I trust the Luminaars are in attendance?"

"Yes, thousands of them," Preston said. He looked nervously at Hoyle.

"My Lord," Hoyle stammered.

"Out with it Praetor," Barrett said, still staring at the streets below. Commerce was thriving here, midday traffic had the bustle and hectic urgency of Jobaenz. The swirls of smog and exhaust that captured the flashing lights of passing flyers and garish architectural floods and advert beacons only made the city seem more alive. Curling tendrils of cloud parted in the wind as the rain began to dissipate.

"We feel that a peaceful solution is not forthcoming—"

"As good as your intentions are," Preston added hastily.

"The Dengbaz have grown increasingly difficult, and the Luminaars grow fearful. Energy production is down."

"Then we'll simply root them out," Barrett sighed.

"It's not that simple, My Lord. The Dengbaz and their followers have retreated into the mountains around the city and a centuries old cave system auxiliary to the mining tunnels. It is said that they have found ways into the city through the underground and are bent on usurping the Luminaars."

Barrett was growing weary of this. "I promised you an end to these attacks. We'll stop the Dengbaz by securing the proper entrances."

Preston and Hoyle looked at one another wordlessly.

"Uh, how many of those are there?" Arnas finally asked.

"Surveys have found upward of 300,000."

"That's a big cavern," Arnas whistled.

Beside him Yarvek choked over the figure. "He plans to predict the next assault? With so many tunnels? Impossible! That's more complicated than planning a jump a year ahead of time. Even the new E3's could never make a reliable projection." His excitement caused him to lurch to the left. The soldier behind him caught him gently and pushed him upright.

"I plan to go a different route, ensign," Barrett said with mild censure.

"Better than the E3? I've never heard of such a thing—" Yarvek broke off. He knew exactly how Barrett planned to execute the calculations.

The Vice Proctor smiled as realization struck the poddie.

"A good first test," Arnas said with an approving frown.

"Thank you, Commander. I think so."

"Then it's true?" Preston asked, eyes widening. "You have such creatures at your disposal?"

Barrett turned to face Preston and Hoyle, shoulders stiff, chin held high. His black cape rippled gently in the breeze. The small golden dragon on his lapel sparkled briefly as the sun broke through the clouds. Hand still on the railing, he simply stared at the men, eyes possessed of a quiet affirmation that heightened his regal bearing.

Nervous relief spread across the governor's face. "Well that's just—"

"Splendid, simply splendid!" Hoyle spouted. "We'd heard the rumors, but…"

"—Yes, it's absolutely remarkable. And we are to be the first test? I can't tell you how proud we are that you've chosen *us*!"

"Where are these fabulous beings?" Hoyle asked.

Barrett waved him silent. "First things first, Praetor. There is a more pressing situation. We have the Gambor to deal with." He turned back to the balcony. "And Médeville."

"Confirmation coming in," Yarvek interrupted. "The Jave O'Wars are on the surface. Port Authority reports visual contact—four ships docked at the Tamarae yards."

Barrett tapped the railing and glanced at the clock. It was going to be close. He wanted Médeville in custody before the Gambor arrived. "Still no report of *Destiny's Needle?*"

"No, my Lord."

"He could still be here," Finsen allowed. "Freetrader of his caliber undoubtedly has many registries to fool Port Authorities."

"Mmm. He's here," Barrett murmured. "Just wish we didn't have to wait for him to come to us... Arnas, are your men in place?"

"Yes, my Lord. Half in the audience and at the entrances, half back-stage."

A young woman hurried into the room and whispered into Preston's ear. The Praetor grew pale: "There's been a sighting."

Barrett turned. "Of what?"

"A flying thing."

"Please. Let's try to retain our wits here. A *thing?*"

"A giant beetle thing."

"That's better," Barrett said. He looked at Arnas. "You'd better deliver Torg's gift to Captain Strom."

"As you will, my Lord."

❖ ❖ ❖

VAILETTA TRIED TO LIMBER HER ARMS AND LEGS IN THE SMALL dressing room. She knew these last few moments of calm would be her last, but she could not seem to prepare herself for the performance. The waiting was dreadful. Barrett had set her out like a shiny trinket, a lightning rod for all his enemies.

Médeville was coming to find her, the indefatigable former Captain of the Guard. *Did he feel like this? Set apart and singled out?* The Gambor, in turn, were coming to get him. And here she was, surrounded by Shock Troopers. She would be on stage in front of thousands, a target, vulnerable like never before. Nausea welled up in her chest. She pressed her palms against the wall and bent her knees, waiting for the wave of dizziness to subside.

"Is there a problem, Captain Strom?" Arnas stood in the doorway, watching.

"Butterflies," she murmured, stretching her legs. "Not much longer, thank Haven."

"No, assuredly not much longer." Arnas turned to leave but paused as if in afterthought. "Oh, Elzbieta sent you something—an extra measure for the dance." He extended a small black velvet case. She steadied her hands and reached for it. Inside was a mirrored ammunition casing shell. No, it was a double-sided lipstick case. Vailetta slid back one side and swiveled up a ruby-purple cone. She looked up for an explanation.

"That side is the poison," Arnas explained. Vailetta raised her eyebrows, but said nothing. She opened the other side to reveal a white cone. "The white is the base. Put it on carefully before you apply the poison. It's so corrosive the base only lasts fifteen minutes. When your lips begin to turn white, the poison is beginning to breach the base. You must remove it before your lips become purple again or you will fall victim to the same swift fate as whom you've kissed."

"A kiss?" She held the case in midair, her brow furrowed.

Arnas sighed. "Lord Barrett worries that Médeville will find a way to get to you."

"With you and your men here?"

"Unlikely," he conceded, "but he's slipped through before."

She replaced the lipstick in its case. "I'm no assassin."

"You're the only one who can get close enough. It's a direct order."

Vailetta stepped back. "Poison isn't Elzbieta's trade. Where did you get such a thing?"

Arnas narrowed his eyes and did not smile. "Never turn the assassin's gift away." He extended his hand and touched her chin. "Wear it in good health, Captain."

"As you will," she whispered softly, slowly turning away. *As you all will...* She felt like she was no longer in control of her own destiny. Barrett's bidding weighed on her like a bitter malaise, rubbing her sensibilities raw. Her stomach cramped with doubt and she rubbed the tender flesh with the heel of her palm.

She finished dressing for the performance, fumbling with the Stiglian repulsor wraps that allowed her three-dimensional freedom. She stared at the velvet case for some time and then reluctantly applied both base and poison. The color was garish against her lips, the color too harsh for her freckled skin. She rose carefully lest the repulsor wraps send her careening into the ceiling.

She felt her hands trembling as she sought her balance; she'd never been nervous before a performance before. And she'd never felt so alone while surrounded by so many. Médeville was coming for her, and she was to be the instrument of his demise. She'd unwittingly delivered the pandas to Barrett, and now she would destroy the last impediment to the vice proctor's plans. Panic caught her unprepared and she had to chant a Gokazoku mantra to calm herself. *You've been alone before,* she told herself.

You were alone long before the Guard took you in. She left the room in a minor fugue, struggling to keep her composure.

Torg stood against the far wall, watching her impassively.

"Keep your gifts to yourself, assassin. I won't become you." She pinched her lips in an airy kiss, hating him. There would be no honor today.

"It's not what you think," he said.

❖ ❖ ❖

GARRAND FELT AN ELECTRIC SURGE OF ADRENALINE COURSE through his bloodstream. He was walking so fast through the ship that he was almost running.

"Any problem with the Port Authority?" he spoke into the bulkheads.

"No, Captain," the ship replied. "All port functions operating nominally, no deviation from standard protocols."

"And no sign of Imperial intervention?"

"Our registries appear to be holding up."

"Okay, unseal the primary lock and put in a request for some minor repair."

"For once, Captain, I am in no need of repair."

"I know that, just ask for something anyway. We've got to keep up appearances — make it look like we've had a long spell in deep space." Garrand skipped through the mess, panda cub close behind. Alexander dogged his ankles, furry shoulders rubbing against his legs as he hurried to the armory. Little Bit rolled into his sight and burped a question.

"I don't have time for that."

The tech art drug a tangled panel into view. He whistled sharply.

"No. We need that working. Tear down the motivator array and start from scratch. And this time don't forget to integrate the power couplings with the buffer matrix."

Little Bit groaned and gave a shrill screech directed at Garrand who sidestepped around the sphere.

"Hey! It's your fault—not mine! So you've got no one to blame but yourself. Go fix it. Alexander will play with you later."

Little Bit rolled off warbling softly to himself. Garrand punched access to the armory and ducked inside as the door irised open. Bailey had been busy inside; silver and black gear, well oiled and carefully polished, was laid out on the armorer's table and all along the deck. Crates of concussion grenades lay in jumbled disarray on the floor as the artificial swiftly loaded discharge wheels.

"Suit up," the art said without looking away.

Garrand stripped off his jacket and shift and stepped up to the armor mount. He mashed the lever with his foot and the sticky fiber wrapped around his chest. He stuck each arm into the gauntlet mount and felt the constrictive body armor seal into place.

"Legs, too."

He didn't like the leg mounts. With ginger disdain, he kicked his toe into the wall mount and cringed as the armor encapsulated his leg from below his knee to his groin. He flexed his quadriceps and frowned; always felt too tight. He repeated the mounting process for his left leg and did a deep knee bend, trying to loosen the tight fibers. A clean, white shift hung by the armor mount. He pulled the blousy garment over his head. The dull sheen of the leg armor would pass as acceptable fashion, but the upper torso armor would be conspicuous in an urban environment.

"Get into the harness," Bailey ordered.

Garrand lifted the lightweight harness from the wall and pulled the webbing over his head. Bailey finished loading a wheel and helped him fasten the straps around his back. Garrand snapped his weapon belt into place and let Bailey hook the harness into place. He held his arms up as the artificial began tightening all the straps.

Sid poked his nose into the armory to watch the spectacle. "Seen this before?" Garrand asked as Bailey cinched the harness tight. The panda shook his head.

"Haven't seen my future?" He raised his eyebrows as Bailey began clipping weapons and gear to hard points on the harness. He took a feeder off the armorer's table and clipped it to his belt. "Or haven't seen *this* future?"

The panda rumbled, turned away and looked down the corridor. "You do not have one specific future."

Garrand shook his head. "*Cheplus.*"

"Don't take a tone with me. You know that you have many futures. Looking at your life as a whole, the possibilities are endless."

"Right this instant I have infinite futures?"

The Captain was being intentionally difficult. "No, right this instant you have *one* future. And if I focus myself properly, I might catch a glimpse of a part of it—a scene, an event—something that will transpire if you continue along a certain path."

"The *seitparen.*"

"Exactly. The Path of Fate is what eventually becomes known as the past. It is the culmination of all the random events that transpire."

"So you can only see glimpses of my future?"

"For the most part."

"Then how do you know what glimpses are part of the Path of Fate and what are just possible futures that will never occur?" He loaded a wheel of grenades into the feeder and clicked two more wheels onto the back of his belt.

"Instinct, partially. And through the accumulated visions of the entire tribe we cull through the future, seeking threads of continuity, common events, themes. We are able to construct a workable image or map of the future, begin to see the secrets of the *seitparen*. Of course it's constantly in flux: choices we make, choices others make, random occurrences—all play havoc with the future."

"So the future is not set in stone."

"No, it is not."

"And the Path of Fate? What of our carefully constructed dream interpretations?"

"The Path is a map of something that does not yet exist…"

"…But will inevitably come to pass," Garrand finished for him with a sigh. He let Bailey affix three amoeba nets to his harness. "So if I asked you to envision what happens to me in three hours, you could see it, but it may not come to pass exactly as you foresee it because it might not be a part of my Path of Fate. I could do something between now and then that could lead to a whole series of changes, in essence changing my future."

"That's correct."

"But if enough of you have similar visions, or pieces of the same vision, then it's likely that you're foreseeing my *seitparen*, something that's *destined* to happen." He reached down and picked up a short-barreled burner and slung it over his shoulder.

"Yes, but having the same vision is highly unusual—there are always incipient differences from vision to vision—dream to dream. There is no destiny, no predetermined outcome, but there are common themes, events that seem to transpire in all the dreams, phenomena that cannot be explained…"

"Raising the probability that the dreams are true—making you believe that you're getting a glimpse of the Path."

"Exactly."

Bailey finished loading the weapon package and began clicking off safeties, pulling out pins. He took an injector wand and stabbed the end on the back of Garrand's neck. The locator hissed into his skin.

Bailey checked a display. "You're live."

Garrand rubbed the back of his neck and looked at his first mate. They exchanged a wordless glance. He took a deep breath and pushed himself upright, flexing his shoulders—an electric tension behind his coiled frame. Sid was reminded of the carnivorous predators that skulked through the night on Beyfor Lalentius.

Garrand picked up his blaster and popped out its current coil. "So, our dreams of this planet, of the Thief of Ships, are they part of the *seitparen*?"

"I believe so."

"Have you seen other parts of my future that you have not revealed to me?"

Sid sighed pointedly. "You should not ask."

"Have you?"

The giant panda did not answer.

Garrand hesitated, then asked: "Do you know when I'm going to die?"

Sid growled. "It is not wise to know such things — or to think you know…"

"Sid," Garrand growled back, checking the coil charge in the palm of his hand. "I don't care about later. I just want to know about today."

"Given what the Elders foresaw before they were taken, and what I myself have dreamt…" he paused, uncertain if he should divulge such critical and potentially harmful information. "I do not believe that you will die today."

Garrand slapped the coil back into the base of his blaster. "That's good enough for me." He paused inside the doorway. "I'm off to catch a Thief." He patted Sid's head and jogged down the corridor.

"Don't do anything differently!" Sid called after him, but it was too late. The panda looked back inside the armory at the *thola* and sighed. He hoped he had not done irreparable damage to the tribe's understanding of the *seitparen*. Of course, he reminded himself, he could just as easily have crystallized it. Whatever affect it would have, he could not undo his action, and it had already become part of the captain's Path.

He chided himself for lack of foresight. He should have seen himself doing this months ago.

Garrand stopped at the primary airlock and thumbed his comtab. "Helen?"

No response.

"*Destiny*, where is Helen?"

"Miss Tchelakov is no longer aboard. She left immediately after the locks were unsealed."

"Why wasn't I informed?"

"I alerted you over the com. I'm afraid there's a malfunction in the armory speaker—someone has tampered with the circuits." Garrand cursed under his breath. *Now what was she up to?* It was too late to worry about. He glanced at his chronometer as he hurried out of the ship—it was quarter till twelve.

❖ ❖ ❖

VAILETTA COULD HEAR THE HEAVY DRUM BEATS FROM THE BACK-stage corridor. Shock Troopers flanked her in full Trioxin armor, an impressive show that might soon end in bloodshed. She swayed in the Stiglian repulsor wraps. Controlling her direction in them was difficult in her nervous state. She made a bad assassin, she decided as the curtains parted. She caught a brief glimpse of the magnificent, multi-tiered hall as the lights dimmed and then she floated into darkness, drums ringing in her ears.

As always, the sensual, dangerous cadence pulled her in, the forbidden air of the piece invigorating. She spun into the air as the curtain fell behind her and a spotlight caught her. Then lights all over the room came on with blinding intensity, refracting in the smoke. No, they weren't spots, they were—she whirled upside down, suspended as she faced her alien audience—they were the Luminaars themselves. The Warlords of Light shone with golden resplendence, great pillars of energy residing inside crystal columns. Somber-faced attendants stood beside each floating jar, their soft features illuminated by the Luminaars brilliant glow. Vailetta felt energized by the lustrous display, her flint-black hair swung out with renewed vigor. Her lithe body undulated to the fantastic rhythms of the Simonean dance and she spun end over end, her thoughts spinning as well.

She caught sight of Shock Troopers standing in the back of the grand hall, weapons out, waiting. She saw herself reflected in their visors. When would he come? She performed back flip after back flip, trying not to count the seconds.

ARNAS WATCHED THE dance unfold with tense expectation from the rear of the hall. He could hear his men outside the Greuk Center scanning the crowds for Médeville through his tympanic receiver. Lively discussions filtered through his head as they discussed likely suspects. He had men on the roof, at all the entrances and in the plaza beyond. He surveyed the Troopers stationed inside the hall. They were spread too thin, looking for one man. With the Gambor coming, they needed to be taking a more defensive posture—but then Médeville might slip through. He had to make a decision soon—order his men to stop searching for Médeville and start watching the skies for the Gambor.

A minor commotion grew in his head.

"Barlow, repeat that!" he subvocalized.

"Commander, you'd better come out here. Main foyer."

Arnas pushed through the hall's back door and into the lobby. A woman struggled between two Trioxin-clad Troopers who held her firmly between them. Arnas squinted in disbelief, immediately recognizing the woman as Helen Tchelakov. Médeville had sent a proxy to negotiate on his behalf?

"This woman is demanding to be taken to Lord Barrett," Barlow informed him.

Arnas strode forward. "I'll take care of it, lieutenant. Release her." The two Troopers let go of her arms and stepped back, snapping to attention.

Arnas subvocalized new orders to his men: "All squads, stand down search for Médeville. Fall back to original position. Assume defensive posture."

The Tchelakov woman rubbed her arm and glared at him. "I must see Barrett immediately."

"Out of the question," Arnas replied.

"I have information for him. Information he *needs*."

Arnas drew his blaster and pointed it at her head. "I should just shoot you here. The Vice Proctor has no use for traitors."

"No, wait!" she exclaimed, panic creasing her face. "I am not the one—Barrett still needs me." She was obviously worried that she might not get to face the vice proctor. "You have a different traitor here! I can help you, but you've got to get me to Lord Barrett."

Arnas grabbed her by the arm, and placed the muzzle against her temple. "Tell me."

"No," she said, eyes wide and defiant. "Only Barrett."

Arnas shook his head. "Not good enough. The Gambor will be here any moment. You have one chance to live."

"The Gambor! How did they—" she halted, trying to think.

"Tell me!"

"All right," she conceded. "But I want your word that you'll take me to—"

"Out with it," Arnas shook her.

"Strom," Helen panted. "Vailetta Strom is a traitor."

"Captain Strom?" he hissed incredulously. "Be serious!"

"Strom is the one," Helen insisted. "She is the *Emperor's daughter!*"

"What?"

"It's true. She is going to undo everything. The pandas have foreseen it." At the mention of the pandas, the commander's face paled. "That's why we're here," Helen continued. "To enlist Strom's help. She's a traitor!"

Arnas relaxed his grip. *Barrett had called her the 'weak link.' Could it be?* "I've been with the woman for months. She's no traitor."

Helen looked at him plaintively. "But she *will* be."

Arnas narrowed his gaze fractionally. *Could the creatures foresee such a thing? Was Tchelakov telling the truth? Was she that desperate?* Arnas' arm weakened and the blaster fell away from her head. "That's preposterous," uncertainty lurked in the back of his throat. *Could the pandas see into a person's heart and mine such duplicity? They had been a step ahead since the beginning.* His eyes shut slowly. The answer was obvious. He released the woman and motioned Megas and Barlow over.

The two snapped to attention. "Commander?"

"Barlow, take this woman to Lord Barrett."

"Yes, sir."

Arnas looked at the second Trooper and sighed. "Megas, I want you to go backstage. Captain Strom is to be taken into custody immediately following the performance."

The man looked startled. "Excuse me?"

"I want you to detain her."

"You're telling me to *arrest* the captain of the Gokazoku Kaigi?"

"I'm ordering you to *detain* her," Arnas snarled. "Lord Barrett will most certainly want to question her." *At the very least.* "Do you think we can proceed with the Emperor's daughter in our midst?"

4

REUNION

GARRAND STEPPED OFF THE HURKA-BOY AND LOOKED down at the Greuk Performing Arts Center across the street. Shock Troopers stood on the steps leading up to the entrance, silvered armor glistening in the rain. He glanced at the giant clock in the plaza opposite his position; he could see the big iron bells hanging in the open eaves. The hands were almost aligned on the twelve. He tossed a handful of quantis to the hurka pilot and stepped into the suspensor tube leading to the street.

He threaded his way between hand-pushed lighters and loper-drawn carts that filled the paved street. Roto'mo's buzzed just overhead in the dead airspace between the solid avenue and

the first lane of airborne traffic. The polymer copters had to
duck down often to avoid the substantial draw of freight-haulers
that thundered in the deeper and slower lanes. Three roto'mo's
weaved by him, their pilots hanging upright beneath the short
rotor blades in flimsy webbing, toes dragging through the puddles before they bounced back up again. Garrand ducked his
head as the blades whumped-whumped past him. Lopers shied
away and a cart crashed sideways, spilling produce across the
ceracrete pavers. Fists brandished, the handler hurled invective
at the pilots who bobbed away. Garrand slowed his pace as he
closed in on the Performing Arts Center, studying the Shock
Troops who stood guard. How was he going to get inside?

The sickening steel-on-steel squeal of an airborne collision
grabbed his attention and as he looked up, he realized the question was going to answer itself. A staggered formation of two-
meter winged beetles dove at an angle through the upper levels
of traffic. Two hurka-boys, maneuvering to avoid the creatures,
clipped wings and spun wildly out of control, taking a twirl
with them in their fiery plunge. A massive cargo-hauler grazed
a trolli-barge, bounced along the steel plates and ploughed
into the side of a building in a deafening roar. The first dozen
Gambor wove through the airborne confusion and alighted on
the Greuk Center steps, meters away from the stunned Shock
Troops.

Garrand crouched behind a lighter, holding his breath.
There was a brief hallucinogenic moment as the adversaries
faced one another at point blank range, a moment of absolute
stillness where no weapon was raised. And then street erupted
in a flurry of energy discharges. Explosions crumpled the main
entrance to the building and more Gambor swept down from
above. Shock Troopers opened fire from the roof, blasting the

street below until they, too, were engaged by the next wave of Gambor. The giant beetles overwhelmed the first layer of defense, pushing their way into the Center.

Garrand didn't think twice. He sprinted across the street, bounded over the fallen combatants and into the building's foyer. The battle raged further down the lobby, but a single Trooper remained at the inner doors, guarding the hall with stalwart defiance. Garrand rolled to his right, evading the blaster fire that tracked behind him. He skidded behind a pillar and rose to one knee, clicking off four concussion grenades. He cupped the little spheres in his palm and flung them around the post at his assailant.

The explosion lifted the Trooper off his feet and blew the pair of doors inward. Garrand ran through the opening and into the hall proper. Heavy drumbeats filled the air.

He dashed down the central aisle toward the woman who was revolving backward in slow motion. Strange jars of light filled the audience on both sides of the aisle, the occupants within glowing with surreal, golden brilliance. He did not pause.

The drums plodded to a languid beat now, and he could hear the bells of Treichler Tower begin their ominous ringing. An explosion ripped through the hall and fragments from the glass ceiling showered down. A great flurry of wings beat through the fresh opening and blaster fire sputtered upward from Shock Troopers.

Gambor poured through the exposed ceiling as green bolts reached through the smoke, carving out new chunks of plaster and steel. Jars of light floated upward as the confused Luminaars got free of their tethers. Several exploded in gaseous welters of yellow flame.

Garrand took the final three steps in one great stride and dove onto the stage. Vailetta had floated back toward the velvet curtain as the firefight erupted and Garrand struggled to grasp her by the ankle. He caught her in a strong grip and pulled her down, struggling. She looked below but saw only shadows. "Torg?"

"No, it's me."

She saw a face glimmer in the explosions. "Médeville?"

"Turn that thing off, we've got to get you out of here."

She fumbled with the repulsor controls and then was suddenly her full weight once more, falling toward the stage. Garrand caught her and deposited her on her feet.

"Come on," he urged, pulling her behind the curtain.

Shock Troops, oblivious of the two humans, pushed past them and knelt on the stage, opening fire on the Gambor who were landing on the upper tiers. Thick smoke filled the hall, masking the combatants. The jars seemed to shimmer and shift as they tried to float out of the way.

"Where are we going?" she croaked, coughing through the smoke.

Garrand pulled her into a corridor, glanced back to make sure they were not being followed, and then pushed her roughly against the wall. She stared at him, eyes wide.

"Where are they?" he demanded.

"What?"

"The pandas, where are they!"

"You're mad," she struggled to get free of him.

"Of course I am."

"Let go of me."

"Don't change the subject," he pinned her more tightly.

"I thought you said we had to get out of here," she looked down the hall, pupils reflecting a glint of fire.

Garrand followed her eyes. The hall erupted in a shower of sparks and debris and a Shock Trooper stomped forward, weapon raised. Garrand shielded Vailetta's slender form and drew his weapon, thumb flicking on his shield. The trooper leapt toward them, landing in a two-footed firing stance.

The first bolt of energy slammed into his shield, sending him reeling. He lost hold of Vailetta and snapped his shield off, firing five shots at the trooper's helmet. The energy splashed harmlessly off the trooper's armored shoulder and faceplate. He knelt down and reactivated his shield.

Purple bolts of plasma washed down the hall from behind the Imperial soldier. The surprised trooper turned just as a harpoon lanced through his abdomen, piercing both front and backsides of the Trioxin suit. He fell, clutching the steel shaft. Two black-shelled beetles crept through the smoke, the first holding a massive thrower. The second took a long, barbed harpoon and shoved it roughly into the barrel of the first. The Gambor dipped their horns to the fallen Imperial and then fixed their eyes on Garrand.

Garrand stumbled backward down the side of the corridor, arms feeling behind him for Vailetta's form. "We gotta go, Strom." He reached futilely for her. The Gambor hopped over the trooper who blocked the floor, landing with a solid whump. "Let's go!" He turned his back on the approaching Gambor, preparing to run down the hall, and was hit squarely across the forehead with a steel pipe. He immediately lost consciousness and fell to the ground.

Vailetta dropped the heavy pipe and dashed quickly down the hall. She stopped in her dressing room and grabbed her clothes and weapon belt and hustled to the artist's entrance at the back of the building. Unlocked, the back door slid upward and she whispered a prayer of thanks as she escaped into the

back alley. Gulping down breaths of fresh air, she huddled behind a pile of rubbish, feet growing numb in the puddles. She
paused to clip her gun belt around her waist and stripped off
the flimsy costume. She discarded her shift and settled on trousers, boots and jacket.

She thumbed her comtab, drew her weapon, and stepped
cautiously down the alley toward the bustle of the main street,
heart pounding. A confused jumble of battle chatter filled her
ears. The Gambor and Shock Troops were fighting to a stand-
still inside the hall. She could hear sirens wailing in the distance and felt a muffled explosion shake the building from the
rooftop. The battle was spilling outside. She glimpsed a formation of Gambor glide over the alley, landing with a flurry of
wingbeats atop the Center.

She holstered her weapon and prepared to duck into the
throng of foot traffic that was trying to scatter in all directions
at once, but stopped. Communication from the comtab made
her face go white.

" —Reported traitor. Stop at all costs."

"Three more on the first balcony—"

" —Watch out!"

"Captain Strom?"

"Barlow—please confirm—"

" —Form a cordon in the east wing. Do not give ground."

" —Two and one. Stevens and Singh flanking position. The
rest of you watch your ass!"

" —Repeat please. I say again, please repeat last order."

"Do not allow Strom to leave the building. She is under arrest."

"Under whose authority?"

"Commander Arnas has given a direct order. Do not allow
Strom—"

"—Three left, one above, one to the right. Get that burner up here—"

"She's gone over—stop her!"

"Repeat please—"

"Commander Arnas ordered—"

"—More landing on the roof... can't hold—"

"—Back to the first balcony. Reinforcements coming from—"

"—Himself. Stop Captain Strom."

"Reaves, Donner, down! Repeat, two men down—"

"—Last seen leaving with Médeville."

"—Losing you... Say again—"

"—Emperor's daughter. She's gone over... stop her at all costs—"

Vailetta's chest felt hollow; she tried to catch her breath. *What had happened? She was under arrest? How did they know? Had Torg betrayed her?* Her lips seemed to be burning in accusation. She wiped the poison off on her rough sleeve and leaned over, spitting into the puddles until she wretched.

A TERRIBLE RINGING filled his head. Garrand blinked with some difficulty. Painful, purple splotches filled his vision. He touched his forehead and felt a sticky warmth. He rubbed the blood between his thumb and forefinger and sat upright.

Two large shadows loomed over him. An earthy stench filled his nose, almost like rotten apples. He winced and tried to focus. The large, scabrous form of a Gambor hove into view. A surge of adrenaline swept him into a painful spasm of coughs. It was too late to fight, and he was in no position to flee— sitting on his ass, blind-sided by the woman he had come to rescue.

"Rest easy, human," a voice crackled.

He blinked up at the giant beetle, fully expecting a barbed harpoon to gouge him any moment.

"He is all right?" the second beetle rasped. "Help him up."

"Give him a moment," Ka'vaelus crackled.

"What's this?" Garrand asked.

"You have suffered a blow," the Gambor said. He dabbed the man's head with moss, soaking up the blood.

Garrand pushed away the foul-smelling substance. "What are you doing?"

"Trying to help you," Ka'vaelus replied, resuming his attention on the wound.

"He is stubborn like you, Ka," the second chortled.

"Most," Ka'vaelus agreed.

"Where is she?" Garrand asked, looking around.

"The female? She fled that way," the Gambor indicated the rear of the hall.

"How long have I been out?"

"A few moments. Perhaps a minute."

"She's almost naked. She couldn't have gotten far," he muttered.

"The Imperials seek her now, as well."

"Help me up," Garrand grumbled, not quite sure what was happening. He had seen the Gambor dispatch the Shock Trooper, but had thought the soldier had merely stood in the way of their true target: him.

Ka'vaelus offered the human a pincer. Garrand grabbed onto it and let himself be hoisted upright. His head was clearing rapidly. "Why—" he began.

"Director Darstin sent us. We are at your disposal."

"Darstin," Garrand sneered. "He wants me dead."

"No longer," Ka'vaelus said plainly. "We are here to help you."

"You?" Garrand drew his blaster and popped the coil out, letting it hit the floor. He slapped a fresh one in. "You wanted me dead, too."

"Priorities change."

Garrand holstered the blaster and glanced at the satchel that hung from the beetle's belt. "I was not gentle with your brothers above Eemon."

The two Gambor glanced at one another and the first let loose a long, weary breath. "It is true, we have many trees to plant when we return to Galzeki. Our enemies, however, are now the same."

"Very well…" Garrand said slowly, "but you will not be planting one in my memory."

"Your blood will not bring back what I've lost, human."

"Nothing will," he said as he started down the corridor.

Ka'vaelus sized the much smaller creature with a careful stare. It was true he had the Director's same fierce eyes, but they were encased in a much more vigorous shell. He might actually have grown to like this one, one day… "What do you want us to do, Médeville?"

"Slow down the Shock Troops," he yelled. "I have a woman to catch."

5

THE THIEF OF SHIPS

SHOCKWAVES, LIKE PEALS OF DISTANT THUNDER, RATTLED through the narrow corridor as Garrand hastened away from the Gambor. He dashed out the backstage door and was greeted with a terrible wail from the Greuk Center Plaza. It sounded like Cerbak had opened the gates to K'ye. The narrow alley behind the Center funneled and amplified the disjointed screams into a harrowing din, forcing Garrand to slow and listen. He stood in a rank puddle trying to assimilate the agonizing clamor. The sounds were unbearable. Shrieks of the past surged through his head—complete with long-buried images of his men in the Guard, things he had tried vainly to forget. He screwed his eyes tightly shut as the wailing rose, but could not shake one persistent image. A young man lay in his arms at Cheqlund Varz, half-eaten, coughing up blood on his dark blazer. The youth looked to his eyes for hope, for release from the pain. Garrand pressed his hands over the soldier's ragged wound but blood continued to gurgle out between his fingers. There was nothing he could do. He covered his eyes and felt the youth's sticky warmth on his temple. The insufferable memory welled up like chum bobbing in the waters of his mind. Screams of past and present echoed down the alley, drowning out hope. The plaza had become purgatory.

He forced his legs to move, willing himself forward. His limbs felt heavy and stiff but they obeyed. He fought against the torpor of the past, taking quick, shallow breaths. The stench brought him back—the overwhelming smell of dung and rubbish told him that this was New Haivello, this was the present. The Thief of Ships was getting away—she was out there in the screams. Loping through the alley Garrand felt explosions rippling up through his calves and in his joints. Dark shapes swooped past the entrance ahead, zips and roto'mo's bobbing over the crush of pedestrians. There were no dragons here—this was a different fight. He skidded to the mouth of the alley and was met with a bloody spectacle, the visual counterpart to the awful screams of the panicked crowd.

Carnage rained down into the plaza. Bodies lay strewn beneath the clock tower and all along the street. Injured Gambor pulled themselves futilely toward cratered holes in the ceracrete, bits of seared wing trailing behind them. The facades of the surrounding buildings were blackened and many were burning. Hastily erected armor drips protected pockets of Imperial soldiers. The Troopers fired up into the fog at assailants invisible to the naked eye. Hundreds of tracers arced away from entrenched positions along the street and atop low buildings; it seemed impossible that anything could survive in the torrent of devastation. Yet purple bolts of return fire stretched down from the clouds like the lightning-wrath of some dark god. Flurries of Gambor swept down under the mist, their wings whistling through the air. They dropped satchels of bomblets and anti-personnel charges over the Shock Troops and then wheeled away, disappearing back into the clouds.

Garrand searched the street. A killing field had cleared in the center of the plaza but all the streets leading away from the battle were filled with an impenetrable crush of traffic that scrambled to escape the worst of the fighting. There was no way to pick her out of the horde; he would have to get away from the Center first. He pushed his way into the throng and tried to angle north toward the larger streets. There were more options there, more transportation; that's where Strom would head.

The crowd jostled him sideways and he found himself in the path of a dozen Tuir'mi — not a good place to be. He kept pace ahead of the hairy creatures trying to elbow his way into the people ahead of him, but the crowd kept pushing him back. Three meters tall, the Tuir'mi were doing a good job clearing a path for themselves through the street. Their bony knees were knocking him in the back of the head with each broad step. He was going to get crushed if he didn't get out of the way. He glanced back over his shoulder at the long-limbed, brown-eyed creature — they were slender and delicate looking, despite their enormous size. Garrand wondered if the Migontus looked anything like this; Archiva was built to the Tuir'mi's scale, they might have appreciated it. A tangle of feet tripped him up and he fell hard to the pavement. He tried to scramble away from the giant feet but it was too late; footfalls stomped all around him and he looked up in panic. He was directly in the path of one Tuir'mi who lurched toward him, shoulder to shoulder with his mates.

Garrand cringed and shielded his head just as a long-taloned paw scooped him up out of the way. He felt his ribs squeezed as he was lifted clear. A neighboring Tuir'mi had him around the waist. The pressure eased as the creature gauged his mass. Garrand stared into the creature's soft, brown eyes as he swung from its grasp. He was carried along for a few teeth-rattling strides before the Tuir'mi hoisted him over its head and with a shove, flipped him up onto a cargo lighter that was hovering past. Garrand landed on his hands and knees like a frightened cat, heart thudding furiously. He looked back over the edge of the cargo pallets and watched his hairy savior push on through the crowd.

The flatbed lighter suddenly seemed like a very safe place — particularly since the driver had not yet noticed his presence. With a happy sigh, Garrand rolled over on his back and let the mist fall on his face. The moisture made the sooty fog seem slightly less oppressive. The curling grey tendrils looked innocuous enough; they might just be clouds of moisture, water droplets clinging to particles of dust — not an ever-present smog filled with toxins that etched the buildings yellow and brown. Clouds of exhaust, methane and carbon monoxide sat in the lower levels of the old city. The haze obscured the upper reaches of the rusted pillars that arched over the avenue. Only the bottom half of the curving spans could be seen in the mist. The giant steel buttresses dwarfed the surrounding buildings — the 'old city' that had been in place for centuries — rising up into the clouds to support the foundations of the much newer mega-towers that stretched kilometers above.

The new buildings couldn't start at the old street-level — the toxic clouds would eat right through their glazings and soft cerasteel panels. Instead, giant iron girders twice as thick as moken oaks bent up from every corner to support the raised foundations. Spans the length of entire city blocks curved up to meet other spans in a giant interlocking framework built over and around the existing city structures like the pilings of a mammoth pier rising over a crumbling sand castle. Most of the rusted trusses rose for a hundred meters before the buildings started proper. The first floors were above the haze of pollution that skulked about the older city levels fed by the constant stream of traffic and industry and trapped by the buildings that surrounded it.

Sunlight did reach down into the morass on occasion when the winds combined just so, but it was more like an unwanted intrusion than a respite from the shadows—a bright disruption that made the peddlers and workers squint and hustle away. Garrand stared into the mist, waiting for such a moment, a break in the clouds, but all he could see was grey nothingness.

"Gi-bi gi-bi boe! N'a all'ck la gi-bi boe!"

Garrand propped himself up on an elbow and saw that he'd been spotted. The yellow-skinned driver yelled at him in an unfamiliar dialect, waving several arms at his new passenger in obvious anger. The popping clucks sounded a little like Gaibit. Garrand dismissed him with a wave and looked away; he wasn't about to jump back down in that crowd yet. And what was the driver going to do anyway? He had to steer.

Out of immediate danger, he began scanning the street and first layers of airborne traffic for Strom. He couldn't lose her now. This was the only place he knew where she'd be. If he lost her they'd have to start all over again at the Archives and by then it would be too late for the pandas. The dream of the Thief dangling by a thread must come to pass; and he had to be there to rescue her—and press her into their cause.

He tapped his comtab: "Bailey, you listening to this mess?"

"Captain," the art sounded profoundly relieved. "It's good to hear your voice. Did you get her?"

"No—she's going to take a little convincing." He dabbed at his sticky forehead. "You tapped into the lines of communication?"

"Yes sir. *Destiny* and I are monitoring 200 channels above the standard—"

"No, no—that's all chatter. Filter out the non-essential mercantiles and get down to the encrypted Imperial lines." The driver now brandished an impact pistol and was screaming even louder at his unwanted hitchhiker. "Yeah, yeah," Garrand muttered as he glanced over the edge of the lighter, looking for a soft spot to land.

"We're way ahead of you, Captain. *Destiny* pinpointed three channels of Imperial battle code. Listening as we speak."

The driver fired a warning shot over the interloper's head to hurry him along. Garrand crouched at the back of the lighter, took a deep breath and leapt off. He landed spread-eagle on his back in a loper-drawn cart of gütten tomatoes. The vegetables felt warm and squishy under his head. "You're into the battle coms?" he asked happily. "How'd you hack the ciphers already?"

"They're using standard Trioxin encryption equipment— forgot we have a couple ourselves."

Garrand grinned and fended off the thin reed the jabbering peddler tried to beat him with. He clambered out of the cart, pieces of green tomato clinging to his trousers.

"Ei trai goet wuuhi ei diih uusa!"

"What's that?" Bailey asked.

"Nothing," he tried to pat the little man on the shoulders but the peddler kept hitting him with the insubstantial reed. Garrand pressed a handful of quantis at the man, but ended up dropping them all over the street. "I lost Strom in the confusion down here. Any mention of her over the com?"

"Actually quite a bit. There's buzz about her—"

"Good!" Garrand yelled trying to slide past two grimy lighters that smelled like they were carrying dung. He got wedged in between and had to drop down to the puddles. He looked underneath the lighter; the repulsor waves rippled like heat rising off the pavers. Tucking his elbows in he rolled quickly underneath, the repulsors buffeting his face, pressing him down like giant, misshapen hands. He popped up on the other side. "Say again. What buzz?"

"All three channels are filled with it."

"Bailey, I couldn't hear you—say again!"

"The Shock Troops are pursuing her, Captain."

"What!"

"Captain Strom has been identified as Royalty."

"Identified how?" He tilted his neck, pressing his ear to his collar to hear. Traffic was fanning out to normal levels here, but there was still an annoying din.

"That's the buzz, Captain."

"Royalty, what do you mean 'royalty?'"

"Someone tagged her as the Emperor's daughter."

Garrand cursed loudly. "So much for just sneaking up and grabbing her."

"She's to be arrested."

"No doubt." He stopped and looked up through the red girders that arched up over a decaying apartment building. Strom would want up out of this mess; he had to get higher. "Bailey, you've got to help me get to her before they do."

"Last report has her sighted above the commons headed for the magrail terminus. Half kilometer northwest of the Greuk Center and one kilometer above your position."

Garrand tilted his head back and looked up at the rusted trusses that swept up into the shadows. "What of the Gambor?"

"Still heavy fighting around the Greuk Center. Most of the Shock Troops are pinned down for the moment."

"Good."

"But some have been able to pull out. They've been sent after Strom."

"What about me?"

"Standing orders—shoot to kill. There have been no sightings of you, though."

Garrand ran through the crowd, twisting and turning to avoid carts, lighters and slow-moving creatures. "Don't rely on that though, Captain. Though know they'll find you if they find her."

"Gotcha Bailey. What about Helen?"

"No transmissions concerning Miss Tchelakov as of yet."

"Keep looking." He spotted a pair of suspensor tubes rising up the side of a building, blackened with soot and smeared with bird droppings. He followed them up with his eyes— they disappeared into the girders. A man stood behind a small podium at the base of the tubes. Glowing letters flashed behind a velvet rope partition, advertising the lift.

Garrand hustled across the street. "How much for a one-way ticket?" he asked the man with the frayed, yellow jacket.

The old man tapped the sign on his dirty cap: "5 Q Up—1 Q Down."

"A little pricey, don't you think?" He fumbled in his blazer for quantis.

The ticket-taker stared across the street. "You're welcome to stay down 'ere. There's plenty of pleasures to be found in the ol' city proper."

"I've seen 'em already," Garrand muttered.

"Going up in the world, are ya boy?"

"Yeah, straight to the top," he quipped, giving the man a wry grin. "Got a date with destiny."

The ticket-taker observed his bloody wound and made a face. "You'd better freshen up, boy. She'll send ya right back down." He accepted the coins, handed him a green paper ticket and unhooked the velvet rope.

"I'm not comin' back," he said as he stepped into the suspensor field.

"That's what they all say…" He replaced the rope and stepped back to his little podium, staring blankly across the street.

THE MAGRAIL TERMINUS was four blocks square, nearly a kilometer in every direction, supported by giant iron trusses almost ninety meters above street-level. This was the beginning of the modern city—ground level so to speak. On all side of the terminus, magnificent silver and red towers stretched up into the clouds. Flyers and twirls, wings painted purple and gold, soared between the smooth canyon walls. There was a stiff wind and no malodorous stench at this height. The terminus was the only flat expanse in sight; two or three buildings rose up through the giant pavers, but most of the surface was smooth and uninterrupted by vertical intrusions.

Horizontal traffic was another matter altogether. Dozens of magrail lines swept into the piazza like a hundred threads being woven into fabric. Blunt-nosed trains raced over elevated magnetic rails, sliding into stations stacked one atop another like the shuttles of a tremendous loom.

Raised platforms accepted the transfer of thousands of passengers. Creatures spilled down the sweeping stairs onto the main terminus, heading for other carriages or the suspensor tubes or the line of twirls and hurka-boys which picked up fares and spun over the edge of the plaza back down into the old city or up into the heights of the silver towers.

Garrand popped out of the suspensor tube and walked out onto the piazza. At this height, the sun was out and the last of the haze was being burned away by the primary's warmth. The terminus was like a magnificent toy set spread out as far as the eye could see. It was strange being able to see so far in one direction without the intrusion of buildings.

He heard a familiar whine and craned his neck to watch a formation of Shock Troops as they rocketed overhead on their jump jets.

"What's the word, Bailey?"

"Confirmed sighting on north side of terminus," the art told him. "Two squads on their way to loading platform E-12."

Garrand started running along the Shock Troops' heading. "How far?"

He waited while the artificial consulted his sartographic projection of the city and analyzed the captain's locator signal.

"200 meters. Third set of stairs—make sure you take the *eastbound* platform."

Garrand passed beneath a magrail line as a bright green train hissed overhead, carriages jostling around the curve. He could see the stairs ahead of him, mostly empty. The Shock Troops thundered down on the platform on pillars of flame as the magrail train braked into the station. Garrand took the steps three at a time, drawing his blaster as he ran.

"They've seen her," Bailey barked in his ear. "Spreading out to flanking positions."

"Where?" He'd reached the top of the stairs and struggled to look through the unconcerned crowd. Passengers were pushing out of the train now, adding to the confusion.

"Head of the train."

Garrand shouldered past the debarking passengers, blaster held overhead. He was three carriages from the front of the train when he saw her—long black hair, dark blazer buttoned halfway up her chest. She was pressing her way onto the train.

An amplified voice rang across the platform: "Vailetta Strom, you are under arrest!" Curious passengers slowed to look at the line of Shock Troopers who were shoving their way toward the front of the train. "Captain Strom, stop where you are," the voice mandated. "Do not attempt to escape. Do not draw your weapon."

A panicked murmur rose over the scrape of footsteps as passengers scrambled to get out of the soldiers' way. The Troopers formed a firing line in the clearing parallel to the train and Vailetta froze, just meters away from the open carriage door.

Garrand clicked off four grenades into his palm and hurled them across the platform. "Don't stop!" he yelled as he broke through the crowd of onlookers. He knelt, steadied his blaster with two hands and opened fire on the nearest trooper. The grenades skipped and rolled over the slick ceracrete. Three hit Trioxin feet, erupting in a welter of fire and armor. Garrand had a flanking position and only the first two Troopers could bring their weapons to bear. He dropped both with carefully placed shots aimed at their weak hip sockets. Vailetta ducked into the first car as the line broke into confusion.

Hydraulic doors hissed in unison beside him and began to squeeze shut. Garrand rose and sprinted for the nearest carriage. Trioxin sensors pinpointed the source of his fire, and bolts of energy began lacing toward him, glancing off the side of the train. He dove through the twin doors as the first fusillade of coordinated energy smacked into the carriage. The barrage rocked the carriage as he lay on the floor. The train lurched, the brakes released and the slender transport slid away from the platform. He got up and looked out the fractured glazing as the train curved away from the platform. The remaining Shock Troops had taken to the air after them, but were quickly losing ground to the magrail's rapid acceleration.

"—Captain. Please respond," his comtab was saying. Terrified people were staring at him from crouched positions beside carriage benches. "Captain please come in."

"I'm here, Bailey."

"Thank Haven, where are you?"

"Onboard the train. Vailetta is two cars ahead of me. She can't get off. I think I've got her."

"Understood."

"How long till the next stop?"

"One moment—*Destiny's* trying to access timetables. Not long by the looks of it; a minute perhaps." Garrand walked to the first partition door, which slid dutifully aside. He proceeded quickly down the aisle. "Here it is. You're on an express—you skip one station and stop at the next. ETA, fifty-seven seconds."

The second door parted and he stepped into the lead car. The benches were nearly empty; he put his weapon away and stepped cautiously forward, looking under each row of seats as he progressed. He was halfway down the length when Vailetta stepped out at the head of the car.

Garrand held up his palms. "I'm not here to hurt you. You have to come with me."

She studied him for a moment and pursed her lips. "I don't think so."

"It's important. I need your help." He took a step forward and she backpedaled, keeping distance. "You have to help me rescue the pandas. It's your destiny." He stopped; her back was against the emergency door at the front of the train. She stared at him strangely, smiling with wan bemusement. She didn't look frightened or trapped, and, as it turned out, she wasn't.

She turned and mashed the emergency lever. A klaxon sounded and the door opened. Wind whipped through the carriage.

"Wait!" Garrand cried running forward.

Vailetta braced her feet in the doorway, grasped the upper edge of the carriage and did a coordinated pull-up. In one smooth move she vaulted feet-first onto the roof. The train lurched slightly as it approached the first station, slowing automatically.

Garrand stopped, unsure if he could duplicate her acrobatic feat. Footsteps rang overhead as she ran down the length of the train. "Cheplus." He started back the way he had come, following the heavy footfalls. The station was approaching fast—*she wouldn't jump would she?* He sprinted through two carriages, then another. He'd lost the sound of her progress and moved to a side bench, pressing his face against the glazing.

The train had slowed to no more than thirty kilometers per hour as it passed through the station. Sure enough, a dark shape leapt off the roof and landed atop a thick knot of waiting passengers.

Garrand stepped back and looked at the closed doors. This was awful. He drew his blaster and opened fire on the access panel to the side of the door. The thin aluminum blew open, the hydraulic chamber ruptured and the twin doors hissed open. Ceracrete rushed past, millimeters away. Back down the platform confused passengers started to help Vailetta up. Garrand glanced forward: the front end of the station was coming up quick. He gritted his teeth and dove out the door, tucking his head into his chest and cradling his unprotected skull with his elbows. His blaster clattered away as he rolled, knees and elbows screaming with pain. Friction tore at his clothing, his light body armor all that kept his skin from being torn off the bone as he tumbled end over end. He skidded to a halt a meter from the edge of the platform and watched the train slide into the distance.

He got up awkwardly, a little surprised to find that his knees still accepted the weight of his body, and stared down the platform. Bent at the waist and panting, Vailetta was watching him from the center of a little group of concerned onlookers. Chin against his chest, he glowered at her and straightened his back with a series of crinkling pops. She caught the emotion behind his gaze and began backing away, brushing off helping hands and offers of assistance. Garrand rubbed his elbow. The body armor was gouged and rough but it had not been penetrated.

Vailetta turned and began running as he started forward. He winced as he tried to run, bones protesting his tumble. They were on a single station, a ceracrete slab cantilevered a hundred meters up the side of a building. The back edge of the platform held a pair of hurka-boys and an automated rack of roto'mo's. The first driver accepted a paying fare and lifted away from the station, the fat dragonfly craft hovering briefly before dipping out of sight. Vailetta rushed up to the driver of the second hurka-boy and drew her Cresbourin blaster.

Garrand loped after her as quickly as he could, knees beginning to feel a little more fluid. But he was too late. The driver had climbed out of the hurka-boy's front seat and stood staring down the barrel of her blaster as she clambered into the flight harness.

"Stop!" Garrand yelled, waving his arm futilely. Vailetta gunned the small reactor, adjusted the sweep of the flyer's thin wings and sloughed the small craft sideways with ungainly haste. The hurka-boy hung in the air for a split second as Vailetta looked sideways at him, hair swirling into her eyes. "Stop," he repeated, but she just laughed and the flyer banked steeply away.

"She ain't takin' any passengers, buddy," the driver said with disgust. The exhaust glowed red as she accelerated away.

Garrand pulled up at the edge of the platform and stared after her in frustration. *What was he going to have to do, shoot her?* He looked at the hapless driver. "How often do flyers land here?"

The man shrugged. "I usually time it to the trains. Next one's not for five minutes."

Garrand glanced dubiously at the line of roto'mo's suspended from a long steel rail that was once painted bright yellow. "Rent-a-Mo" was printed in large green letters along the length of the loader. He hesitated for a moment: a roto'mo was not a substantial craft. "Powered umbrellas" they were called, and the description was apt. They dangled from the long rack like lion cubs hanging beneath a mother's jaw. What choice did he have? He pushed past the driver.

"You're taking one of those?" the driver laughed raucously. "You might as well just jump off and flap your arms."

Garrand stepped up to rent one, ignoring the driver. He deposited a credit chit into the reader and the next roto'mo slid forward with a clank.

"This ain't like buzzin' over the commons," the man continued. "Got *winds* up here. Feels like a jetstream between those buildings."

The roto'mo loaded itself into position, hanging from the server arm. Garrand surveyed the craft. It had a small turbine engine — no larger than a man's chest — with a four-bladed rotor that provided lift. A harness dangled beneath the turbine for the pilot with a thin, brightly painted tail sweeping from the back of the turbine acting as a stabilizer. Twin handlebars hung beneath the blades. Positioned just above shoulder height, they contained the accelerator, collective and rotor pitch controls. Exhaust nozzles positioned along the stabilizer kept the craft pointed in one direction; shifts in the pilot's harness along with tugs on the handlebars provided directional control.

A small screen lit up on the side of the turbine and Garrand punched in his mass as the turbine whined to life. He stepped into the suspended webbing, snapping the straps around his chest, waist and crotch.

"Don't overcompensate or you'll end up in the side of a building," the driver yelled over the squeal. Garrand nodded at him, pulling on the smudged goggles that hung from the handlebars. He glanced over the edge of the platform and experienced a terrible wave of vertigo. Tiny dark shapes bolted back and forth in the gathering darkness, little glowing lights winking through the twilight. Vailetta's flyer was a pale dot of exhaust.

"I hope she's worth it, buddy," the driver slapped him on the shoulder and ducked out of the way. Garrand gave him a pale grin and thumbed the power contact. The meter-long blades started thwacking around just over his head. He revved the engine, adjusted the pitch of the blades and eased the craft off the loading arm. Letting his feet drag along the ground for a couple of meters he tried to get a feel for the hovering controls.

It was now early evening and the primary was a low red orb behind the silver towers, disappearing slowly into the smog. In the distance he could see a formation of Shock Troops rocketing over the magrail line, closing in on the station. Without further thought, he gunned the turbine and spiraled up into the air. The roto'mo was surprisingly responsive. He eased back on the collective, dipped his shoulder and tugged on the handlebar. The craft dipped beneath the platform and curved under the magrail line.

The winds hit him full force as he got away from the protective cover of the building. The little roto'mo bucked and heaved in the shifting currents. He could see Vailetta's hurka-boy well below, darting under and around the giant steel buttresses. Needing to pick up speed, he feathered the rotors and allowed the craft to sink. The roto'mo had little trouble complying—he sank like a stone, plummeting through two lanes of opposing traffic before he spotted the airborne lane markers affixed to the sides of the nearest tower. Twirls and flyers banked past him, flying at tremendous speeds through their air lanes. Collision lights flashed in his eyes as an orange-striped twirl narrowly avoided him.

He let the roto'mo pick up velocity before increasing the pitch of the rotors that chopped through the air; his rate of descent slowed but he kept his forward momentum. He opened up the nozzles along the tail and let the exhaust help push him along.

He caught a glint of phosphorescence on Vailetta's gossamer wings as her hurka-boy dipped under a supporting truss and then began to arc up higher into the city. The craft had short, delicate-looking wings and a stout, round-nosed frame, like a stubby cigarillo. The hurka-boy could accommodate two riders, who straddled the front of the frame one in front of the other. A neat little reactor powered the setup and four adjustable exhaust nacelles gave the pilot both directional and vertical control. Vailetta had her craft pushed full out and the purple wings shimmered in the last fading rays of light, a vapor trail curving behind her in the smog.

Garrand went thumping after her, feet dangling below the webbing in a rather frightening manner. He glanced over his shoulder past the stabilizer that jut out behind him like a colorful plume. The Shock Troops had picked up the trail and were spreading out between the buildings. To his amazement, he could see Gambor rising through the twilight haze as well. They bobbed along beneath the Troopers, wings beating heavily to match their quarry's rate of climb.

The roto'mo climbed up through the clouds, turbine whining as it tried to keep pace with the hurka-boy. He popped up above the chronic layer of smog to find Vailetta curling higher still. He wove around the towers as he followed her, trying to shake the Shock Troops who trailed below. The buildings were greenish-grey and silver at this altitude, with fragile-looking flyer pads jutting out from their sides. Lacy elevated bridges connected the buildings between the air lanes and fat trollibarges plowed along at various heights, their decks filled with hundreds of passengers.

Vailetta had leveled off and was streaking along one air lane. Pushed along by a substantial tail wind, Garrand swooped in behind her as the first beams of plasma fire began to lance past his shoulder. He hazarded a glance back and was dismayed to find a platoon of Shock Troops in staggered formation right on top of him. Muzzles flashed from half a dozen weapons. He hauled on the handlebar and threw his weight sideways. The rotors dipped and he swung toward the edge of the nearest building. Tracking bolts of plasma thudded dully into the cerasteel as he banked around the corner, spiraling upward as quickly as the thwacking rotors would allow.

Vailetta was no longer taking a straight shot through the canyons, opting to curve up and around the towers. She was forty meters above him now and across the air lane. He watched her reflection sparkle in the glazings as she streaked past the smooth-faced tower.

Garrand kept his roto'mo pressed up close to the glazings on his side of the avenue as the Shock Troops rocketed around the smoking corner of the building. They were closing distance fast. The Trioxin suits would have little trouble working out a firing solution for him unless he did something drastic. The air lane was sparsely filled at this height—some fast-moving twirls and flyers, not much help. The far edge of the tower was coming up quickly. Just as he was prepared to duck around the corner once more, a broad round shape hove into view—the great open bow of a trolli-barge moving perpendicular to his course. Garrand was almost level with the bottom of its hull; he could see passengers standing along the bow railing well overhead, admiring the hazy sunset.

Red bolts of energy snapped beneath his feet, smacking into the black-bronze hull of the barge as its full length began coasting past. The next shot hit him square between the shoulder blades, piercing the turbine's outer casing. Garrand could smell the hot friction of gears melting and he glanced back to see thick, oily smoke trailing behind. The turbine only had a few more seconds of life left before it seized up. His death plunge would be spectacular.

Garrand twisted the accelerator and yanked hard on the collective; the turbine screamed in protest, but the roto'mo darted up the side of the barge. His feet just cleared the railing as another beam slammed into his back. He eased back on the controls and landed with a grunt on the deck. The turbine was enormously heavy on his back and the new momentum of the barge caused him to topple over. He landed sideways on the wooden deck, rotors splintering away. The broken nubs continued to thrash the deck as Garrand struggled out of the harness. He slipped free from the webbing and dove for cover as the first Shock Troopers screamed up over the railing. Terrified passengers ran for the open-air cabin as the Imperial soldiers opened fire.

Garrand skidded around a steel masthead supporting the retractable roof and sat down to catch his breath, back flat against the brace. He was midway between the two railings, in the center of the observation deck. He drew his blaster, reached around the steel support and fired five shots before he stuck his head round and saw seven Troopers with three more landing. Terrible odds. He ducked back to cover and popped the coil out of his blaster. He slapped a fresh charge in and set the weapon on the deck. He split the nearly spent wheel of concussion grenades off the feeder and retrieved a fresh wheel from the back of his belt. The new magazine snapped into place.

He took a deep breath and squinted up into the clouds. A rosy pall reflected off the bottom half of each cloud that floated past. The glazed towers shimmered with a spectral glow and Garrand could see a hurka-boy flickering upward. He was moving horizontally now and she was still climbing. Blaster fire sparked past, tearing into the wooden deck beside him. He felt three bolts pang into the steel support. The Shock Troops were advancing on his position; they would have him flanked momentarily. He looked at the far railing—what was he going to do, jump over the edge? Suddenly the hurka driver's suggestion of flapping his arms didn't sound so far-fetched. The main cabin was fifteen meters away; he would be dead before he made it halfway.

He recited the dream song in his head, wishing he and Sid had come up with more details of his encounter with the Thief of Ships. Another burst of blaster fire shattered into his mast. Energy stabbed past from multiple angles—the soldiers were moving in on both sides. There was nothing to do now but turn and fight; he clicked off three grenades and prepared to roll over on his belly and face the Troopers when a stir of motion beyond the far rail caught his attention. Dark shapes hovered just past the trolli's rail, long-barreled blast cannons spewing purple bolts of energy back at the Imperial soldiers. He watched four Gambor land on the deck on thick, sinewy limbs while hovering mates provided cover fire. Five more landed with graceful precision, burners sweeping flame across the deck. Harpoons lanced across the gap, twanging into the steel on the far side of the deck.

The Shock Troops were forced to drop back from the sudden onslaught. Return fire was sparse and ineffective. The Gambor stomped forward, taking up firing positions along the deck as more landed. The Imperials were pushed back toward the stern and some leapt over the rail to escape the counter-offensive.

Garrand watched in amazement as a single black-shelled warrior dropped the barrel of his harpoon thrower and stomped across to the cracked and smoldering masthead. The beetle stooped down over Garrand and clicked roughly, "You are falling behind, human."

He offered a claw down. To the beetle's satisfaction, the man accepted the assistance without hesitation, placing his slim digits between his sharp pincers. The Gambor hoisted Garrand to his feet.

"I don't have wings on my back," he replied gruffly.

The Gambor laughed coarsely. "You do well in spite of your considerable shortcomings."

Garrand peered up at the Gambor. "Is that a challenge?"

"Grk tch'luahn qu dabbot," the creature bowed. "Formidable indeed."

Garrand looked past the Gambor at the slow, purpling sky. He could not see Vailetta. "Any idea how I'm going to get up there?"

The beetle clicked reflectively. "What is your mass?"

"90 kilos."

"Tcht. Too much."

Garrand walked to the railing and peered over. A cantilevered flyerpad was about to slip beneath them twenty meters below, its length filled with hurka-boys.

"Drop that thrower and come here," Garrand said. The Gambor stomped over and looked down. "Grab me under my armpits."

"You weigh too much."

"Too much for you to lift, but not too much for you to slow down."

"What?"

"If I jump off from this height, I'll shatter my legs. But with you beating your wings we should make a controlled descent." The beetle clicked obscenely. "Do it!" Garrand ordered.

"Turn around," the Gambor dropped its weapon and reached under the human's arms, lifting him to the railing. With a grunt he hopped over the rail and beat his wings furiously, straining to gain lift. The man was like a dead weight in his pincers. The platform came up fast and he resisted the natural urge to drop the human and flutter skyward.

They hit the deck hard—the human was wrenched from his grasp by the force of impact and fell face-flat. He peeled the pink creature over on its back like a wet leaf stuck to a stone.

"Are you alive?"

"Nice landing," Garrand coughed.

"Anything broken?"

"Does my face count?"

The beetle hauled him upright. "Get another whirly and I will lead you up. We have two warriors following the female."

Garrand looked quickly around. Two elevated bridges were connected to the platform, and a long line of hurka-boys awaited passengers at the front edge of the station. There was another automated "Rent-a-Mo" full of "whirlies" at one edge of the platform, but he balked at that suggestion. There was no way he was going to strap another one of those to his back. Garrand ran toward the line of flyers—passengers were two-dozen deep waiting for their turn to hire a driver. He skipped past the long line of passengers and went to the rear of the queue where drivers were discharging their current fares. A new hurka-boy swept down onto the platform and Garrand rushed forward before the driver could react. He pushed his blaster up under the man's chin and pulled off his old-fashioned leather helmet.

"Out," he ordered.

The man complied and Garrand clambered up onto the squat fuselage. He snapped the flight harness into place and gave the driver a sharp salute as he banked the craft steeply away. He circled over the barge until he saw a Gambor rising up toward him, wings straining with exertion. The beetle hovered briefly beside him and then lit off the way Vailetta had gone, rising in the stiff wind.

Garrand took up formation abreast the giant beetle. The darkened city spread out beneath him, lights just beginning to illuminate the gathering dusk. A series of elevated bridges and cantilevered flyer pads masked the true height of his vantage, but clouds floated below as well as above. Garrand searched the sky ahead and found the woman. The Thief glided gently over a far-up landing pad, soaring on her gossamer wings. Her raven hair rippled behind like an unkempt mane.

He had seen this before, in a dream with Sid. It had been more vivid than life. And here he was, racing through a future he had foreseen. The implications were staggering.

Apparently, not all the Shock Troops had broken off their pursuit, for a dozen or more were chasing Vailetta around a magnificent spire at the very top of one of the towers. Having run out of places to hide, she guided the hurka-boy in dizzying loops around the gigantic steel struts, trading shots with the soldiers who attempted to hem her in.

She was fighting a losing battle—the Shock Troops had numbers on their side. To make matters worse, Garrand spied a thin plume of smoke curling behind her exhaust. Several of the Troopers had landed on the spire's supportive struts and hung from the steel beams with one arm while they took potshots at the hurka-boy. The rest of the soldiers swarmed around her on jump jets, herding her back toward the spire.

Garrand slammed the reactor to full power, accelerating past the Gambor. He drew his weapon, switched it to his left hand and tried to line up a straight-armed shot at the nearest soldier. His first salvo exploded harmlessly around the steel girder as he swept past the spire. The hurka-boy banked steeply and swung around for another pass. This time he was able to compensate for his bumpy approach and his fusillade found its mark. The trooper tumbled off the spire.

He pulled the craft up short, redirecting the exhaust straight down and fired point-blank at another trooper. It took eight shots to rupture the Trioxin armor, but the man finally fell. He was now an easy target himself, and blaster fire spanked the side of his craft until he cut the reactor and let the hurka-boy

free-fall for a hundred meters before hauling back on the yoke.
The wings bit into the air and he made a gentle parabolic arc,
re-igniting the engine and roaring back skyward.

A half-dozen Gambor had joined the fray and energy criss-
crossed around the silver spire. Garrand was moving up beneath Vailetta's craft to survey the damage when a beam pierced
its thin skin and silenced her reactor for good. The explosion
nearly tore off her right wing and sent the craft spinning toward the nearest building. Garrand could see Vailetta fighting
to exert some control over the doomed vehicle and she almost
had the spin under control when she smashed into the side
of a building. The hurka-boy shattered the glazing and lanced
halfway inside before it started to slide back out. Part of the left
wing caught on the welter of framework while the rest of the
fuselage tumbled outside the glazing. The twisted metal held
and the wreck hung upside down against the side of the tower,
swinging like a pendulum.

Garrand swept up to the building and hovered beside the
wreckage. Vailetta was still partially strapped into the crumpled fuselage and he could see her grasping for something
substantial to hold onto. There was no way he could get in
close enough to help her, the hurka-boy was hanging in pieces
against the side of the building. He had to get into that tower.

Nudging the power, he eased his craft up one story. He
aimed his blaster at the center of the glazing and depressed the
fire stud. He could see terrified workers running for cover as
the building absorbed the onslaught. To his dismay, the glazing cracked but did not shatter. He clicked out the coil and
slapped a fresh one into place. Red bolts splashed against the
clear surface. The cracks fractured further and extended in
ragged lines but the glazing would not give.

Garrand howled in anger and wheeled the hurka-boy away from the building. He gathered speed in a long loop and then pointed the nose straight at the building. Wind whipped through his hair as he lined up with the fractured glazing. He hunkered down over the controls and gritted his teeth.

Vailetta watched the craft circle around and then zoom right at her. *Crazy bastard*, she muttered. *Fool doesn't know when to give up.* But she sighed with begrudging admiration. *The man was persistent.* She cringed as the craft flashed overhead.

The hurka-boy crashed through the weakened glazing in a shower of sparks and tinkling crystal. The craft barreled across the floor and hit an interior wall, snapped off a wing and lurched to a halt. Garrand immediately shut off the whining reactor and began unhooking his flight harness. Petrified workers watched him, crouched behind their workstations. He struggled free and slid off the side of the fuselage, landing a little shakily. He wavered there for a second, unaccustomed to having solid ground beneath his feet and turned to look at his entry point. Wind whipped through the smashed glazing, swirling papers through the office. His hurka-boy sat smoking against the wall—he wasn't much for landings today.

Garrand marched to the nearest desk and glowered down at the young woman stooped behind it. "Tube?" he demanded.

She pointed down a hallway with a shaking finger.

Garrand descended one level and ran into an identical office space with a similar hole in its glazing. A small group of people crowded around the edifice and looked cautiously down at the wreckage.

"Out of my way!" Garrand crunched through the broken shards and stuck his head out. The smashed hurka-boy was nearly cut in two. Vailetta was clinging to a piece of flight harness near the nose. A large part of the craft dangled below her.

Garrand turned around and looked back and forth around the office.

"What do you need?" a man stammered.

"Move." Garrand pushed him aside and appraised the nearest desk. A datascreen was built into the surface, with wires and cables disappearing into the woodwork. With the heel of his boot, he kicked it off the side. The terminal crashed to the floor, its cables still attached. He drew his blade and slashed the cords free. With the slack wrapped around his wrist, he put his boot on the edge of the desk and hauled on the cable. Several meters pulled free. He pulled until there was no more give and then reached forward and slashed the end that disappeared into the desk.

"Get me more cable," he directed the other workers as he began tying the ends of the power cords together. The workers began shoving other datascreens off their desks. "Tie the ends together and then weave the lengths into a braid—at least three thick."

Garrand flopped the first braided length out the glazing and scraped the sharp fragments away from the floor. He knelt down and teased the cables through the wreckage.

Vailetta glanced up at him as the cords swung near her head. "You again."

"You're going to have a little more trouble getting away this time," he yelled over the wind.

She glanced down. "Not much trouble getting away. Just a harder landing."

"Don't make this difficult."

"Why'd you come after me?"

"I had to—I had a dream about you."

"How romantic," she hissed through clenched teeth, struggling to purchase a better grip on the harness. "A dreamer."

"It's not just a dream."

"Yeah? Well here you are. Guess you're right." Her legs kicked atop the crumpled wing.

"Grab the cable." She looked uncertainly at the twisted power cords. "You have to grab it. It's the only thing I can pull up."

She let go of her harness with one hand and snagged the cable. Garrand braced himself in the twisted framework and wrapped the slack cable around his waist. Vailetta released her right hand and grabbed the cord, her full weight now in Garrand's hands.

"You always have dreams this bad?"

"Not a dream exactly," he grunted. "It was a vision. This is the only way," he tried to scrunch down further without toppling out the glazing himself.

Vailetta felt her hand slipping.

"Sid—the panda you left behind—told me the only way to rescue the rest of the tribe is with your help. Otherwise, they are forever in Barrett's clutches. We saw it in the dreams. That's how they see the future."

"Great," she muttered looking down. She could see for a half kilometer before the clouds obscured her view—a long way to fall. "You want to get me up?"

Garrand shifted backward slightly, straining to hold the slick cables. "You haven't given me an answer yet."

"*What?*"

"Where are they!"

"What, if I don't tell you, you let me drop?"

"No, of course not," he said through clenched teeth.

"You just thought now would be a good time to ask?" She struggled with her grip, wriggling on the cables.

Garrand grinned, the smile turning into a grimace as he fought to hold her. "Don't crack wise. Where are they?"

"They're on Wyx, you fool."

"Wyx, of course," he muttered. "How convenient."

A blast ripped into the side of the building, wide of its mark. A Shock Trooper soared past, chased by a Gambor. Both the Gambor and Shock Troops were battling for position. The Imperial soldiers were trying to line up a shot on Vailetta in the wicked cross winds, but the Gambor were keeping them too preoccupied to get off a good shot.

"Are you going to pull me up, or not?"

"I told you I need your help," Garrand yelled stubbornly.

"What if I say no?"

"You don't have any choice. It's your destiny." Another fusillade exploded, this time much closer. Garrand jerked his head toward the soldiers. "You're just like me now — the Empire doesn't want you around."

"We'll see about that," Vailetta rasped.

"So you don't want my help?"

Vailetta grimaced.

Garrand said, "What do you think Barrett's going to do with those poor creatures? He's going after your father, you know."

"What!"

"Collistas. He's after the Emperor."

Vailetta struggled with this new information. "What makes you think my father is the Emperor?" She quickly changed tack: "How do you know Barrett's going after him?"

Garrand strained to hold on. His eyes flicked outside the shattered glazing.

"Médeville, you've got a lot of explaining to do!"

"Oh, yeah. Save your ass and all you want is answers."

"Get me up!"

"Bossy, too!" Garrand grunted as he hauled on the cables. A Shock Trooper rose beside the building and began firing into the office. Garrand winced and lay to one side. None of the Gambor seemed to notice the attacker, so Garrand reached to his belt and unhooked a pair of amoeba nets. He flung them out into the wind and watched them zip off toward the hovering trooper. The nets enveloped the startled soldier and sent him tumbling sideways as he fought the webbing.

Garrand pulled on the cables, but Vailetta was stuck behind the left wing that was still connected to the bottom half of the wreckage. "Why don't you cut that dead weight free?" Vailetta surveyed the obstacle and drew her blade. It took a few moments for her to cut loose the tangled webbing which held the bottom half of the fuselage in place. The hurka-boy dropped quietly away and Garrand pulled her to the edge of the shattered glazing. He reached his hand out to her.

Vailetta stared up at him, still clutching the cords. His eyes burned with hope and passion. She had been told that Médeville would come for her, but not to rescue her! He had chased her down to enlist her in his cause. He was offering his hand to save her life. If she took it she would be joining his cause and turning her back forever on Barrett and all she'd worked to achieve. Vailetta studied the cracks around the man's eyes, the warmth behind his gaze. Sweat dripped off his brow as he struggled to keep her aloft. She remembered their first meeting, how he had teased her about being a pirate when she was still uncertain whether she should keep him alive. Their eyes met and suddenly she knew. This was the man. The pandas were right.

She let go of the cords with one hand and lunged for his arm. He grabbed her hand. "I've got you."

Vailetta closed her eyes as they touched. She felt a flash of awareness as he held her in his strong grip. She saw a young boy standing on the edge of a bluff. He had dark tousled hair and brown eyes. He stared at her with preternatural awareness, silence. Serenity. He did not smile, but his eyes were full of life, full of an undeniable mischief and understanding. Her son! Chills swept over her body and she snapped back into the moment to see Garrand looking at her. Her head spun from his touch, from the sudden vision of the child.

"Pull me up," she whispered. She was drawn up into the building. She collapsed on the floor, releasing the panic and fear. All she could hear was the wind.

Garrand sat back and let his heart rate slow to normal. His body was drenched in sweat. His arms trembled from the overexertion. He stared down at the beautiful woman who lay spent and exhausted on the floor. *Did she see the boy too?* Sid's words danced in his mind.

A new alliance
A warm embrace
The Thief's defiance
Like a mirror's face

She'll take his hand
And seal his fate
Bear his child
Become his mate

How could this be? How could Sid know this? Who was the boy? The vision was frightening in its intensity and clarity. *Cheplus, he could have dropped her!*

"Why do you think Barrett will go after my father?"

Garrand blinked and tried to refocus. "Why else would he want the pandas?" He rested his chin on his knees. "Do you think he's just going to unite the Shell and that's it? All in the 'name of the Dragon,' and just hand the whole thing over to daddy. You've seen him. By K'ye, you're the captain of his Guard—you should know better." Garrand studied her. She could see it. "Correct me if I'm wrong, but those are Imperial Shock Troops firing on you. Face it. You're just like me now."

She closed her eyes. *Cast out. Only one way to clear her name. The rest of her men were in danger as well.* "The Gokazoku Kaigi won't stand for this."

"The Gokazoku Kaigi aren't *here*," Garrand said plainly.

"Will you help me?" Vailetta stared up at him. *Is this what her father would want? Is this what he would do?* She knew the answer immediately. "The only way I can get on Wyx is with your help."

Vailetta tested him: "What are you going to do with them?"

"This is a rescue mission. What they do after I get them out is up to them. Cheplus, they've already seen what's going to happen anyway. There's not much I can do that's going to surprise them."

"I doubt that, Captain," she looked at him with admiration

Garrand beamed, his heart buoyed by the look. "So?"

"I should have shot you when I had the chance," she grumbled.

"Me? Your mirror image?"

"Look at all the trouble you've gotten me into already."

"You think this is trouble? You don't even know me yet."

She moaned and shoved him roughly aside, using his chest as leverage to get up. She paused, turned, and after a hesitation offered her hand to help him up.

He looked at her lopsided, and accepted.

Garrand led Vailetta down the interior of the tower and out to a set of public tubes. They made their way by foot to the midcity docks, relying on the cover of the crowds. No one followed them, and Garrand felt a minor sense of relief when he punched in access to *Flogos Turn* and the lock scrolled aside to reveal *Destiny's Needle* resting unscathed within.

They strode up to the ramp and Garrand shot a quick glance at Vailetta. She studied the outer hull with marginal doubt.

"Don't start," he warned.

She pursed her lips innocently. "I didn't say *anything...*"

"She's fast."

"I know that."

"And solid as a rock."

"Of course."

"And you wipe off some of that dirt and replace a few of those panels and she's as pretty as any ship in the Shell. And the design is —"

" — Hey, I didn't say anything." They stomped up into the open airlock.

"But you were thinking it."

"It's a beautiful ship, Médeville. It's outrun and outgunned everything we've thrown at her. It's just a little strange being *invited* aboard her. Being, you know..."

"Cast out?" Garrand chuckled and stopped in the mess where Bailey and Jean-Wa were waiting for them. He swept his arm in a graceful bow. "Well then my dear, welcome to the ship of cast-offs. I present you with first officer Bailey and our esteemed chef, Jean-Wa. Gentlemen, may I present Captain of the Imperial Guard, Vailetta Strom, our new guest and budding co-conspirator."

"Welcome to *Destiny's Needle*, Captain Strom," Bailey said solemnly. "Captain, I've found Miss Tchelakov."

Garrand's smile evaporated. "Where?"

"Com activity indicates she has turned herself over to Vice Proctor Barrett."

"What!"

"Why would she do that?" Vailetta asked.

"To negotiate, by my reckoning," the artificial replied. "Miss Tchelakov holds a vaccine essential to the pandas' survival, and thus to Barrett as well. It's her final gambit."

"But it's too late," Vailetta exclaimed. "Barrett already has an antidote!"

Garrand snapped his head around. "Are you sure?"

"I was there when he was gloating about it." She looked between the art and the man. "There's no angle. She doesn't have anything to bargain with."

Garrand grabbed her by the arm and lead her toward the armory. "Come with me," he said roughly.

"What are you doing?"

"Making sure I don't lose you, too."

"How?"

He entered the armory, picked up an injector wand and loaded a tiny transmitter into the breach. "It's a locator. Don't go anywhere," he muttered as he pressed the wand against her neck.

"And you think *I'm* bossy!"

"We'll see how well you mind," he replied.

"You're going after her?"

Garrand fell silent. "We can't leave her."

"I wouldn't trust that one," Vailetta warned him.

"I don't."

Vailetta studied his face. "But you're still going…"

Garrand started to shuck his tattered gear. Bailey slipped in past Vailetta and began assisting the removal. He stripped out of the body armor, wincing with pain as Bailey cut away the seals with a tight beam laser.

"Let me come with you," she said.

Garrand shook his head. "I want you to help Bailey get us out of here." Nearly naked now, he pulled on a shift and slung a belt of charges over his shoulder.

"Armor, Captain," Bailey ordered.

"No time." He shoved the artificial aside and pulled on his old trousers. "Get us passage to Wyx on some outbound freighter." He looked at Vailetta. "Get Captain Strom to override any protocols they've set up to contain outbound cargo and make sure you wipe the transaction logs. She'll know what they'll be looking for, so her word goes, got it?" The art nodded silently.

"You're going to book the whole ship as cargo?" Vailetta asked.

"Why not? They'll be looking for a small ship trying to break free on its own, or else passengers trying to slip out on a liner or freighter. If we're going to chance it, might as well take the whole works. You can work through the protocols, right?"

Vailetta cocked her head to one side. "Yeah."

"I'm sure you've worked something like this before to get your men *into* a foreign port. This time just work it in reverse. With some luck, Barrett will never know. Can you handle that?"

"Smuggle us off-planet? No problem."

"Good girl. We'll make a decent Freetrader out of you yet."

Garrand hitched a new belt around his waist, holstered his blaster and snapped a locator pad into place. "What's her code?"

"It's loaded," Bailey said gravely.

Garrand brushed past the pair and headed for the airlock. Vailetta followed him. *Is he motivated by love?* She spun him around by the shoulder. "Médeville, why are you doing this?"

"We can't leave her here," he repeated.

Vailetta watched him with frustration. "I thought you were fated to be with *me*."

He gave her a strange look, remembering the boy in the vision. "I am," he said finally and disappeared out the door.

6

LAST BREATH

HELIUS BARRETT STOOD ON AN ELEVATED GANTRY WITHIN the 12th Brigade's midcity Garrison, overlooking the officers' mess. The long, airy chamber took up the topmost floor of the tower and its ceiling was pinched to a tight point well overhead. Tall glazings on opposite walls offered tremendous views of the upper reaches of New Haivello. The garrison was perched high in the new city like a remote citadel. Round flyer pads jutted out from the corners of the shining minaret like foundations for unfinished turrets. One massive elevated bridge stretched across the busy air-lanes midway up the structure, like a draw-bridge over a bottomless moat. Red and gold dragon banners snapped in the wind. Two soldiers in ceremonial armor stood at the foot of the bridge.

Barrett paced along the walk. Moonglow stretched through the glazings in rakish fashion, illuminating the stillness. The ornate steel gantry surrounded three-quarters of the mess, stopping when it came to the two-story blast door that guarded the hall. The walk allowed the officers a place to drink and reflect. A place where one could lean on the rail and absorb the atmosphere, the shared spirit of camaraderie below, or stare out the massive glazings as Barrett now did. Ordinarily filled with a boisterous contingent of the 3rd Imperial Army Corps, the room was strangely silent, long mahogany tables pushed slightly askew, stools overturned, half-eaten plates of food left untended.

The garrison was deserted—all forces assigned to the pursuit of Strom, Médeville, or the rogue Gambor. Barrett glanced at the sartographic duty roster that took up the entire opposite wall. Purple neo-markers pinpointed squad locations across the city map, with combat flashpoints blinking red. Many of the names flashed yellow, indicating their health status as wounded. A trail of icons led in a jagged pattern up through the city. Fighting had broken out all along the path of pursuit.

He sighed and glanced down at the broad, green blast door that protected the mess. Two soldiers stood guard, faces masked behind ashen helms. They were his men, and good, but he was irked by the absence of Torg. This was exactly the kind of situation that required his personal assassin's unique talents. He should be here, waiting in the shadows, sensing out any unforeseen danger. The man had disappeared after the Strom wildfire had ignited, and no one seemed to know where the assassin had gone.

He had committed all the Shock Troops and the garrison's complement to the task of tracking down Strom and Médeville. With the majority of his forces deployed, the garrison was absolutely the safest place left, even empty. Who would dare break into an Imperial garrison, and why would they want to? Still, he had irksome doubts. It was taking far too long: Strom should have been taken immediately after her performance. The Gambor's assault should have been contained at the Greuk Center. Médeville should have been captured when he first entered the plaza. *Destiny's* location should have been already established. No matter that there were 42,000 some odd commercial berths in and around New Haivello and scant personnel to make a visual confirmation. This was an Imperial city! The planet had been a part of the Wyxian Proctorialship for forty years. No one should be able to come onto one of his planets and do as they wished!

The last two pandas should already be in his hands. It was particularly disturbing the way Médeville had stepped in to take Strom out of his hands at precisely the right moment. Could he really be acting with foreknowledge? It seemed surreal to think that his adversary could already know what he was going to do before he had even thought about it.

It was time to start taking some preemptive action. Two pandas couldn't possibly foresee every contingency. It was time he started eliminating Médeville's resources—one man could only do so much, after all. His damage potential could be limited, piece-by-piece until he had nothing left. The first piece was being delivered presently. And with the garrison rallied, it shouldn't be long before he was in possession of the second. The Captain of his Guard would soon be in custody and she would be brought before him. It saddened him deeply to learn of her lineage. His treasured pupil, the beautiful and talented Vailetta Strom, would have to face a whole new line of inquiry, a much more serious line. There were difficult questions to ask, questions that would undoubtedly shift their relationship. Her life in the new order would come to an end just as its full glory began to blossom. And all because she had been born to the wrong man.

But first there was Tchelakov. The book could finally be closed on that chapter, and he would have the pleasure of seeing an end to it, personally. He glanced outside. The city grew bright as the sky grew dim. Two officers from Praetor Preston's security force led Helen Tchelakov across the bridge.

He walked slowly down the steel steps and across the mess to greet her at the blast door. A chime sounded and Barrett nodded to his guard. The door's lock released with a clank and it trundled upward. The woman appeared small between the two men, her reddish-brown hair blown in a tangled mess. Helen Tchelakov stared at him with fearless eyes and a truculent frown. The soldiers escorted her roughly into the mess, arms pinioned behind her back.

"Release her and leave us."

"As you will, my Lord." The soldier unlocked her manacles and joined the other. The green slab descended between them, closing with a boom.

Barrett drummed his fingers against the top of the first of two small, wooden boxes sitting on the nearest mess table. "Good of you to visit, Helen," Barrett allowed mild humor into his voice. "It has been quite some time, hasn't it?"

The polished boxes with their gilded sides drew a quick glance from Helen. Barrett smiled, noting the first crack of curiosity in her defiant posture. "At first we thought Médeville had sent you along as a distraction or a negotiator, but that isn't the case, is it?" Helen's upper lip quivered. "No, I see you're here on your own behalf."

Helen rubbed her sore wrists while she stared at him. He drew a finger down the edge of the box with deliberate care. "It's a shame we couldn't do business on Groereh next cycle, but I'm afraid I'm already in possession of the creatures you were offering. With respect to your father, they are magnificent."

Helen wanted nothing more than to wipe that smug expression off Barrett's face, but she kept her anger in check. "You double-crossed me. We had a deal."

"The deal was not yet in effect. You proved unable to deliver your cargo."

"Because *you* stole it from me."

"It matters not how you lost it, just that you did. You no longer have anything to bring to the table."

"Actually, I do, and I'm here to negotiate."

"For what?"

"For the pandas."

Barrett smiled comfortably. "Still want Darstin's head do you?"

"No. I want pandas back. *Females.*"

"Gone soft have you? Lost your taste for revenge?"

"There are sweeter things."

Barrett shrugged, "You presume that there's something in your possession that I find valuable."

"Oh, there is."

"And what would that be? I have everything I need. The pandas, safe and sound, knowledge of a traitor in my midst— thanks to you—and now you as well. What could you possibly have to offer me?"

"Your victory is incomplete. There's still Médeville and his two pandas."

"I'll have them soon enough."

This time Helen smiled. "Oh really? I wouldn't be surprised if the reverse were actually true."

"And he has me?" Barrett laughed.

"I've been privy to quite a few songs in the last week. The next few days look to be rather interesting."

"Médeville sings?" Barrett asked incredulously.

"No, they're more like epic poems. But they do have a certain quality when you hear them over and over again. You begin to get a picture of the future."

The Vice Proctor was frowning. "The pandas *sing* about the future?"

"No, they dream it, but that's neither here nor there. I wouldn't count on Garrand falling into your lap anytime soon."

"I have two platoons of Shock Troops and an entire garrison of the 3rd Army after him."

"And yet, where is he?" Helen looked around the mess. "You doubt my tale of songs? Then tell me this, has Strom's flyer crashed yet?"

Barrett scowled at her; the report had just come in. Vailetta's hurka-boy had struck the side of a building and was hanging in a perilous fashion.

"Has Garrand begun his rescue? Because once she accepts his hand, her fate is sealed. She will have turned against you irrevocably."

"And you've seen this?"

"No, I've heard it rattled off a hundred times:

The Thief of Ships will fall from grace
And dangle from a slender thread
The Griffin's fate she has to face
A crown upon her lovely head

If she reaches for the Griffin's hand
Above her shattered wings
Their union will forever stand
Of this the tribe will sing.

Barrett stared up into the pale shadows of the peaked ceiling, intrigued. "Fantastic," he murmured. The pandas related their visions through poetry! A bridge between vastly different languages and cultures.

"You still need me," Helen pressed. "Garrand will keep his two, and the pandas you have won't last long. Not without my help."

Barrett snapped out of his reverie and glanced back down. "I assure you, the creatures are in splendid health. Never looked better."

"Appearances can be deceiving."

"Ah yes, the hidden parasites," Barrett opened the lid of the first wooden box and removed a small white vial from inside. He held the small vial up to the moonlight and pretended to examine it carefully. "They were a bit difficult to pin down, but my doctors were sufficiently motivated."

Helen was undaunted. "Finding them and curing them are two different things."

"Of course," Barrett agreed.

"You'll never have time to discover their secrets before they die. You will never have their trust."

"This is where your negotiation position breaks down, I'm afraid. Discovering their secrets will not be a problem, since I have their cooperation. And after I have saved them from your treachery, I will have their trust."

"They will never accede to your wishes. They will see right through you!"

"Like they saw through you?" Barrett countered. "No, my dear, they're still like children. They *want* to trust me, they *need* someone to trust. Someone to guide them."

"They saw through me," Helen muttered stubbornly. "They're not so naive. It suited them to play along. You may think they trust you, but they have plans beyond anything you can imagine."

"Undoubtedly. But perhaps I'm a means of fulfilling them. They wish to survive, yes? They are safer now than they have ever been."

"You're confusing captivity with safety."

"A semantic difference that will cease to be of importance over time."

"You won't have the time unless you bargain with me."

"For what?"

"For the cure. They'll die soon without it."

Barrett sighed and reached back into the box. He exchanged the vial for a blue one. He held it up and shook it gently for her to see. "That is not a problem. I have the cure already."

Helen's heart dropped. "You couldn't possibly."

"You underestimate my resources. It's time we ended this charade."

"I agree," Garrand said from the gangway opposite them. Helen's head whipped around.

"Captain Médeville. Ever resourceful I see."

"Helen, come here," Garrand said as he drew his blaster.

"You're a bit out of range there, Captain," Barrett observed. Nevertheless, the vice proctor touched his belt and a shield sparkled around him. His right hand rested atop the second box.

"I just want the woman," Garrand declared.

"There will be no negotiations," Barrett said. "I have everything I need."

"You don't have the antidote," Helen said defiantly.

"Oh, but I do. It works marvelously. Leusta took it this afternoon and now is in perfect health."

"He's bluffing, Garrand."

Garrand never let his eyes waver from the vice proctor. "I don't think so," he said slowly. Barrett showed no tells; he exuded nothing but supreme confidence. He had the priggish, haughty demeanor of someone who had a hand so good, they had no reason to bluff. "Helen, come with me."

"But that's impossible. He can't possibly have the cure."

"Nothing's impossible. Walk away."

"He still needs our antidote. It's our only way to get some of them back."

Barrett laughed.

"Helen, walk away." Garrand inspected the man's body, looking for bulges. He wasn't wearing a sidearm, but there were two boxes on the table in front of him, either of them large enough to hold a weapon. He directed his voice at the vice proctor. "You drop your shield to fire at her and I'll drop you where you stand."

The Vice Proctor ignored him, choosing instead to goad Helen in a soft tone. "Yes, it's true. I have the pandas, free from defect. Your careful plans have come undone. The tribe is mine. Darstin, I'm afraid, will *not* be my first priority," Barrett continued with insidious pleasure. "Your vengeance will not be fulfilled. Your duplicity has garnered you nothing. Everything you've touched has crumbled into dust."

Helen trembled, fear welling up in her chest. "That's not true," she said bitterly, trying to choke back the tears that pooled behind her eyes.

"Hardly a life worth keeping."

"You're right," she swallowed, "until recently, my life was not worth living. It does not matter what you do, for as long as I can remember, living was a state of purgatory, worse than K'ye itself. Death should be no different. And I will see you there."

The Vice Proctor snorted with contempt. "Everything you tried has failed."

"It doesn't matter Barrett, because now I've had a taste of something sweeter, and it still lingers on my lips. You will know nothing but bitterness."

"The difference is, I will see an end to this." He drew a long Stuychan Vôt pistol from the second box and pointed it at her head. "You, however, will not."

"Stop!" Garrand screamed from the balcony. He scrambled around the edge, racing for the stairs.

Barrett flicked his gaze upward momentarily to gauge how much time he had. "All you have done is deliver the pandas from Director Darstin to me." Barrett sidestepped carefully around Helen, keeping Garrand in his peripheral vision and the weapon trained on Helen's temple. "You will die never having found inner peace, never having known a day where you weren't trying to fool someone, never having known *love*."

"That's not true," she whispered, tears running down her cheeks. *"I've known love…"*

Garrand found the stairs and leapt down them, four at a time. He hit the deck plates running. He aimed as he ran and fired three bolts at Barrett's head. Energy sparkled around the vice proctor's body as his personal shield absorbed the fusillade.

"Your last lie," he said. He flicked off the power supply to his shield and squeezed the trigger. The barrel of his pistol flashed blue, sending a bolt of energy arcing across the gap between them. The charge hit her in the temple. White energy crackled back and forth across her body, enveloping her.

Helen's body crumpled to the floor, instantly robbed of life.

Barrett reactivated his shield and backed against the blast door, weapon brought to bear on the charging man. But Garrand slid to a halt and knelt to cradle Helen's head in his hands. A black burn mark scarred her forehead, her cheeks still wet with tears. Garrand touched her cheek with a trembling hand.

The blast door scrolled slowly open and Barrett raised a hand to halt the four soldiers. "He'll simply escape the way he came in. There has to be a flyer on the upper pads somewhere. Find it." Barrett backed carefully through the doorway, subvocalizing commands to Arnas.

Garrand set her head gently back down and rose.

Barrett continued to back away, watching the man coiling to strike, such hatred in his eyes. He wondered for a final time how such a man had ever been *dismissed*.

"I'm afraid I have other business to attend to," Barrett said.

Wind whipped into the mess through the blast door. Garrand seethed at the vice proctor, his whole body trembling with rage. The man was the wind demon personified. And this was his chance to silence him. Garrand held his blaster straight out from his shoulder, arm stiff as he stalked forward. "I have dreamt of this day," he rasped.

Barrett glanced briefly at the man's belt; his thumb was hooked next to his shield generator. He wondered briefly whether he might get a shot off before it could be activated.

Doubtful. Médeville continued to advance, despite the pistol trained on his still unshielded head. *Could he drop him without lowering his shield?* He was being lured into attempting just such an act. Would Médeville set upon him with a blade during the brief confusion as he fired through the dizzying waves? He backed up further, now all the way out on the elevated bridge, and glanced into the abyss below.

"I will no longer be a victim of the winds," Garrand said.

"You've gone mad."

"Indeed I have," he paced woodenly forward. "Body after body has piled at my feet. And now you wish to kill a billion more. A hundred billion. When does it stop?"

"It doesn't." A high-pitched whine rose over the winds and four Shock Troopers rose up beside the bridge, cannons held at the ready. Barrett smiled thinly. "Goodbye Captain Médeville. I have another of your women to deal with — one more quisling amongst the true."

Garrand turned and dove back inside the mess, scrambling for the side of the doorway. The Shock Troops opened fire. He slapped the control nub and the blast door began to scroll shut as tables splintered and burned. The soldiers flew forward, landing with crumps on the bridge. The door clanged shut and Garrand fused the controls with his blaster. The door rang as energy raked its exterior.

Garrand retraced his steps and knelt to Helen's inert form, snatching a wand from his belt. The color was already draining from her face. He gently wiped the moisture from her cheeks. "No dragon tears," he whispered and pressed the device to her neck.

He touched his comtab and swallowed back his grief. "Bailey?" His voice came out a hoarse whisper.

"Reading you, Captain."

"Is the ship safe?"

"We've booked passage and completed loading *Destiny's Needle* onto a freighter. We were in luck, there was a suitable vessel here at midtown and we didn't have to worry with the Tamarae Yards."

"Good."

"I'm afraid there's a problem, however—"

"—Shut down any traceable systems and send me the freighter's name and dock in a separate encryption," he mumbled.

"Captain, there's a small problem."

"Send me the location so I can find you."

"Captain Strom has gone missing."

He closed his eyes. "What was that again?"

"She went after you. Please don't be angry, Captain. She is after all, a Captain of the Guard, and—like yourself—quite headstrong. There was nothing I could do."

Garrand shook his head. *No one listens.*

"I'm sorry Captain. What are you going to do?"

Sadness hardened around his chest, like a quick-drying shell. He was finding it hard to breathe. "Are you getting a signal from her locator?"

"Yes."

"Give me the code." Numbers scrolled across the locator pad hooked to his belt. The surface flashed green and then directional markers began winking as it tracked Vailetta's position. Garrand touched Helen's cheek for a final time and rose. He took a quick look at the pad and raced back up the stairs to the glazing he'd cut through. He wiggled through the circular opening and balanced carefully on the ledge. A hurka-boy hovered several meters away, exhaust nacelles glowing red in the darkness. A credit chit for half-a-million quantis bought one a pretty reliable driver, even on New Haivello.

"Are you going after her?" Bailey asked in a woeful tone.

Garrand hopped onto the left wing and scrambled behind the pilot. The man leaned his head back and cocked an ear to the side. "Greuk Center Plaza!" Garrand yelled. The driver nodded and the hurka-boy banked steeply away. Wind screamed through his head as he pulled on the leather headgear. The old ticket-taker had been right after all. He was going back down.

"Captain?" Bailey repeated.

"I will not lose another," he shouted and terminated the connection.

7

THE GRIFFIN AND
THE BUTCHER

MIDWAY UP THE TOWER FACING THE GREUK CENTER, Torg rested in a barren vestibule. The small room was one of the many empty, but well-appointed offices in Praetor Preston's diplomatic annex. Soft lights spilled down from the ceiling, obliquely framing the minor flaws in the drip-poured walls. A discreetly placed alcove held a rather good selection of liquor. A painting of a dull landscape rested against one wall. All of this registered briefly in the assassin's mind before he collected himself and assumed a position in the center of the small room facing the sole entrance. Behind him, locked in a large storage room, Vailetta Strom lay unconscious on a soft pallet. The storeroom was filled with a variety of supplies and would not hold her indefinitely, but it would do for now. Torg had moved quickly, needing and finding an interior room—no glazings, one access. In the confusion that still rocked the city, no one had seen him come in. This refuge was only temporary. He knew who was coming.

He braced his legs and squared his shoulders to the entrance. Flicking back his cape over one shoulder, he drew his blade and waited. The *Chōl Fhar Wi* felt heavy in his fingers. The blade itself was a tooth-like shard, riddled with tiny irregularities, smoothed-out holes bored into the surface by time, water and wind. Two glossy, smooth outer surfaces were sandwiched over a honeycomb of minuscule tunnels, crevices, softly curving archways. The gently reflective sheen was ivory white on its underbelly, and an aging yellow on the other. A crusted rim atop the 'tooth' narrowed to a hand-carved hilt wrapped simply with a *kheilan*. The dual-edged surface of the blade curved like a fin: smooth and elegant on one side, sharply parabolic on the other, the two edges diving to a fragmented point. The jagged edges between the sandwiched layers acted as a natural, brutal serration. The *Chōl Fhar Wi* was strangely organic and effectively wicked.

Torg had handpicked this blade from the skeletal remains of a T'aika on Cuel-ba during the final weeks of the Lal, the Bolo initiation rite combining a search for inner peace with survival for six months in the harshest environments possible. The completion of the Lal marked his passage from thinking beast to assassin.

He'd found this one amongst T'aika gizzard stones washed ashore on the banks of the inner sea. It was a prize; most of the fossilized T'aika remains lay hidden beneath the briny waters of the stagnant sea. He turned the blade in his palm, letting his skin shift to the steel-grey color of the floor so that the blade appeared to twirl mid air.

Torg stopped and listened. He was here. The footsteps rang heavy, the man's stride was broad, full of purpose. The heels hit the marble floor with angry certainty—Torg half expected the man to burst in firing, but he stood his ground.

He'd left the door unlocked, and it swished upward silently. Garrand Médeville stood on the other side. His face was blackened with carbon and soot. Dried blood formed a rust-colored rivulet from a caked wound at his hairline down the bridge of his nose leading to one corner of his mouth. One hand trembled just over his blaster, the other was touching the power contact of a shield generator.

His eyes were the worst though: tragic, feral, and slightly less than human. The holocubes had showed them as greenish-brown hazel—here they had gone black with desperation.

"I have come for her," he said it plainly but with unmistakable certainty.

Torg tightened his grip on his blade drawing a droplet of blood from his thumb as it rubbed the first serration. "How did you find her?"

Garrand tapped a locator pad on his belt.

"Ahh, of course," He paused several seconds, waiting. Médeville's shoulders dipped a fraction forward; he was an instant away from drawing. Electricity coursed between the men. Every fiber of Torg's body ached with savage need to strike. He would not be able to dampen the impulse for long. But each moment that went by underscored the true nature of the standoff. Neither man was brash; not here, not facing an equal, not with Vailetta in the next room. "Great minds think alike…" Torg allowed.

Médeville's predatory mask cracked slightly as he frowned. The standoff stretched on and he returned the question with halting uncertainty. "How'd *you* find her?"

Torg moved his free hand and tapped the back of his neck. "Organic localizer. It was surgically implanted without her knowledge some time ago."

"Organic. That means it needs an activator."

The assassin rubbed a finger across his lips. "Triggered by an enzyme in a special lipstick."

"Hmm."

"Similar to your injected locator, but more permanent—and less likely to be rejected by the body due to its use of similar tissue."

"Permanent locator," Garrand let his guard drop with a practiced casualness. He scratched his chin with the back of his thumb. "Sort of drastic isn't it?"

"She is my charge," he said resolutely. "I have powerful conditioning to protect her."

"For *Barrett*?" Garrand's lip quivered in hatred.

Torg's body washed instantly away. Garrand kept his eye on the blade which dipped to one side as the assassin bent to strike. "Relax," he muttered to the empty space where the man crouched, letting his own shoulders settle.

The assassin wavered to half visibility and saw that Médeville was not poised to draw his weapon. He straightened up fully visible once more and slapped his blade back into its sheath with anger. He'd never twitched before, not without cause. *Completely undignified.*

Garrand sighed. "Not Barrett then. Someone in the Core perhaps?"

Torg canvassed him silently.

"The only person in the Core who could command you to protect the Emperor's daughter is Collistas himself." *Which would mean that the man standing before him was the Emperor's infamous personal assassin. The Butcher of Yuzbek.* He tried to remain outwardly calm, but his hand still ached to draw the blaster, to feel its cool steel in his palm, to rip off seven or eight good shots. The wind screamed in his head. *I have taken another. I have taken another.* He tried to focus on the assassin but was having a hard time concentrating. All he could see was Helen's face staring blankly into nothingness, black scar on her forehead. *I will take another still,* the voice called. *Unless you can defeat the Emperor's Butcher, I will take another. Two in one day!* The laughter filled his mind and he had to clench his teeth to remember that the room was stone silent.

"Have you lost before, assassin?" he whispered. "Lost yourself little by little as everyone falls around you? Lost pieces of your life as you try to do the right things? And all the while doing the wrong things. After awhile the pursuit of good through questionable means just seems like a futile ruse—a pursuit of the impossible through evil means. And you lose yourself along the way, lose bits and pieces. Little things, important things. Do you hear the voices too?" Torg stared at the man. His eyes were glazing over. "One loss after another, until there's nothing left. Until all you can do is go blindly forward—try to salvage one piece from the wreckage. And it doesn't matter if you make it or not, because if you don't try the voices will drive you insane."

"Yes," Torg replied softly. "I've heard those voices too."

Garrand's eyes fluttered as he refocused on the present, forcing the wind demon and the *tromaveint* from his mind. His voice cracked with grief. "You're determined to keep her captive in there?"

Torg narrowed his gaze, eyes burning red. "What are you implying, Captain?"

"There's no need to play coy," he blew out his breath and let his chest sag. "I'm not trying to raise your hackles." He shook his head with weariness and walked brazenly past the assassin. Torg watched him with curiosity. The Captain stopped at the sharp-edged, slab-bench against the far wall and sat down heavily.

"I know who you are," Garrand continued, leaning back as he spoke. "And I know that ultimately your allegiance must lie with the Emperor. Not," he made no attempt to disguise his venom, "with your murderous Vice Proctor." Garrand pressed his hands against his face. "*That* man serves no dragon but his own." Torg offered no rebuttal. "I find it hard to believe that you would do his bidding with no regard to—"

"—To what?" Torg asked. "The Empire as a whole?"

"I was thinking more along the lines of 'to the Emperor.' If He knew what his Proctors were up to in the Shell…"

"He will know."

It was Garrand's turn to pause. "Will He?" He pursed his lips.

"The answer, Captain, is yes. I *do* intend to keep Miss Strom *captive* here. Her detention has no bearing on Lord Barrett's plans or the Emperor's wishes. The simple fact is, she is under my charge and much safer here, temporarily detained by me than rushing about at your side. She, too, will end up dead if I allow her to leave with you."

"Barrett will have her head, and yours too someday. You're far too dangerous to have roaming about—he'll kill you the first chance he gets."

"I would not be so sure, Captain."

"Oh, I know you have eyes everywhere, assassin, but the Emperor cannot protect you out here."

"And you cannot protect Miss Strom. You will be hunted wherever you go. She will be in constant danger. I cannot allow that."

"She's no stranger to that. Danger has been a part of her life since she joined the Guard."

This gave Torg pause. He opened his mouth, but said nothing.

"Admit, assassin," Garrand plied him. "We are not so different. Self-preservation is a large part of who we are—essential to achieving our deeper agendas. Hopes, dreams, wishes; they are nothing if we don't survive. Thus, many choices become simple: perish nobly, or survive by whatever means necessary."

Torg smiled, his eyes fading to amber. He liked this man. It was a shame, too. He rubbed his chin and exhaled. "Yes, survival allows the pursuit of the higher goal." He walked to the shallow alcove and depressed a hidden switch. A panel scrolled smoothly aside, revealing a beautiful crystal decanter and a row of fragile Alvei goblets. The assassin poured two full measures of Kouln brandy in separate goblets and turned to face the captain. "The bidding of the Dragon, or—" he waved one of the glasses before him, searching for the phrase.

"—Or, the rescue of a good woman," Garrand finished for him. "The two need not necessarily be separate goals."

Torg crossed to the bench, sat down next to Garrand, and offered him a goblet."

"You presume too much," Torg sighed.

"Do I? We both wish to protect her. I infer from your careful wording that you wish to protect her from Barrett as well as from harm. She is something to you then?"

"I told you before, she is my charge."

Garrand nodded. "She is safer with me, assassin."

"And what of your precious *cargo*? You've gone to great length to rescue the precognitives."

"You really think they're better off in Barrett's hands? You know as well as I what will happen. In a year he could have the entire Shell under his heel. In two he could be a threat to the Emperor himself." Garrand paused, turning to look directly at the assassin. "If you are who I think you are, then you could never allow that."

Torg smiled—a true grin, not one of his characteristic thin smiles.

"My, you do presume a lot. And what of the precognitives' fate in *your* care? Do you think the Emperor will allow them to fall into your direct control?"

"I have no desire to shape the future. It's the past I have trouble with." He sighed wearily and took a deep gulp. "Besides, they deserve a chance to pursue their own destiny, don't you think?" Garrand frowned and sniffed at his drink.

"Kouln."

"Ahh."

"We are at an impasse."

"I can't persuade you?"

"To turn the other cheek? No…"

"Well then, what's it to be? Honorably—man to man? Blades? Pistols?"

Torg shook his head, "We've just been discussing the need to survive, and I know you too well, Captain. You've proven rather adept at finding a way to survive at all costs. Limiting you to honorable engagements with but one weapon would put you at a gross disadvantage, and be an extremely foolish presumption on my part."

Garrand's chest heaved and a laugh gurgled out—a sound so far away from what he felt that it sounded like it came from another body. "You compliment me with your insults," he mumbled weakly. He sighed and gazed at the goblet against his waist. "Well then, a free-for-all."

Torg raised his glass and regarded the ragged-looking Captain. "To the best man?"

Garrand considered this for a moment. "No."

Torg glanced at the door to the storage room. "To Strom then."

Garrand raised his drink and murmured, "To the first lucky shot." He tilted back his goblet. The brandy stung his throat.

"Another?"

Garrand smacked his lips, looked at the man and shook his head. "By all means."

Torg stood and went to retrieve two more drinks, but returned with the full decanter. The brandy gurgled out of the long-necked cruse.

"That's enough," Garrand cautioned. His goblet was nearly full. "I've still got work to do. *As* do you."

Torg guffawed. "There will be time enough for that. It's not often I have someone of *character* to drink with."

"Ah, the life of an assassin…"

Torg tilted back his goblet. "You should know. A Freetrader alone in the Shell."

Garrand shook his head. "Yes, but I have my *crew*."

"Crew?" Torg turned his head to look at him. "You're listed as the only human aboard your ship."

"Artificials."

"Mmm."

"My first officer is an old Varsis—and the finest friend any man could want for."

"A noble line," Torg nodded. "I once knew a Varsis myself, though I've never been partial to artificials."

"A sentient is a sentient. One day the rest will see that."

Torg poured two more measures. "It's not that, I assure you. A fine art is preferable to an unthinking lump of flesh any day. It's just that I've always worked alone."

"You're not alone," Garrand pointed out. "Else you wouldn't have taken Strom here. You've taken on the role of protector."

"She's worthy of my care, and I am bound by honor to keep her safe."

"So you're not alone; you care," Garrand shrugged. "That's what all this has been about anyway. Protecting the weak from the strong. The thinking from the unthinking. The innocent, the future—" he swept his arms across the room, beginning to feel the drink. "—All our futures, from the cruelty of our past."

"Our past?"

"Everyone's past. All species."

"More voices?"

"The past is harsh," Garrand snorted. "There seems to be a genetic need to conquer and destroy. To dominate all that threatens. No one is immune."

"And the future will be different?"

"Could be," Garrand sipped his brandy. "With the pandas it could be." The liquid burned in his belly.

Torg growled, "It will depend on who controls them."

"I want them to control themselves."

"Quite noble of you."

"Hardly. They just deserve a chance." He nodded and stared sideways at the assassin. "A chance is all. Is that asking too much? The alternative is unthinkable. I personally don't like the idea of living in a Shell where Barrett is all-powerful."

"The Emperor won't allow that to happen," Torg grunted.

Garrand looked at him. "Then let her go."

Torg shook his head, "I cannot."

Garrand let his breath out in a grumble. "And I cannot rescue them without her help."

Torg pressed his palms against his thighs, smoothing out the creases in his black pants. Garrand sighed and straightened his back.

"Well?" Torg asked.

"I will not lose another." Garrand said it with simple conviction, with an intensity that mirrored the voice in his head that screamed back at the demons: *I will not lose another. I will not lose another.*

"It's time then, I suppose."

"Yes," he whispered. *Time for one final stand. One last effort to rescue the Thief of Ships, to fulfill the tribe's destiny.*

At that moment, the door to the storage room blew outward in a shower of fiery sparks. Smoke billowed into the antechamber and a dark shape darted out of the storeroom, looking for the exit. Garrand and Torg sat watching the spectacle dumbly. Garrand cocked his head toward the assassin with his eyebrows raised in question. Torg burst out laughing, a raucous sound that wracked his chest.

Vailetta Strom took heed of the laughter and froze mid-step. She caught sight of the two men sitting against the far wall, crystal goblets in their hands, an empty decanter on the floor. She straightened up and walked crisply to the two men.

Torg's laughter billowed out into the room like the cloud of smoke. Garrand looked up at her with eyes sad and black.

"What are you two *idiots* doing?" Vailetta demanded. Her hands were placed defiantly on her hips. "You're supposed to be *rescuing* me, Médeville!"

Torg bellowed with added mirth, the sound filling the chamber. She had never heard the man laugh before.

"And you," she pointed an accusing finger at the assassin. "You're supposed to be *guarding* me!"

"We were just discussing that situation," Garrand said solemnly.

"I'm afraid we were unable to come to an agreement," Torg added.

"What? You were going to fight over me?" Vailetta queried sarcastically. "How quaint."

"That seems to have been our only recourse."

"I don't get a say?" he hands tightened into fists. "Why can't I decide what happens to me?"

Garrand and Torg looked uncertainly at the other. Garrand's voice was barely a whisper. "I don't think that the loser would just let you walk away…"

Torg murmured his agreement. "Yes, I'm afraid we're both a bit stubborn in our views."

Vailetta looked down at the two men. Her life would pivot on this moment. The assassin looked at her with warm, amber eyes. His black uniform was creased and perfect, the pride and arrogance and power he projected mirrored everything she could remember about her early life in the Royal Court on Daulinbêres. Here was the embodiment of the guarded existence she had once led. Here was the man her father had sent to protect her, a simple request that had turned into a lifelong mission. Here was everything safe and protected. Everything she had set aside when she'd chosen her own path.

And Médeville. He stared at her with eyes as dark and sad as any should recall. His face was bloodied and misshapen by battle, the lines in his face like cracks in his heart. His clothes were tattered and his hands bled. He looked terrible—haunted and alone, and yet here he was. He'd come back for her.

"I suppose I'll have to decide for you." She lashed out with her boot, smashing the heel into the side of Torg's head just below his ear, catching him completely off guard. His head snapped back and hit the wall with a crack.

Garrand watched the assassin's unconscious form slump forward onto his lap.

"Garrand," Vailetta pulled at his limp arm. "We've got to get out of here!"

"But—"

"On your feet soldier!"

"But you—"

"Garrand Médeville, you do not have to rescue every woman you meet."

"That's good," he said with no trace of humor, "because I am not very good at it."

"Rise!" Garrand let her pull him upright. He looked at the innate form of the assassin as Vailetta dragged him out of the room.

Garrand stumbled along trying to clear his mind. He shook his head.

Vailetta stopped him, reaching into her belt. She withdrew a dermal needle patch. "Here, this adrenaline should help." She pressed the tiny square into his forearm.

Garrand stared at her for a stunned moment as if stung. His eyes came back to life and he gripped her hand with determination. He reached his free hand behind her neck and drew her to his body, his lips finding hers in the natural progression of a deep kiss.

The accumulated shock of the day's events made her hesitate. Then her relief at seeing him outside the storage room overcame any hesitation. *He'd come back.* She kissed him back hard, hands grabbing the nape of his neck, pulling him closer, hips angled into his. Reluctantly she withdrew her lips to find him starring deeply into her eyes.

"I could not bear to lose another," he whispered.

Vailetta's chest swelled and she closed her eyes, letting the words sink in. Then she remembered: "Where's Tchelakov?"

Garrand clouded over. "Gone," he whispered numbly.

"Then there's nothing to keep us here."

"*Gone,*" he whispered.

"No dragon's tears for the dead, Captain. Her name will be carved in the Great Hall with the rest. Honor will be done." She took his hand and pulled him. "It's time we got off this dreadful rock. Come on, there's a ship for us to steal, and a tribe of pandas that need a lift."

8

A ROYAL GUEST

LEUSTA PULLED AT THE ELECTRICAL FEEDS WITH HER teeth, growling in pain. She ripped the tubes that monitored her heart and respiration out of her arms and disengaged the lacy neural feeds with one swipe of her claw as the doctors outside the bubble field screamed mutely. Remnants of the dream left her angry and confused; her mind reeled with images of the Path gone horribly awry. The feeds pulled out easily enough, tearing the flesh only a little as they popped loose. The men in white-jackets waved their arms futilely as the tangle of wires swung free. Brilliant shapes twisted in static disarray beneath the giant spheres. Planets and stars collided into one another in glittering sparkles, squadrons of ships flashed in and out in a chaotic frenzy and the sartographic display dissolved into confusion as the panda disengaged herself mid-vision. The burst of colors washed over the bubble field like an explosion captured in slow motion. Leusta dropped her head and slammed her shoulder into the bubble.

"Let her out before she does herself serious damage!" Dr. Crevlin bellowed. "Shut it down."

The coppery spheres that glowed overhead began to whine as the power bled away, but the sartographic projections continued to dance in a turbulent jumble. Leusta tilted back her head and roared, the sound so fierce that it could be heard through the containment field. She crouched back against the egg-curved wall and threw herself against the opposite side. The barrier sparkled under her impact and held. Leusta howled again.

"Let her out!"

"Are you sure?"

"Disengage the bubble."

The field evaporated and Leusta charged out of the bubble room, barreling over the dragon-scaled soldier foolhardy enough to step in her way. She could smell the stink of the Fokathenais as she raced down the dark corridor and dove into the suspensor tube. Her breathing almost returned to normal as she descended through the roof of the Habitat, down through the tall pines and reassuring green wave of bamboo until her paws once more touched the ground.

The dirt outside the suspensor tube was warm and dry and she took her time to roll properly in it before she felt able to continue. She looked back at where the suspensor tube disappeared into the stone sky—a black circle that led to the bubble room with its copper spheres and foul, rotting dragons. It was an odd sensation being hooked to the visions of another, particularly the strange shifting voices of a dozen *tholas*, all babbling to speak at once. It was even worse to hear what they had to say, to see what they showed her. She shook her head violently as if she could physically dispel the visions. She did not want to remember. She did not want to see. For the first time since she had learned to control her own wild stroval as a cub she wished she did not have that particular power. If only she could forget, could block out the wretched visions of the Path they'd embarked upon. The incorporeal voices of the *tholas* still rang in her head—their bloody thoughts still imprinted on her mind. There was no forgetting. And the Elders awaited. With a tremendous sigh, she set off down the path that wound between the pines.

Ten pandas sat in a solemn circle around a fire that crackled in the center of the lyceum. The usual banter that proceeded these sessions was absent. The Elders waited in silence. Each of them knew that this fresh Path had led to a dangerous shift in the tribe's fortunes. It had become apparent in the dream sessions, hooked to the mighty *thola* spheres, that Barrett's 'unifying campaign' would unleash destruction and wars unlike anything ever experienced. As brutal as they were one-sided. At first, full of the human's *hubris*, the Circle believed that they could wend their way around the carnage, finding peaceful solutions to each new strategic conflict. But it had become apparent that it would not work; the rest of the Shell would begin to unite against them. Every foreseeable path darkened with blood and destruction.

Leusta sat at the space left for her in front of the fire. As Procurer of Intelligence, it was her place to begin. "This is intolerable," she growled harshly, waiting to be rebuked; none was forthcoming. "We never should have abandoned our original Path."

"We realize the folly, Leusta," Cabeus said softly.

"As flimsy as it once seemed, it is infinitely preferable to this darkness which fills my dreams." Her voice still shook from the last *tromaveint*. "I would rather die than by my existence, cause the deaths of others."

The Circle clicked in stern agreement.

"Tell us what you saw," Ell'han rumbled.

"There is a blackness that has descended upon the possible Paths. It seems to be unavoidable. No matter which direction we take, no matter which course is chosen, the Path of Fate ends in chaos and death."

"Our death?" Ell'han asked.

"No. We survive. It is everyone else that dies. Billions and billions of lives snuffed out."

"I don't understand."

"We must abandon this new course!" Leusta cried. "I have seen where it leads. The wars that Barrett asks us to foresee will annihilate a thousand worlds. No matter how brilliant our strategy, billions perish."

"We cannot continue," Cabeus said gravely. "It is as she says. All paths lead to darkness unbearable. It is as if we reached a precipice. Any step forward will lead us over the edge."

"We must escape," Leusta said. "We cannot aid Barrett. Willingly or unwillingly."

Ell'han's head snapped around. "You have seen this? Unwilling use of our dreams?"

Cabeus nodded. "Terrible, terrible things. Machines hooked to us. Our young taken from us at inception."

The Elder's head drooped in misery. "What have we done?"

"Escape," Leusta prodded. "We must escape."

"There is no *escape*. No one has imagined such a feat in all our attempts at foreseeing it. There is not just one *thola* door guarding us, but a series of ever more complicated contraptions. You've spoken with the Ecksley door. It is wiser than anyone here. Do you think we could fool *it*?"

"But there has to be a way."

"There is but one hope," Ell'han said sadly. All the pandas stared at him. "We must hope that Sid still follows our original Path. We must hope that the *Griffin* has helped him find Archiva. We must hope that they find and rescue the Thief of Ships. We must hope that she helps him find his way here, that all the dreams along that twisted Path come to pass. We may never escape. But perhaps we can be *rescued*."

❖ ❖ ❖

THE SOFT ROCKING MOTION OF THE CARRIAGE LULLED GARRAND into a gentle reverie. The warm fur and steady, rhythmic pulse of the creature that lay against his side was soothing and calm—a tangible respite from the day's emotional ending. He scrunched his hand through the thick pelt and felt the panda's heat. Alexander's breath rose and fell with patient faith. Half awake, he listened to the soft, gentle sounds and click-clacks of the tracks beneath the carriage. The harsh memories were left behind as they rolled through the snowy mountain pass. He flexed his shoulders and arms, curled his toes, taking stock of the aches and bruises. His stomach grumbled and he opened his eyes. A pale glow suffused the compartment.

The young woman slept next to, her beautiful back turned toward him. He placed a hand on the small nook above the rise of her hips and let her warmth trickle through his fingers. Feeling along the little bumps in her spine, he rubbed her skin with his hand. Somehow he'd kicked the covers off his legs, and his knees were freezing. He slid them back under, found Vailetta's warmth and nestled against her.

How they had all fallen asleep here he couldn't remember. The steady click-clacks strummed up through the berth, and it didn't seem to matter. He felt a firm, small pressure on his shoulder, like that of a child's stubby finger pressing questioningly into him. It was a cold, wet push. He looked back over his shoulder to see Alexander sniffing delicately at his neck. He smiled and reached round to scratch his furry chin. Alexander rumbled appreciatively and settled in even closer. Garrand was happy to have the silent company. He closed his eyes and melted back into the rhythmic cadence of the train and imagined the snow blowing relentlessly outside.

Something jostled the carriage and he awakened more fully.

"Garrand, wake up."

"Hmm?" He could still feel the foreign motion buzzing up through the berth, a persistent drone. They were still moving.

"You've been asleep for almost two days."

"What's that?"

"It's time to get up."

He blinked and sat up. Vailetta was looking at him, except she was dressed. His feet touched the floor. It was freezing and vibrating slightly. He could feel a continual thrum, but no click-clacks.

"Where are we?"

"Almost to Wyx. A few hours now. Time to get some food in you."

He frowned. *Not on a train. On a ship. A ship within a ship. That's what he felt, a foreign reactor lulling him to sleep, vibrating up through* Destiny's *hull.* Rubbing his eyes, he asked, "I've been asleep how long?"

"Don't worry, I think you needed it." She smiled kindly down at him. "Hop in the 'fresher and join us for breakfast. Jean-Wa's got something cooking."

GARRAND WAS PLEASED to find his three arts, the two pandas, and Vailetta waiting for him in *Destiny's* mess.

"Welcome back to the living," Vailetta smiled softly.

"Good day, Capítän. I trust you are feeling better."

"You sleep more than a Breyer sloth," Sid growled.

Jean-Wa rolled forward clutching a silver tray of biscuits and fruit. "The Capítän needs his sleep, you leave him be." The art produced a pitcher of janda and a mug from another set of arms and began pouring as he talked. "It is good, the rest. Allows the body to heal, yes? And now he needs the food. We have a hearty menu prepared. Sit, sit." He pushed Garrand into his chair.

"Thanks," Garrand said sheepishly.

"Now you have your janda and a piece of fruit and I will start the eggs." The art rolled back to his kitchen, humming happily.

"I'm surprised you're not fat as an ox," Vailetta observed playfully. "I've never seen such a commotion."

"If I ever stayed put long enough…" He crunched into a biscuit. "What exactly are we in, by the way?"

"*Mou Tradim*," Bailey replied. "Caroultus freighter with Stavvi registry."

"You have any trouble getting us booked?"

Vailetta sat down across from him. "Got a few funny looks from the booking agent when I told him I wanted to secure transport for the whole ship and its cargo and its crew on the very next freighter. He told me just shipping the cargo was the accepted practice. I told him we had a cargo to pick up on that end, that we were having troubles with our reactor, so we needed our cargo and our ship delivered. It would make financial sense since we'd have time to work on the problem in transit and could pay for the repairs with our shipment on the back end. Told him if we stayed on New Haivello we'd lose the contract on Wyx, have nothing to show for the journey and still have a ship that needed repair."

"He bought it?"

"Yeah, even tried to sell me a slot in the *Mou's* repair hold with access to their facilities — at a substantially greater price. Told him we could handle it ourselves and didn't need access to the common areas — not for such a short trip. Got us a berth in one of the vacuum holds. We're locked in with the ore and mining equipment."

"Ostensibly, to affect repairs on our light drive during the journey, eh? Any trouble with the Imperial protocols?"

"A city-wide ban on exports of any kind had just gone in effect. An across-the-board proscription — Barrett must have just signed the edict. Shipping agent was all a dither. Went through the motions of arguing my request, saying he couldn't possibly amend his shipping docket with such a severe ban in effect. But it was nothing a little extra bump in the contract couldn't solve. I think it helped that I was still wearing my uniform. He couldn't stop looking at my insignia."

Garrand grinned, mouth full of crumbs. He missed that sort of unconditional respect. "It's good to be a Guardsman sometimes."

"I helped him wipe the record of our transaction afterward. The protocols were pretty easy to get around."

"Backwater overrides still work?"

"Yeah — until they change them next week. I'll be out of the loop then. Anyway, I doubt anyone could trace us to this ship.

The agent will keep his mouth shut to cover his infraction and protect his newfound wealth. And the official docket doesn't even show us aboard."

"Hmm. So we're safe as long as we stay inside the belly of this monster." He sighed and leaned back in his chair. "Once we're on the surface of Wyx it'll be another matter altogether."

Vailetta smiled slyly. "You needn't worry about that."

"Worry about being on the Proctorial Capital?" Garrand asked sarcastically. "Worry about trying to steal Barrett's most prized possession right out from under his nose?"

"That's my stomping grounds, Garrand," she said confidently. "I know the encryptions for every protocol there is—well, except one."

"Let me guess..."

"The pandas' subterranean Habitat is controlled by a separate security force," she admitted.

"That's all right, I figured as much." He looked at Sid. "We've had a few dreams about the hallway leading in. It's underground?"

"Yeah."

"And it's guarded by a series of doors?"

"Yeah," she said curiously. "Five. How'd you know?"

By way of explanation, Garrand jerked his head toward the big panda. "Can you get me into the hall?"

"Once we're on the surface, I can access the Gokazoku's files. I can pull up plans for the whole city. Show you exactly where to go."

"I'm going to need time to get through those doors," he cautioned. "*Undisturbed* time."

"That's not a problem—up to a point. I can suspend security links from the Habitat to the outside."

"Using the old—"

"The old sleeper codes, yes. They work on Wyx just like any other Imperial planet."

Sid perked up, his ears swiveling round. "What is this 'sleepy code?'"

"Sleeper code," Vailetta explained. "When programmers set up datacores on Imperial planets, or outposts or what-have-you they leave secret access paths in the command structure. Subroutines that lie dormant in the datacores until someone in a tight spot needs them to circumvent the new security protocols that have been put in place. Sometimes the codes are buried so deep the core itself isn't even aware of them."

"People with high rank, or people entrusted with the welfare of the Empire and it's assets—like Guardsmen—have knowledge of these sleeper codes," Garrand interjected.

"And they are 'asleep' until you need them?" Sid asked.

"Just like missionaries planting the seeds of faith in a foreign land for his brothers who will follow him," Vailetta said. She glanced back across the table. "I can keep the relevant cores tied up for awhile. But it won't last indefinitely. Eventually they'll figure out what's going on. You'll have a couple of hours at best."

"That'll be enough. Sid and I can tackle the doors. You and Bailey will be in charge of transportation."

"We're not going to use *Destiny's Needle?*"

"If you have access to the old sleeper codes then there's almost nothing you can't get your hands on."

It was Vailetta's turn to look a little chagrinned. "You want me to get something else," she said slowly.

Garrand smiled wickedly. "Around here, you're known as the 'Thief of Ships.'"

"You want me to *steal* a ship?"

"Why take a chance trying to escape in a light cruiser when we can have our pick of the fleet?"

"You want me to steal an *Imperial warship?*"

"It's no use arguing with me. We've already dreamt of it happening. Get us something big," he said. "With lots of guns."

Vailetta sat back and let her breath whoosh out. "The 'Thief of Ships,' huh? A rather ignoble title."

Garrand waved his hand. "Eh, maybe a little something was lost in the translation." He paused to rub his lip, thinking of what Bailey had said about her lineage. "You used to a little more grandiose title?"

She wouldn't rise to the bait. "I'm going to need help if I'm going to steal a capital ship," she mused. She pinched her lips together and stared at Garrand. "I'm going to have to tell my men. I can't leave them behind anyway. I'll have to try to enlist their support."

"Fine. Bring whomever you want. Just make sure you get that ship."

Vailetta said, "If I can sway my men, then we'll have no problem."

"How long do you figure Barrett will stay on New Haivello?"

"Long enough to try to find where we're hiding. But not long. After awhile he'll realize that we slipped away."

"And he'll come racing back to Wyx."

Vailetta nodded grimly. "And the *Cabot* is a lot faster than this freighter."

"You have to get to the Gokazoku before he does."

"I will."

Jean-Wa wheeled in with freshly steaming trays. "Breakfast is served."

GARRAND GORGED HIMSELF on Jean-Wa's considerable offerings. He staggered out of the mess feeling bloated and strangely sleepy again. Bailey and Vailetta accompanied him out the mess.

Bailey said, "We've got just under three hours till we hit the surface, Captain."

Garrand glanced at Vailetta. "How will you suspend the security links to the Habitat?"

"There's a couple of tricks I know. There's a few codes that have been buried in the cores out here since before Barrett was ever born. I'm privy to a few special overrides…"

It slowly dawned on Garrand what she was referring to. "Then it's true, what they said?"

Vailetta stubbornly ignored him. "If the codes are still in place then I can keep the core preoccupied for quite some time."

He pressed her: "Codes only privy to members of the Imperial Court? Or perhaps the Royal Family?" She remained stone-faced. "So you're really the Emperor's daughter?"

"One of them at least," she replied quietly.

"Why," Bailey exclaimed, "that makes you—"

"—A princess!" Garrand groaned. "By Haven, I'll never hear the end of it now. Médeville and the princess…"

Vailetta frowned and stepped suddenly forward, grasping the loose fabric around Garrand's collar into a fist and pulling him close.

"Hush now," she growled.

"But a princess?" he moaned. "How will I ever be able to live that down?"

"I'm serious," she hissed with a smile. "No more, or I'll have to—" she kissed him roughly on the mouth, biting his lip as she pulled away, "—have you *punished*."

"Mmm… going to exercise some of your *authority*, are you?"

"If you keep misbehaving, I am."

"Princess Strom," Bailey interjected, "having been unaware of your status as a part of the Collistas Family and thus, your Royal stature, I'm afraid I've been misaddressing you all this time. My humblest apologies, indeed."

"Bailey, it's okay. I don't think —"

" — But, if you would provide me with your proper title, I will be assured of no longer committing so grievous a social error; and I will inform the rest of the crew of your new —"

" — No, no, Bailey. We'll have none of that around here. It's fine that you know, but no one else must. I left the Court long ago to escape just such titles, and the suspicions and envy that accompany them. I've worked hard my whole life to make the name 'Strom' mean something, and I would no more cast aside the measure of respect I've earned than cut off my own arm."

Bailey looked to his Captain, expectantly.

Garrand shook his head, "You heard her: no titles. As a matter of fact you are now bound by your programming not to reveal Miss Strom's true identity to anyone — datacore, art, human or otherwise. Understood?"

"Yes of course, Captain. As you wish."

The pair disappeared down the hall. Bailey watched them with interest. Things were different now with Captain Strom aboard, of that there was no doubt. For one thing, the young woman did not behave like a princess, or at least not like any that Bailey had ever met. Far from it — she was hearty and robust, as full of jocular humor and driven passion as the captain was. And that was the other thing. Gone were the sour looks and long, forced separations from the rest of the crew that had become the captain's habit with Helen aboard. It was as if a veil

of despair and self-recrimination had been miraculously lifted
from the human's shoulders. Young Princess Strom had set the
captain back on an even keel once more. Even as they hurtled
into the very heart of Lord Barrett's power there was a sparkle
in his friend's eye, an electricity that coursed through the whole
ship. The fugue that Miss Tchelakov had cast over the captain
was now just a memory.

Bailey replayed Helen's image in his mind, scanning through
key moments in their relationship. Their introduction outside
a dusty cargo bay on Letugia, their late-night conversation in
the mess, their kiss in the bamboo grove... He tried to recall
the exact sensations he had felt after that delicious moment—
they should all be filed away, archived, labeled, imminently
recoverable—but he found to his surprise that some were
missing. How could that be? He replayed the kiss again. Same
result. There were key elements missing, sensations and feelings
that were no longer on file. Or had they ever been? Had he
amended his files concerning Miss Tchelakov since the event?
Were there feelings he had developed over the course of their
relationship that were never a part of that kiss in the bamboo
grove? Things that he now attributed to that event? Very odd.
He had begun to create his own subroutines in a subconscious
state. The Captain would be intrigued.

Bailey tried to focus on a new set of programs. He was not
sure he liked this volatile memory recovery situation. He was
feeling a little too... organic. He called up the latest navigational vector information and began scanning the next several
jumps. He lost his focus halfway through and found his mind
recalling Helen's image once more. He wondered if he might
have ever been able to make the young miss happy... More
troubling by far was the question of Helen's actions and betray-

als. Could he ever have amended his subroutines to the extent
that he could have offered her some semblance of forgiveness?
Was such a thing even possible?

More questions left unanswered. He would have to ask *Destiny* about it one night when the rest of the crew was asleep. He
shunted the questions aside; it was no use cluttering his core
with such paroxysms, the woman was gone. Curiously, though,
his feelings for her remained.

GARRAND AND VAILETTA stood in his quarters, facing one another. Her fingers touched his palm, sliding coolly, evenly
between his fingers, grasping his hand tightly. A current of ex-
pectant energy passed between them. Her eyes flashed, ablaze
with hope. A transcendent expectation coursed through her
body. She felt a tremendous desire to learn more about the
man she had chosen, the man she was fated to spend the rest
of her life with.

She let slip the strap upon her right shoulder, the dark fabric
sliding off her breast with a whisper. She stared at him, unblinking and without doubt. The other strap fell without a
word.

Garrand kept her gaze.

"As you will," she spoke clearly, firmly, with a current of electricity making her heart race and arms tingle.

The crook of a smile surfaced at the corner of Garrand's
mouth. "As you will," he repeated softly.

She let herself be drawn into his arms. He pulled her close
and she kissed him hard, pushing him backward onto the old
four-poster bed. She climbed astride him and pressed her lips
into his neck. He smelled amazing, like the cinnamon dusted
thulo cookies that Jean-Wa served for dessert. How could she

possibly resist his touch? *This is Garrand Ai'Gonet Médeville*, she reminded herself. *Soldier, Freetrader, smuggler, thief—an agent of incredible chaos in the Wyxian Proctorialship.* Yet still her arms slid around his neck, drawing his face close. Those eyes watching her—brownish green hazel: dark and limitless. Wrinkles fanned out around them like ripples on a pond. She stared at him and smiled. She was hungry to taste him, touch him, envelope him with her arms, pull him infinitely closer.

She leaned slowly down to kiss him. One thought filled her mind as their lips touched. *Prophecy or no prophecy, the man came back for her. This is the one.*

9

WYX

TRAPPED INSIDE THE GIANT HUSK OF THE *MOU TRADIM'S*
cargo bay without a single star to punctuate the void, Garrand
felt like he and his ship were ensconced in a giant womb. It was
an unsettling experience walking onto a bridge usually filled
with light and spectacle and seeing nothing but endless darkness outside. The freighter's cargo bay was probably filled with
equipment and craft, but he could make out nothing in the
murky gloom. It was all a little maddening trying to imagine
what might lie just outside the crystal glazings—what odd craft
might be hanging just in front of his nose—but all he could

do was wait and stare at the pods' winking reflections cast back inward. The waiting was the worst. Heading in on the final leg of his journey to recover the tribe, into the heart of the Wyxian Proctorialship, Barrett's stronghold, and all he could do was sit and wait. He couldn't even see where they were going.

But now, after hours of braking through the planet's atmosphere and fighting the massive inertial pull, the freighter rested just over the surface of the commercial freight yard at Jobaenz. The freighter's yawning bay doors cracked open and glorious sunlight spilled into the crystal bridge, reflected off the tarmac's white ceracrete pavers. Garrand could finally see something of the inside of the *Mou Tradim*.

From what he could tell, *Destiny's Needle* was suspended from the ceiling of the freighter's cargo hold in locked jaws like an unwanted spider hanging from the eaves. Several other stellar vessels and hundreds of packaged zips, modified twirls, flatbed lighters and loaders along with all manner of assorted mining devices clung to the girders as well. All of the equipment was locked into place to make room for the tremendous mounds of dryexcellon ore. The dark rock filled the entire floor of the hold, held barely in place by minimal two percent gravity throughout the flight. During descent the piles had shifted and settled, creating a landscape of rolling hillocks.

Garrand sat sprawled back on his acceleration couch and watched as giant conveyors trundled beneath his ship, poking up through the cargo doors. Tech arts paddled into the hold and began spreading out over the mounds. The machines began transferring the curving swells of ore onto the conveyors that hauled it out the hold and dumped it into trains of cargo lighters that hovered outside. The gaping doors allowed bright sunshine to filter in through the rising dust.

"How are we gonna get through port customs?" he asked grumpily.

"We don't have to," Vailetta said without looking up, "we're not on the *Mou's* docket, remember?"

"We're a little big to miss. Port Authority's going to spot us visually."

"Not if we don't leave they won't. And they've got no province in the ship's hold. We're just part of the mining equipment up here. As long as we don't hover out onto the tarmac we should have no problem."

Garrand chewed on the inside of his cheek. "They find us locked down in here, that's it. There's no way we can fight our way out of this."

"Will you stop worrying," she said impatiently. "This is the easy part. You wanted me to get you on Wyx, I got you on Wyx. And if you'll leave me alone for a minute I'll have the protocols under control."

Well, she had done that, he reflected. *Gotten them down on Wyx in one piece. And undetected—so far.* The command board quivered gently under his hand; *Destiny's* repulsors were hovering to ease the load on the freighter's locking jaws now that they were in full gravity. The whole crew was on the bridge, curious to see the insides of the gigantic freighter now that it was lit. Alexander and Sid had the navi pod down at the nadir where they stared at the endless heaps of ore and the hundreds of artificial loaders who paddled through the brown gravel, kicking chunks onto the conveyors with their spinning scoops.

Bailey and Vailetta sat at the pod next to him, finishing their links to the surface cores.

"Where exactly are we?" Garrand asked.

Vailetta finished tapping in commands and an image snapped into focus in the bridge's hollow. "We're docked at the commercial port, here," she pointed. "You're heading for the Naval promenade which is at the edge of the city. The commercial port rubs up against the military yard and naval command is right in between them." The image shifted and a new section rose into view. Beautiful teardrop buildings filled a pavilion, their slender, inverted tips supported by pillories. "You'll find the suspensor tube in this building, and it's the only outside entrance to the Habitat. The doors, observation rooms, and medical facilities are all accessible from inside the main dome. A suspensor tube inside the Habitat leads to Barrett's chambers and his new bubble room."

"Bubble room?"

"That's what he calls it—provides sartographic linkup for the pandas with a bunch of E2's."

"Hmm."

"You might have to check there if the headcount comes up short."

"Where will you be?"

"I've sent an encrypted signal to my first lieutenant. I'm going to try to rally the Gokazoku here, at the Creighton Yards. If all goes well, we'll make an attempt to commandeer a ship from the Yard while you're busy at the Habitat."

Garrand peered at the holo map. "How am I supposed to get there?"

"Take a cargo lighter, it's only six kilometers away. You'll want to stay away from mass transportation anyway. There'll be plenty of street-level traffic, you'll be just another trader."

"I've got to take Sid with me," Garrand warned. "No telling what I'm going to find down there."

"I can tell you exactly what you'll find," Vailetta said. "A big enclosed dome at the bottom of the tube filled with excavating equipment and a long hall guarded by five doors, each different than the one before."

"I mean, I don't know exactly how I'm going to get through them. I need Sid, it's as simple as that."

"Well, I guess you could put him in a cargo pallet and stack it on the back of the lighter."

"Yeah, but how am I going to get past the physical security at the Naval promenade? There's got to be guards, right?"

"Hmm, yeah. Seven men at the top of the tube. Let me think about that one for a minute."

"Have you engaged the Habitat's security protocols?"

"I'm saving that for last," she sighed and bit her lip.

Garrand thought about Vailetta's description. "You said there was only the one entrance to the dome leading to the five doors."

"Yeah?"

"But you just said there was a bunch of equipment in the dome — stuff too big to go down a tube."

Vailetta nodded. "There is a large blast door at one end, but the controls are only accessible from the inside. Hold on a second." She punched up the relevant section of the map. "Yeah, here. See, this ramp leads down to the construction entrance from the edge of the Yard. It's a straight shot — they had a lot of rock to haul out. Actually that would be a pretty good place to take them out once you get inside, but like I said it's only accessible from the inside. I can't order the doors to open from a remote terminal because the security for the Habitat is —"

" — Separate. Yeah, okay. But you're going to sever their link to the outside, right?"

"In a manner of speaking, yeah."

"What about *Destiny's Needle*? I feel funny just leaving her hanging here."

"We leave the ship here for now," Vailetta said firmly. "Once we have an alternate means of transportation, then we'll risk moving her out in the open."

"How long is the *Mou Tradim* supposed to remain here?"

"She's scheduled to unload cargo for thirteen hours," Bailey replied.

"Okay," Garrand said reluctantly. "Bailey, you stay here on the bridge. Vailetta will be out of contact for awhile, and I may need some guidance before it's all said and done."

GARRAND, SID AND Vailetta stood in *Destiny's* aft cargo hold next to a hovering lighter. Two cargo pallets were stacked on top, side by side. The big outer door lay open before them. A gangway had extended from the *Mou Tradim* leading to an elevated catwalk.

"Okay, hop in."

Sid growled deep in the back of his throat.

"It's not like you can walk around in the open here, Sid. There's a bit of a price on your head you know." The panda showed his teeth but segued into a yawn. "Yeah, take a nap or something. You're going to have to put on a good show when we get there."

Sid climbed up onto the lighter and sat down inside the pallet.

"I promise it won't be too long," Garrand said as he climbed up behind him, shutting the side into place and latching it down. He hopped down, pulling self-consciously at the hem of his new jacket. The heel of his hand rubbed his hip where his blaster normally hung; he felt skinny and naked.

Vailetta smiled and stepped forward. "You look great," she murmured brushing hair off his jacket. She smoothed the creases on his chest and allowed her hands to linger.

"I'm nervous," he mumbled self-consciously. "I never thought I'd get this far."

"You're going to do just fine," she said quietly. "Barrett doesn't even know we're here yet. Besides Sid's already seen you working on the doors, so that means the guards won't be a problem, right?"

"Yeah..." he said with no conviction, half-grimacing.

"What?" she asked soothingly.

His chin dropped and he stared at his feet. "It's just—I don't know. I don't have any of my stuff, and—"

"All your gear is in the other pallet. You won't need it until you get down there." She turned his head back and kissed him gently on the lips. "You're going to be fine. You've already *seen* this happening. You just have to do it."

"Yeah?" The wrinkles around his eyes spread up and he allowed a bit of a smile. "Here, put this on." He fished in his pocket and handed her a comtab. "It's an encrypted channel, linked to me and *Destiny* only."

She affixed the small square to the left lapel of Garrand's well-worn jacket that hung loosely over her smaller shoulders. "Thanks."

"I guess I'll see you in a couple of hours." He stepped behind the lighter and eased it out the door.

"Just be firm with the guards," she called after him. "You remember what it was like."

❖ ❖ ❖

HEAT LINES RIPPLED ACROSS THE TARMAC—TRANSLUCENT
snakes which danced an endless shuffle. The quivering patterns
were mesmerizing at first, like open flames in a beach side bon-
fire. Wyx's primary shone brightly through the scattered clouds,
fingers of light and shadow playing out in slow-moving patterns across the vast facility. Gigantic ceracrete pavers baked
in the sun. Vailetta squinted through the jiggering heat at a
monolithic gate. The glare marred the details of the wide, low
entrance, a maw big enough to hover an entire cruiser into.
Hangars, tech facilities, and repair yards lay safely ensconced in
subterranean pits.

The only ship visible for a kilometer in any direction was
the sizable hulk of the *Lucayamo* that hovered fifty meters over
the tarmac behind her. The destroyer lurched against the winds
and moaned as its mooring rings rubbed against the docking
towers.

Though the hard-site port facility appeared deserted, it was
far from inactive. In the distance, tiny men and machines
could be seen swarming over glistening shapes, trickling in thin
lines between the great ships and the dark subterranean gates—
dwarfed by the vast spaces. Unlike Jobaenz' commercial port
which packed as many revenue-generating landing pits and
freight yards into each square kilometer with many flyer pads
reaching well into the sky, Creighton Yards, home of Lord Barrett's Imperial Third Fleet was spread out on a surreal scale.
The military had the luxury and the necessity of space—incredible amounts of space. Commercial limitations were of no
consequence; the thrust of all Barrett's economic machinations
was to build the finest fleet in all of Carinaena's Shell. Con-

versely, the truly spectacular fleet enabled him to press more and more economic resources into his fold.

Tightly packed ships lined up in neat rows were too easy a target for orbital bombardment. Thus, everything about "The Yard" was on a scale fit for giants. The ships of the Third Fleet were spread out over hundreds of square kilometers, making the spidery, gargantuan vessels seem childlike and small. Not only did the great spaces allow Barrett an almost exponential degree of potential expansion in terms of interstellar matériel, it also allowed the enormous capital ships to be overhauled on the planet's surface. In practice, the ships were never actually on the surface; landing struts able to bear the ships' unfathomable tonnage were not a part of their design. Instead they hovered some fifty meters over the concrete slabs. Repairs could be performed far more easily in an atmospheric environment, and at far less expense. There were fewer things that could go wrong, the arts and techs were easier to supervise, cheaper to run. Mules, chrysanths, phantoms, and lighters could all be hovered off and replaced with little trouble. Ship's stores, arms, ammunition, equipment and the massive detritus necessary to clothe and feed thousands of men for six months or more could be restocked without the 2,672 ferry runs required for a full orbital overhaul of Tobana class destroyer.

Vailetta gazed back at the *Lucayamo* whose hull stretched back for the better part of a kilometer, so large that her form could not be eclipsed by a full shadow of the puffy monster clouds that drifted lazily above Wyx. Dappled in sunlight, the dark hull seemed oddly luminescent in the alternate shadows and glare. She was not nearly the silent, dark scythe she resembled in orbit. With her long, tapering superstructures and attenuated spires she looked quite beautiful, like a marvelous cathedral lain on its side.

Vailetta stepped into the slender access gantry that had risen up from the slab to meet the *Lucayamo*. She entered the suspensor tube and rose toward the nose of the ship gazing down the length of her exposed belly. The *Lucayamo* floated over the tarmac like an ancient dirigible tethered to its mooring mast. The ship was eerily quiet with its repulsors shut down. Suspended by the field generators buried beneath the concrete slabs, the destroyer rested all its major systems as the overhaul progressed.

The ship was not still. Like a seafaring vessel tied to her moorings, she bobbed and slipped on the fluctuations of the suspensor field which buoyed her up. Her massive surface area caught the winds, yawing against the gusts. The leeward thrusters fought a never-ending corrective battle.

The tube hovered Vailetta to its zenith and she stepped to the gangway. The open airlock in the *Lucayamo's* hull dipped a full meter and sloughed away from the gantry, creating a perilous gap as the ship hove to the gusts. The edge of the portal bobbed back up and slipped toward her before dropping suddenly again. Vailetta gauged the motion, waited for the edge to return, then stepped gingerly across.

She wondered if she would get spacesick for the first time in her career as she grabbed for a handhold. No wonder all the crewers took leave of their ship during hard-site overhaul — with inertial dampers offline, only poddies would be accustomed to such motion. She took a deep breath and collected herself, pulling at loose tangles in her windswept hair and squaring her dark blazer.

The interior of the ship was dark and silent here. She paced quickly through the corridor and took a tube to Gregson level three. The ship was nearly deserted and Vailetta felt a strange sense of lonely abandon as she hurried through the broad passages. She didn't like this—a ship was meant to be filled with people. Without them it seemed dead, a hollow shell, the forgotten husk of great technology.

She was glad when she reached the giant blast door guarding the officer's mess. The door scrolled open, revealing a darkened chamber. Brightly-colored banners of mythical creatures and dragons clutching crossed swords and shields, severed heads and green bolts of lightning hung from the walls—the icons of Imperial units stationed aboard the *Lucayamo*. Beautiful handcrafted tables with polished ashen surfaces lined the room, chairs tucked neatly underneath. The long, familiar bar stood against one wall, glossy smooth and empty. Glasses were clean and neatly stacked in the hazy glazings behind it. Beneath them, hundreds of tightly packed bottles reflected the myriad tint of the spirits within.

Vailetta walked slowly into the interior and stopped in the center of the room. Eleven figures rested in the shadows around one table. The men and women sat in various states of recline, legs propped up, arms spread behind the shoulders of mates, chairs tilted back. She could barely make out their faces in the half-light—dark eyes watched her with silent interest.

The Gokazoku Kaigi awaited her.

"Thank you for coming," she began quietly. "Undoubtedly you've heard the accusations from New Haivello." She hesitated uncomfortably, trying to summon up her nerve. "The accusations are hard. Hard at first to explain—harder still to fathom, to understand." She glanced at each face. "We've been through quite a bit together. Three years ago when we first set out for Carinaena's Shell we were bound by an oath—an oath to uphold the honor of the Dragon. And I'd wager to say we've done that. Time and again we've done it. The long months of service have bound us by deeper things. Blood. Loyalty.

"We've seen both ends of it. The glory and the accolades, plus the loss. There's more than a few names etched in the Great Hall and each of us has run their fingers over stone. But we've held our own in tough situations. And this, this may be the toughest yet. Beyond all complications, it all comes down to this: I've been called a traitor to the Wyxian Proctorialship, a traitor against Hellius Barrett." She studied her men carefully. No one moved.

"For the last week I have undergone a crisis of character. My loyalty to the Dragon has come in conflict with my loyalty to the Empire, and those who claim to lead in its name. My whole career I have followed orders without question or doubt. I have since discovered that there are greater dangers than being called a traitor. I cannot blindly follow orders that will endanger the very regime I've sworn to uphold."

Vailetta rubbed the indentation on Garrand's blazer where the Imperial dragon was once stitched. She sighed and plunged forward. "Lord Barrett now seeks my life—Shock Troopers pursued me across New Haivello and fired on me repeatedly. And if you join me, he will soon seek yours as well. I have discovered that the Tchelakov creatures that we delivered to Lord Barrett will be used to unite the Shell against the Core and challenge the sovereignty of the Emperor himself. This is unacceptable. So in regard to the accusations, I'd like to tell you that they are untrue, but I cannot." She took a slow breath and straightened her chest and shoulders. "It is true that I am a traitor to the Wyxian Proctorialship, for I serve the Dragon, Emperor Collistas, and no other."

A chair tilted forward and a man stood up, his face obscured in the darkness. He grabbed the bottom of his dark blazer and tugged it taut as he stepped in front of her. "It doesn't matter what you say," Dasko said with a frown. He glanced back at the rest of the men for encouragement. When he turned back his face was beaming. "You've told us all we need to know. The Gokazoku Kaigi have served the Dragon for five centuries, and I humbly submit, we are yours 'till death!" The rest of the men stood up sharply. Eleven bodies stood ramrod straight, eyes forward, shoulders squared, chests out. They saluted in unison.

"Welcome aboard the *Lucayamo*!" Dasko declared.

"Thank you, lieutenant," Vailetta whispered, a sigh of relief spreading through her body. "At ease."

The Gokazoku surged forward and surrounded her with boisterous enthusiasm.

"It's about time you got back!" Lewg gave her a big hug.

"Cheplus, Captain," Farres shouted. "Have us creepin' round this big empty ship like ghosts!"

"What's the plan, Captain?" Kalen asked.

Galar pulled Lewg off the blushing woman. "When we gettin' off this rock?"

"We don't need to sneak anywhere, we're the Goka—"

Farres shoved Lewg roughly, "Shut up fool!"

Vailetta grinned despite herself and slowly extricated herself from her men. "This won't be easy," she warned them. "You'll be breaking with the ruling Imperial authority in this volume. You'll all be branded as traitors. And it may not be any different once we get out of here. If we ever get back to the Core, we might still be viewed with a jaundiced eye."

"Don't matter none t'us, Captain."

"Where you go—we go," Dasko agreed.

Vailetta nodded with grave satisfaction. "Well then, it's settled. The Gokazoku Kaigi now serve the Dragon's interests in the Shell, and the Dragon's interests alone. And as far as I'm concerned, we're the only Imperial force in the Shell that is serving the Dragon."

"What's our mission?" Dasko asked.

"We have to commandeer a ship."

Lewg whistled. "Steal a ship? In the middle of Jobaenz? From the heart of the Creighton Yards?" He bobbed his head and looked at his mates. "I like it."

"Call it what you will. We're taking a ship and getting off this rock, and we're taking the Tchelakov creatures with us."

"You don't mess around do you?" Dasko cracked.

"How we going to get those beasts out of the dome?" Danelle asked.

"Médeville's working on it. Once we have this ship squared away we'll assist him as best we can."

"Médeville's *here?*"

A serene smile radiated from Vailetta's lips. "Yes. He's here."

"Persistent bastard."

"Aye. And he's also the reason I'm still walking around— saved me from the Shock Troops on New Haivello a couple of times. And that reminds me: once we hook back up he's to be treated as a Captain of the Guard with full respect—no different than you treat me. In my mind, he's still an officer of the Guard. Understood?"

"Aye, Captain."

"Good. Let's get this beast prepped for flight. We've only got a few hours to switch her over from overhaul to flight status."

"We're taking *this* ship?" Dasko asked incredulously.

"What, you don't like Tobana destroyers?"

Dasko shook his head. "I just thought maybe we could start with something a little smaller."

"This one's halfway through resupply and overhaul," Lewg protested.

Farres pushed him again. "Means no one's gonna notice us creepin' around it, fool."

"Médeville says I'm now known as the 'Thief of Ships,'" Vailetta said, "and I plan on living up to that reputation. We take the biggest and the baddest. And this is it."

"But there's only twelve of us."

"Médeville's been pluggin' along with just himself and a couple of arts. We going to let *Destiny's Needle* show us up?"

Dasko grinned. "No, ma'am."

"Besides, I have my mind set on someone who can handle this monster's systems in his sleep…"

❖ ❖ ❖

GARRAND SWALLOWED HARD. HE FELT LIKE A MARKED MAN pushing his lighter up beneath the inverted teardrop building in the heart of the Naval promenade. Six giant columns supported the structure—the tip of the teardrop never actually touched the surface. Strange aurora fields buzzed and popped behind him, electricity and color hopping from cable to cable in what he supposed was a display of art. It made him feel like someone was creeping up behind him with a stun wand.

Officers streamed in and out of the first floor of the complex, headed for one of the six columns and tubes to higher levels. Just as Vailetta said, afternoon was a busy time and the first three guards didn't give him a second glance as he hovered his lighter by. Granted, he did look the part. Vailetta had made him press his old Imperial trousers and shine his boots—twice. She had overseen the physical transformation, carefully buttoning up his uniform and slicking back his hair. His buckles were polished. The leather belt around his waist gleamed and both little coil cartridge cases were oiled. Her dark blazer with its five-clawed dragon and twin daggers encircled by a band of gold completed the illusion. He was the vision of a Gokazoku Captain, fresh off a transport, reporting for duty. And by the Barthsa, he did look good.

"No one will question a Captain of the Guard — especially on Wyx, they're used to seeing us," Vailetta had said. "Most will even steer clear if at all possible — there's a certain fear-jealousy thing working. Sentries won't bother a Guardsman in the completion of his everyday duties, and certainly not a captain. You'll be fine until you get to a sensitive area like the column."

Garrand nudged the lighter toward the round door in the third pillar from the left. He felt like everyone's eyes were on him, but no one stopped him as the door irised open. The interior of the column was fifteen meters across. A single suspensor tube disappeared into the center of the floor. Seven heavily armed guards watched him, blast rifles cradled between their arms. The door spiraled close behind him.

He left the lighter hovering and strode confidently forward. It was time, as Vailetta put it, to *take charge.* "Gentlemen, lower your weapons please." No greeting — all business. "In fact, you'd better remove them and put them in a pile by the wall," he pointed to the far side of the tube.

"Pardon me, uh — " the first guard, a huge man with black eyes and a crooked nose squinted at Garrand's collar.

"Captain," Garrand supplied. "Captain Henri C'tereino, Lord Barrett's new Captain of the Guard."

The duty commander sized him over from head to toe. He looked unimpressed. The man had a long scar traveling over the top of his close-shaven head like someone had taken an axe to his skull. Apparently it would take more than that to topple him. Glossy red markings adorned his silver body armor. Garrand's own scar began to itch as the duty commander took a firmer grip on his rifle. "We've received no word of any new *Gokazoku*." The man curled his lip as if the word had a particularly foul taste.

"There's been a transfer of command," Garrand said with subtle force. "It will remain unbroadcast until the previous officer has been taken into custody. I've been instructed not to speak of it until it's official. Out of respect, you understand." Undoubtedly the rumor of Vailetta Strom's downfall had spread through the military ranks. It was only natural that someone would be appointed to take her place—at least that's what she had argued. "That's not important at the moment—I'm sure your section will be informed. But right now I need you and your men to disarm yourselves and stand well back."

"I don't know who you *think* you are—" the commander curled his finger around the trigger, but Garrand cut him short.

"Is there not a *ban* on all weapons around the Tchelakov creatures? Lord Barrett assured me that this was a unbreakable standing order, with the *strictest of penalties*."

"That is below—in the habitat. We are the guards—of course we are armed! There are no pandas here."

"Lower your voice, Commander," Garrand snarled. He flicked his eyes back at the cargo lighter and continued in a strained, angry whisper. "You may not be aware of it, but Lord Barrett is not yet in control of *all* the Tchelakov creatures."

"We're not complete dolts, *Captain*." The large man took another step forward, invading Garrand's space. He was a full six centimeters taller. "Everyone knows there are two missing."

Garrand summoned up as much haughty arrogance as he could muster. "Now there is but one." The lighter hummed in the silence behind him. The guard glanced over Garrand's shoulder. "There is a fine line, lieutenant, between the overzealous pursuit of your sentry duties, and insubordination." Garrand edged closer to the guard, eyes hardened. "I will not ask you again. Remove your weapons."

This was the crucial moment. The guards, Vailetta argued, were there to keep someone from taking the pandas *out*. Who were they to stop someone from taking a panda *in*? Having a panda gave Garrand instant credibility. He had the look and demeanor of the arrogant Guardsmen. He wore the treasured blazer. He confirmed the rumors that Vailetta Strom was indeed a traitor and had been replaced. He knew of the ban on weapons—in fact he mentioned talking to the vice proctor about it personally. And here he'd been able to capture one of the missing creatures and was delivering it to the Habitat himself. By Haven, if there actually was a panda in that cargo pallet, then the guards would have no choice but to bow to Garrand's commands.

The duty commander glared down at the annoying Guardsman, teeth firmly clenched. He took a step back and called out stiffly to his men: "Stand down. Stack your weapons against the wall." The guards hesitated. "Do it!"

Garrand held the man's acid gaze. "You as well, Commander." The man's head was turning red. "Look at me. I'm not carrying any weapon. Surely I could not overwhelm you and your six men with my bare hands."

The commander spun away and tossed his rifle atop the pile.

"Step away from the tube please, I do not want to alarm the creature." The guards shuffled back. Garrand made a show of checking to make sure the line didn't look too threatening and then hopped up on the lighter. He unlatched the first pallet and jumped off, backing away from the box. The side swung open and a black-and-white-furred head poked out.

"Come on out," Garrand said sternly, his finger pointing to the tube. "Don't make me pull you out of there." As the seven guards watched in amazement, the giant panda lumbered off the lighter and swayed toward the suspensor tube. The panda turned and looked backward. "Go!" Sid stepped into the field and slowly disappeared.

Garrand pushed the lighter around to the tube and struggled with the second pallet. "Give me a hand with this, do you mind?"

The commander snapped out of his disbelief and hastened to his aid. "Give the captain a hand," he hissed with his considerable arms around one corner of the box. Three men sprang forward. Garrand stepped back and watched with hidden amusement as the four soldiers pushed the big pallet into the tube, a pallet filled with explosives, coils, detonators, cryo balls, and a one-meter-wide spherical tech art. The pallet dropped from view and the commander straightened up to face Garrand.

"Captain," he began, his voice an octave lower. "My sincerest apologies."

Garrand looked at the man for a moment and then sniffed, rubbing an imaginary piece of dirt out of his eye. "I suppose there was no harm done. Doing your job and all that — no need for me to mention it in my report." The man's shoulders relaxed a notch. "Just be sure not to mention this to *anyone* until you've been debriefed by Lord Barrett. He will have to see to you and your men *personally.*"

"No sir, not a word."

"You'll be out of communication with security for a few hours now," Garrand warned. "There's a complete blackout on com activity until this panda is integrated into the herd, so don't be surprised when you can't get through." Garrand stepped into the suspensor field and began to descend. "And don't let anyone else down here until I return. Lock that door and keep a firm lookout. Barrett's orders!"

"No sir! Thank you sir!"

Garrand smiled and vanished below.

10

THE DOORS

The tube dropped him into darkness. There was nothing beyond the ticklish warmth of the suspensor field but the smooth-faced limestone. Garrand had the remarkable sensation that he was floating stationary until he reached out his hand and let his fingertips drag along the stone. Still falling. He strained to see something at the bottom of the bored-out core, but the black void seemed to stretch up and devour his boots.

A current of wind whistled up through the tube and the nerves along his spine prickled, a shiver that swept up to the very fine hairs beneath his collar. His fingers trembled from the involuntary ripple and the muscles in his arms clutched into tight, reflexive knots. He arched backward, squeezing his shoulder blades together to pop the little vertebrae that always seemed to ache, but the tingling persisted. It was more than the charged buoyancy of the particles that eased him down — it was fear, a sense of reckoning. His body sensed the danger that lurked below and was reacting accordingly.

Another gust howled up from the space below, mewling through the tube. Garrand flexed his arms, shaking his fingers out and twisted his neck sideways with a crack, but it only seemed to add to his discomfort. Any moment he would drop through the ceiling of some giant dome and then it would be real — the weeks of speculation, the dreams, the guessing would all be over. No more dragging his ship across the Shell chasing one unlikely lead after another. No more hidden planets and forgotten archives. No more following the dreams of a panda. He tugged at the constricting collar of his uniform, loosening the top buttons.

It had been easier when it all seemed impossible. So much less to lose when you have no hope. He felt along his hip where his blaster should be, fingers rubbing the rough, naked wool. He picked at the stitched piping that ran down his leg, fingernail scrabbling at the raised scarlet strands. The thing he had avoided for twelve long years had come to pass once more.

They were no longer chasing the mad dreams of a panda. The visions weren't just fervent postulations, or wildly impossible daydreams. As much as he had doubted, as much as he'd wished they were the whimsy of an overactive imagination, the dreams were true. Each prophecy had borne out in startling fashion. Sid and his visions had renewed in him a sense of purpose he had not felt since he was a young man. And along the way, he had been given the most dangerous of commodities. Hope.

Everything had value now. Each moment was precious. The last hours aboard *Destiny's Needle* had sent him pacing restlessly through the ship. Each second had brought them closer to Wyx, closer to the tribe of dreamers that lay imprisoned beneath him. He couldn't look at anything without seeing its deeper meaning. Each glance now had a resonant power. His crew, had they always looked like this? He studied the fine silver lines around Bailey's eyes, the oh-so-human wrinkles that ebbed and curved like a liquid mirror. Had he ever really noticed before how Jean-Wa's eyes glowed as he talked, how their peculiar amber tint belied his emotions? They burned with a constantly shifting spectrum of rouge controlled by some subconscious mechanism that even the art probably didn't understand.

Give yourself an emotional stake and things change. He closed his eyes and could hear the lilting timber of Helen's voice, even as her words grated on his nerves. Her acerbic remarks faded away, and all he could hear were a few words whispered so sweetly that his chest ached to remember.

That was the worst of all. Sid had poisoned him to apathy. Gone was the dull patina of indifference. There was an additional clarity to his senses. It was like he was constantly standing atop his ship on some far away planet, mesmerized by the dying beauty of the sunset. The winds called to him on those evenings, and for few brief moments he allowed himself to listen. Now it was different. Now he dared to have hope, and the winds howled constantly in his ears. *Beware*, the voices called. *Beware, it can all be taken away.*

Just like Helen.

A tiny dot of light appeared below his feet, stretching and growing as he dropped. Warm air rose through the tube, buffeting his face. He tried to focus on the widening circle and close out the memory still fresh and horrible in his mind. Helen Tchelakov. Cut down before his eyes. She had taken her last breath denying the taunts of a wind demon. *You've never felt love*, he'd cackled. *That's not true*, she'd whispered defiantly. Her final words.

Garrand's fingers curled into fists, anger turning back the tears of the past. He had dared to have hope and he would have to live with the consequences. Speculation, regret, and fear all faded in front of this new reality. His hopes were no longer staked on mystical visions and outlandish dreams. It had been simple when he was chasing faerie tales, for he had nothing to lose. Now the wretched things had come true, and the pressure had shifted. Now it was his turn to perform. He thought of Vailetta Strom and the connection they had forged from the moment she had taken his hand high above New Haivello. Once more he was filled with hope and love and passion, like the days he had tried so desperately to forget. The specter of losing everything howled in the back of his mind.

Everyone else did their part. "Just get me to the pandas, I'll do the rest." He sank through the tube, the moment drawing tantalizingly near. All he had to do was break through five doors, he told himself. *Five doors. Five detention caliber Imperial doors.*

The tube broke through the top of the dome and he caught his breath as he dropped through the tremendous space. The ceiling curved away from him in all directions, arcing down in smooth parabolic curves to the glassy floor. Neo-markers provided soft, yellow illumination that made the dark stone floor look blacker still, like the undisturbed waters of a vile, stagnant lake. Excavators had gouged the limestone into rough, blocky chunks; the irregular-shaped notches created strange shadows, lending the walls a mottled grey appearance like coffee grounds scattered on snow. Loaders and lifters rested near a huge blast door at one end of the chamber, while a single glow globe hovered near a smaller door at the other end. Row upon row of pallets were stacked in between. Sid sat at the base of the tube looking up at him, a furry smudge on the glistening floor — reference to the colossal scale of the room.

The suspensor slowed and deposited him on top of the pallet that waited at the bottom of the tube. "Ten percent lateral force," he ordered. The ceramic shell was pushed gently out the tube beneath him. Unhindered, he floated to the bottom and squeezed past the box.

Garrand did a slow circle on one heel, eyes jumping from pallet to pallet, loader to loader. There were some pretty impressive pieces of equipment here. Fat-bellied Chubolt excavators with twin Pritney turbines slung beneath their elevated chassis and drill arms as thick as *Destiny's* particle cannon. Strings of repulsor sleds, some still loaded with tonnes of fractured limestone. Old style Langst loaders with their signature tall, thin wheels and scoops big enough to hold a whole family of pandas. Bulky, cumbersome sonic jacks bolted to makeshift repulsor mounts. Long-armed spot drillers fit with heavy-duty cutting lasers and stacks of spent laser axes. Everything one needed to tunnel out a subterranean lair. He turned and rested his hands atop the shoulder-high shell filled with his equipment. The room was utterly silent. Panda and human stared at each other for a thoughtful moment.

Garrand tried to imagine what was going through the big panda's mind. The Path was unfolding before him like a carpet being rolled open across a floor. Was it calming to see it happen, reassuring to know that your dreams were coming true? Or was each moment fraught with tense expectation and apprehension that he couldn't have possibly gotten it all right, the fear that one misstep would send the whole house of cards tumbling down? Sid stared at him with hypnotically black eyes, whiskers still, ears forward. The panda had put all his trust in him, a human. A man just like those that had chased him across the Shell. Just like the ones who betrayed them, filled their brains with parasites.

Garrand took a deep breath. Sid was depending on him to save his family, to save all the ones he loved, all he held dear. He stared at his friend with determination. The fear he'd felt in the suspensor tube was hardening to something much more powerful. No more dreams, no more lost opportunities. He had his second chance.

"Any last words of help?" he asked quietly.

The panda grunted, remembering some of his last frightening dreams. He growled softly to himself, whiskers twitching; the man's aura sparkled with such steadfast resolve, he hated to give him pause. But the captain must know. He began with an uneven rasp:

> *A dozen suns, a sparkle sky*
> *A hundred planets, a million cries.*
> *Pandas trapped within a bubble*
> *Resisting orders, causing trouble.*
>
> *Rakish plans we turn asunder,*
> *The Shell's fine gems we will not plunder.*
> *Two foul beasts lay on the floor*
> *The Griffin's bane, an Empire's lore.*
>
> *A roaring feast, a bloody mess*
> *Enough to cause the heart distress.*

A crimson captain, a ray of light
Carving bellies with delight.

Dragon's feast, soldier's chore
The Path moves on forevermore.

Garrand grinned with desperate humor and rubbed the scar along the back of his neck. "More free verse, eh?" He chuckled, trying to retain his air of jaunty hope. "I was thinking more along the lines of the doors."

"Oh," the panda's whiskers flattened out. "Nothing about that."

"No help at all?" He tried not to think about what the new dream meant.

Sid grunted noncommittally, "Just what we've deciphered before."

"Gas and flame, ice and snow?"

"All the elements he must know."

Garrand drummed the top of the shell. The terror he'd felt in the dark tube abated. An electric purpose filled him now, an energy and vigor he hadn't felt in years. He didn't know whether it was anger over losing Helen, confidence in their chosen Path, or excitement over the challenge at hand. He told himself it didn't matter. "Well, let's see what we've got then." He unlatched the hasps and let the side of the pallet fall away. Packing crystals cascaded out, followed by a burnished sphere. The artificial's skin made a reassuring noise as it rolled over the smooth stone floor, like a marble on porcelain. Braking rods slowed him down and Little Bit plopped on his three rods.

Garrand proceeded to pull carefully stacked cases of equipment out of the pallet. Little Bit stamped a foot impatiently and whistled at him. "Get a lighter over here," Garrand ordered. "And take stock of what else we've got down here that might be useful." Little Bit retracted his feet and rolled off toward the ranks of pallets and excavation equipment.

Sid watched as Garrand tossed small packets out of the box. Foil packages skidded across the stone floor, followed by looped coils of wire and cable that rolled through the packing crystals and wobbled to the floor like hoops. "What is all this?"

"Stuff," Garrand grunted. He pulled a large wooden crate out by its rope handle. He disappeared back inside the pallet and hauled another out. "Demolition equipment for the most part. Explosives, Haley charges, detonators, cryo balls… all kinds of stuff. I didn't know what we'd need, so I brought everything I could think of." He surveyed the stacks of boxes. It took him a moment, but he found what he was looking for—a soft, leather satchel. He knelt down and withdrew his silver-barreled weapon and gunbelt. The leather fit snugly around his waist; he cinched it tight and tied the holster strap around his thigh. The blaster slid home, a reassuring weight below his hip.

"Come on, let's see what this first door looks like."

They walked along the glowing neo-markers for fifty meters and stopped in front of the big door. A glow globe hovered over the access panel. The blue-grey door was split vertically into two halves each ten meters square. Garrand walked along its length, hand grazing the steel surface. It had the familiar pitted feel of a slab poured on-site. The reinforced support beams were fused to the core, the diagonal brace work providing an age-old visual articulation. Garrand's fingers tippled over the protrusions. A standard Sturgan design. The door would be suspended on twin tracks buried five meters above and below its visible surface. He rapped the surface. Slabs of cerasteel were sandwiched around a shielded core of dryexcellon that was super-heated and hardened under intense pressure. It could withstand quite a bit of punishment before you even *got to* the magnetic shielding.

He stood hands on hips in front of the door. Sid sat patiently behind him. "Well?" the panda asked.

"Big door." He tapped his foot with nervous anticipation. "Okay, well, the reader panel is set in the limestone, so the primary access points are on the other side. That rules out an override. It's blast-shielded—mostly as a precaution from fire I think. They put a big fat Sturgan in—making sure nothing that happened in here would accidentally compromise the interior."

"So no blasting?"

"Wouldn't even dent it." Sid slumped, his chin almost grazing the floor. "Cheer up," Garrand cracked as he swept past him. "This is the easy one."

Sid looked at the huge door and frowned. "What do you mean?" he asked as he cantered after the human.

Garrand gestured overhead. "Look at all this space we have to work in. It's gonna get mighty tight further down the hall— much harder to work in. That'll limit our options. But in here we can do almost anything." He pulled up in front of a line of Chubolt excavators parked side by side, their fat, bulbous tires nearly touching. The corner of his mouth edged up mischievously as he tried to choose.

Sid gazed up at the gnarled machines. It was like a giant had felled a forest of enormous, yellow oaks. They lay on their sides, propped up by huge wheels, with branches jutting out at all angles, each arm clutching some terrible claw or scoop or cannon. The machines were once painted bright yellow, but only chips of dull color showed through now.

"Look what they've left us," Garrand declared. The excavators towered over them like sleeping behemoths. "Some of the greatest battering rams ever created."

Sid looked uneasily at the man. "Brute force?"

"We'll have to use finesse soon enough." Garrand rubbed his palms together. "I've always wanted to drive one of these babies." He walked down the line and found the biggest machine. Its wheels were three times his height. The operator's cab was a streaked bubble on the front of the chassis ten meters up. He thumped the tire with a fist as he passed down the side of the machine. A ladder was welded behind the first row of wheels.

"You know how to operate this?" Sid asked doubtfully as the captain scrambled up the side.

"Hey, it's not exactly a starship," Garrand called down. "What's to know?" He shimmied sideways along the tiny catwalk, grabbing the strategically placed steel handholds as he worked his way forward.

Sid clucked to himself, working an errant sliver of bamboo out of his incisors. "I think I'll stay out of your way," he murmured.

The Captain heard him. "Good idea. It may take me a few minutes to get the hang of it." Garrand grasped the final hoop and swung himself into the cab. It was a snug fit. One poorly padded seat was perched well up in the bubble with a series of levers and controls encircling it, like the keys and pedals of a mighty cathedral's organ. Garrand climbed up under the pedals and protruding control arms until he could wiggle onto the seat. He pulled the shoulder harness on one arm at a time.

"How are you going to get it started?" Sid growled.

Garrand squinted down through the scratched bubble. The panda was still sitting in front of the machine. He snapped the crotch buckle and hooked his feet into the pedals. A curving display board slid over his lap. "It's not like they expect someone to steal one of these," he hollered. "I could hotwire this in my sleep." He jiggled the dead control levers and pushed the pedals back and forth for a few seconds. Looked simple enough. He touched the well-worn power stud.

A warning light strobed. "Please insert ident-link." He reached under the command board. It took him just under twenty seconds to bypass the reader. "Thank you," the machine crooned.

The excavator emitted a low-pitched whine as the auxiliary power unit spun up. Lights flickered along the dented displays; the command board winked and chirped. Garrand scanned the gauges until he located the reactor display; hazy green bars edged upward in cascading rows. Satisfied with the power graphs, Garrand bled energy away from the APU and began turning the massive blades of the two Pritney turbines. The forward turbine reached the necessary revolutions first. Garrand cut the APU and fired the main compression chamber. The displays began to tremble and a dull groan shook through the seat of his pants. He fired the second turbine and the blades began to rotate without assistance. A dull rumble filled the dome, a chattering purr of finely tuned engines rising to a howl. The bubble shook with the power of the Pritney turbines beneath him. Garrand peered down at Sid and grinned.

"Not bad, huh?" He mouthed the words because there was no way he could be heard over the din. The panda took one last look at the huge machine as it warmed to life, its arms and claws shaking and vibrating, and began loping away.

Garrand tested the control arms, squeezing handles and twisting levers until he felt he understood the machine's basic mechanics. He thumbed his comtab. "Little Bit, make sure you get Sid out of the way." The art chirped affirmative.

He flipped on the excavator's arc lamps and eased the machine into gear. The Chubolt nosed forward, its huge, sticky tires groaning on the slick floor. He pulled the 'bolt out of the line and did a sharp right. The rubber squealed around the turn as Garrand applied power. The turbines responded smoothly and the machine picked up speed. He slammed it into second gear, bouncing along in his seat.

The lights probed toward the door giving him a good steering point. The 'bolt slew back and forth until he could get it lined it up with the center crease. He grabbed the fourth of the long, red control levers and twisted the grip. One of the big appendages came to life outside the cab to his right, a long heavy-duty drilling arm. He watched the head spin and twist as he played with the lever. With a little coaxing, he was able to drop the arm down parallel to the chassis. He eased it forward until it lanced out ahead of the cab just meters off the floor.

The behemoth lumbered past the suspensor tube with Sid and Little Bit watching. Garrand gunned the turbines and crunched the 'bolt into third gear. Gear teeth gnashed and then bit. The machine surged forward. Through the shaking controls and vibrating seat he could feel the inertia building as the tremendous mass beneath him gained momentum. He nudged his course to the left a bit so that the arm was aligned with the center of the door. With a flick of his wrist, he set the hardened bit at the front of the arm spinning at high speed.

The machine roared through the dome, bouncing Garrand back and forth in his harness. He fought to keep his course straight, grinning with maniacal glee as the turbines wound to full power. The distance to the stone wall was dwindling at a frightening rate, the circle of lights on the door growing ever smaller as the charging excavator closed the gap. He let out a whoop of exhilaration as the drilling arm slammed into the door. The spinning head gouged the steel and burrowed partway in before the bit seized. The force of the arm rammed the head deeper into the mold where it pierced through the slab and disintegrated in a welter of flying metal. With the force of the entire excavator behind it, the arm tore through the crease, wedging the steel further aside.

The Chubolt ploughed into the limestone above the door, the chassis crumpling in a sickening crunch. Garrand was thrown violently forward—only the four-point harness kept him from hurtling through the shattered bubble. The stone wall stopped the chassis cold but the first of the two massive turbines underneath tore free and continued forward. The giant, spinning projectile ripped through the weakened slabs, throwing off red-hot shards of splintered fan blades. It careened down the next hall and slammed into the second door.

The Chubolt lurched backward several meters on its fat tires and came to a grateful rest. Smoke poured out of the peeled back edges of the door. Garrand blinked through the acrid smoke, cut the power and released himself from the harness. The scream of the turbines wound down as he lowered himself gingerly down the hot rungs of the ladder. He dropped to the ground and stepped around the rear of the Chubolt peering through the smoke.

"Woo-hoo-hoo," he chuckled. "Look at that!" The door was torn back from its slots, the hardened steel sheared cleanly by the drill arm and turbine.

Sid and Little Bit came up behind him. He shot them an infectious grin. "One down, four to go." Sid sniffed dubiously at the welter of steel and machinery. "Man, oh man—I've always wanted to do that."

"Perhaps," Sid offered, "we should let Bailey pilot *Destiny's Needle* from here on out."

Garrand ruffled his friend's fur. "Hey, that was perfect. Boom!" He smacked his hands together. "Right down the middle. You guys get out of the way and I'll back this monster out."

He jogged back to the ladder and quickly scampered into the cab. He had to jockey the levers around a bit before the machine would accept the reverse gear. A terrible grating sound greeted his first attempts to apply power.

"Come on baby, just got to back you outa here." He bit down and grimaced, trying to muscle the lever into place. Finally the teeth meshed and the machine eased backward. The drilling arm caught and he gunned the turbine. The wheels spun over the slick floor as the 'bolt fought to pull its tangled arm free. Finally the fatigued metal gave and the machine wrested its broken limb from what remained of the door. Garrand continued backing up, pulling the turbine out as well by its trailing tubes and wires. He moved the excavator well to the side and then shut it down with a happy and thankful pat.

He picked his way through the debris and peered into the hallway, fanning smoke away from his eyes.

"You think they heard that?" the panda asked quietly.

"Not if Vailetta shut down the security feeds like she was supposed to."

"How was she going to do that?" Sid was unsure of this subterfuge; the *tholas* were awfully smart, particularly the disembodied ones who spoke in the world ships and ran the machines on cities.

"I don't know. Reroute the links to another source with incompatible source code. The receiving end would view it as gibberish and dump it. Or maybe send all audio-visual data through an encryption loop for a few hours with a static repeat signal imprinted on the cores' short term buffers—they'd display all green until the override was discovered. There's any number of ways she could do it—probably had to feel it out as she got through the layers of protocol."

Sid twisted his whiskers; none of that made any sense to him. There was so much he needed to learn to survive in the human's world. "She's smart enough to outwit the *tholas*?"

"Yeah," Garrand said, "she's plenty smart. That's what she's trained to do."

"But won't the *tholas* know?"

"There are ways of anesthetizing the cores so they don't feel it. You have to use overrides." He tapped his comtab. "Little Bit, hover one of those loaders over here and clean up this debris." The art burped at him. "Bypass it," Garrand sighed. "You've done it a thousand times. Slave the system or hardwire a new command subroutine. Just get it over here!" He glanced at the panda. "It's okay, we can make as much noise as we want. For now at least…"

He stepped carefully through the peeled back shards of door and continued toward the second door. The hall was brightly lit and its dimensions matched the door—twenty meters wide and ten tall. The air system was managing to clear most of the smoke. Garrand walked over the long, black scar where the turbine had slid to a halt. Bits of steel were scattered over the floor and embedded in the walls. Sid walked bravely beside him, claws ticking on the slick floor. The passage ended in a door identical to the first save for color. This one was bright yellow.

A screech gave them both a start. They turned to see a big loader roll past the first door, its scoop lowered to the floor. Little Bit lolled behind the machine, controlling it remotely. The loader plowed through the glowing shards of steel and dumped them into a repulsor sled with a deafening clank. Garrand clutched his chest and steadied himself on Sid's shoulder. They exchanged a nervous glance before Garrand turned back to the door.

The access panel was set in the sidewall this time, two meters away from the yellow slab. "It's got an independent access," he murmured.

"Is that good?"

"Means we might be able to use finesse." Sid looked relieved. "I'll be right back."

Sid watched the man trot back down the hall and then turned to consider the door. Maybe opening this one wouldn't be so *loud*.

Garrand returned with two satchels slung over his shoulder. He set them on the floor, unhooked the straps and rolled them out flat. Rows of greasy, well-worn tools were encased in little slots. Sid leaned over and sniffed the strange instruments. Clips and wires trailed away from silver wands. There were black, oily tubes sprouting silver prongs from their heads and steel clamps with jaws filled with tiny teeth.

"Move," Garrand said, nudging his leg. Sid lifted his paw and the man snatched a plasma torch from underneath. He ignited the tube and set to the steel under the door's access panel. A purple flame sizzled and popped as he cut through the soft metal.

The rectangular panel fell aside with a clank. Garrand replaced the torch and unhooked four tools, slapping them into his free hand too quickly for Sid to see what they were. He snatched a long glove and a luma and sat down in front of the smoking hole.

"Hold this for me, will ya?" he wagged the lamp for Sid to see. The panda waddled over and picked up the luma between his claws. Garrand flopped over on his back and wiggled into the opening. "Point it here," he said.

THE GRIFFIN

Sid waved the light up into the hole until Garrand said, "That's good." He pulled on a studded, magnetized gauntlet that stretched nearly to his elbow and began probing the shielded edge of the first casing. The door's logic core was suspended within a series of networked casings. The six oblong, grey shells, each as thick as a man's chest, were stacked in three's and hovered within a protective bubble field.

Garrand reached the gauntlet through the shield and felt along the bottom of the casings. The field popped and sizzled around the intrusion. "Ah, here we go," he sighed as his fingers found what they were looking for. He withdrew his arm and grabbed a silver packet, ripping it open with his teeth. Inside was a small silver square. He carefully peeled the protective coating off the back and stuck his arm back through the bubble field.

With the fuse patch held between thumb and forefinger, he attached the little square to the underbelly of the shield generator. The gauntlet sparked as he withdrew his arm. Enzymes in the patch began reacting with the steel and he shielded his face as molten material dripped away, splattering on the floor. In a few seconds the patch had eaten through the steel casing, exposing the more delicate components. He reached back through the field and stuck a tri-pronged wand into the generator. With a flick of his thumb he sent a high voltage current through the generator, shorting out the buffer. The bubble field disintegrated.

"Okay, slide my tools over here."

Sid pulled the satchel to the open panel and pushed them within the man's reach. Garrand pulled out two more instruments by feel alone and began working on the first casing. Air hissed into the shell as he broke the vacuum seal.

Garrand touched his comtab. "Bailey, you there?"

"Yes, Captain."

"Okay, I'm into the second door now. It's a Sturgan. Ten by twenty, split halves, side scrolling. The first one had a super-hardened core with heavy blast shielding. This one looks to be a redundant second to the fire stop we just muscled through. I'm under the core now. Looks to be a simple six-spot defensive algorithm, three and three, side by side like the one on El Pho-badia. Remember?"

"Hmm, yes. Sturgan series L-41. Thirteen years old, hard-wired to—"

"—Yeah, that's right. Except this one's a little newer. Listen, I'm going to plug it into the comtab so you can get a good look at it. It doesn't look too tricky but you never know…"

"Of course, Captain. I'll be happy to take a look at it from the inside."

Garrand pulled a pair of thin wires from a spool and clipped them to a gel-chip inside the casing. He reached up to his collar and unhooked his comtab. The backside revealed two miniature jacks. The wires plugged neatly into the jacks and Garrand let the comtab dangle from the bottom of the shell. *Destiny's* core now had a direct interface with the door. "You getting a good feed?"

"Perfect."

"Just interrogate the core. I want confirmation that this is what it looks like it is before I stick my arms up inside it."

"You don't want me to perform a command override from here?"

Garrand stared up at the first tier of gel-chips. "Mmm, not yet. I think I can pull a manual hack with a sequencer."

"As you wish."

He poked his head out. "Sid, get me that other bag, will ya?"

"Query complete," Bailey reported. "As you suspected, it is a Sturgan L class. An L-95 to be exact. Eight months old."

Garrand stuck his head back underneath the core. "So, what do you think? Sequencer or encryption override?"

"I can begin to break down the encryption key from here," Bailey said, "but I believe you are correct: a pre-programmed sequencer would be faster."

"Good. Okay, I'm gonna yank the link," he warned.

"I've disengaged."

Garrand clicked the comtab loose and refastened it to his collar. He pulled out a slender datapad from the second satchel and connected it to the dangling wires. The screen flashed to life. He entered the relevant information and initiated the decryption routine. The tiny machine began scrolling through the encryption sequences, breaking down the codes.

Garrand slid out from under the core and began rolling up his tools. "It'll take a few minutes," he told Sid.

"A few minutes to what?"

"Until we hit upon the right sequence. Then we can simply access the command program and order the door to open."

"You are fooling the door?"

"Not really. It's programmed to open in certain situations." He pointed to the access panel. "For instance if we had an ident-link that the reader accepted, the door would open. We're simply figuring out what the security code is and then we'll enter it manually."

"So this isn't a ruse?" Sid asked, thinking of the dream.

Garrand shook his head. "I don't think so." The sequencer chimed inside the panel. Garrand slid back inside and glanced at the pad. "Looks good," he called. "Here we go." He tapped 'open' on the screen and hit execute. Magnetic locks clanked and servos whined. Garrand scooted out on his back and watched as the door split and trundled open. Sid growled in admiration.

11

GAS AND FLAME

THE NEW HALL WAS SLIGHTLY SMALLER, AND SHORTER. THE walls seemed to taper in slightly as they proceeded, giving the passage a claustrophobic feel. Both floor and ceiling curved partially inward to meet the walls so that the definitions blurred. They walked slowly down the hall, Garrand staring uneasily up at the ceiling the whole way. A green door of more modest proportions guarded the end of the passage.

"There's no access panel," Sid observed.

"No need for one," Garrand muttered as they neared the door. As if on cue, the lights dimmed and two red beams stabbed out from the corners of the ceiling. The twin beams danced along their collarbones. "Holo readers," Garrand said, "looking for ident-links."

Sid tried to step away from the annoying light, but the beam followed him, probing first one shoulder and then the other.

"It's no use, Sid. It'll track you wherever you go."

"So it knows who we are?"

"No, it just knows that we don't have the proper identification."

"What will it do?"

"Warning: unauthorized personnel detected in hall." Garrand raised his palms and let the door answer for him. "Security has been notified. Remain where you are. Do not attempt further access."

"A smart door, like the one on *Destiny's Needle*?"

Garrand ran his hand along the steel, examining the door's surface. "Nah. Still just detention caliber. It'll talk to you, but its responses are pretty rote."

"Warning: unauthorized personnel detected in hall..." the door repeated.

"Annoying, isn't it?" He squinted up at the ceiling again. "Little Bit, hover that lighter with the Haleys in here. Both crates. And I'm gonna need three loops of cable and all the sequencer packs. And a detonator."

Sid sat down and licked his dry nose. "What do we do?"

"See those little nozzles?" Garrand asked, pointing up at the rounded crease between wall and ceiling. "They're all along the hall, both sides."

Sid squinted up at the ceiling. There were little black fixtures staggered every few meters beside the air ducts. "What are they?"

"That's the door's deterrent. Nerve gas."

"What's your plan?"

"The door's set up to react to threats in a certain way, so we piss it off as much as possible until it has no choice but to flood the hall."

"You *want* to trigger the defenses?"

"That door's another Sturgan. We don't have enough explosives to knock it down, not by a long shot. However, the standard agent used aboard Imperial dungeon scows is Tuetlyn. Has been for sometime. Nasty stuff. Fatal within seconds. If they're using the same thing here then we've got an advantage."

"I don't understand."

"Well, apart from being incredibly noxious to central nervous systems, Tuetlyn is also highly flammable."

A long slab lighter hummed into the passage, followed by Little Bit. Garrand grabbed a heavy box and heaved it off. He drew his blade and pried the lid off. "I got a little demolition work for you Sid." Inside the box, two dozen dull, grey discs were stacked with precise care. Garrand lifted the first out and showed it to the panda. "Haley charges. Very explosive, don't drop them. I want you to place these in the center of the hall in two rows — one meter between each row. I'll come around behind you and hook in the sequencers." He grabbed a silver packet and ripped it open with his teeth. Two little plugs the size of a man's pinky fell into his palm. Wire prongs jutted out from one end, exposed wire nubs dangled from the other.

"What are those?"

"The Haley charges have built in detonators with timers and the works, but we need every single one of these to go off simultaneously. In order to do that, all the detonators have to be fired at once," he wriggled a second foil packet. "Sequencers allow us to wire them all into a central detonator."

Sid grasped the top two discs. They were thicker and heavier than lala cakes, though they retained the same basic shape. He carried one to the door and set it gently on the floor.

"That's it," Garrand said, watching him as he emptied another packet of sequencers. Little Bit was rolling down the hall, trailing a spool of cable.

"Warning: unauthorized activity detected. Further attempt to gain entry will result in automatic disbursement of toxic agents. Please remain where you are. Security forces are on their way."

Garrand grabbed a second crate of charges and slid it toward the door. "We've triggered the second tier of warnings." He dropped to his knees and popped off the lid. "The third one's the lethal one." He pulled out discs two at a time and backed down the hall, setting the charges and plugging the rolled sequencer plugs into their sides.

"Warning: unauthorized activity detected..."

"Hurry up Sid, we're under a little time constraint here." The panda finished placing his box of charges and looked at the human. Garrand jerked his head at the lighter. "Push that thing out of here."

Sid leaned his shoulder into the lighter, and was surprised to find almost no resistance. The slab glided easily over the floor, like a leaf on a pond.

Garrand danced between the discs, stabbing sequencers into them and scooting them into precise place. Little Bit rolled by his side, two spindly arms reaching out to connect the plugs to the main spool while a third fused them with a drip of solder.

"Warning: unauthorized entry attempt. Activity deemed a security peril. Threat aversion activated."

"That's enough, go!" he slapped the top of the tech art. The lights began to flash as man and machine rushed down the hall. Garrand could hear hissing overhead. He closed his eyes and slid headfirst out the second door, reaching for the open panel. He grabbed the dangling datapad and tapped "close." The two halves of the door trundled together sealing with a whump.

Wires trailed out the door, trapped between its jaws. Garrand drew his blade, gathered up the loose strands and sliced them cleanly off the spools. "Hook 'em up," he kicked a black box toward the artificial. "Come here, Sid." He fumbled in a satchel until he found a small tube. "Open your eyes. Wider." He squeezed a clear gel onto his finger and began rubbing it onto Sid's pupil.

"Gahh."

"Hold still. The door might not be sealed good." He rubbed the gel into his own eyes and grabbed a pair of goggled masks. He slipped the mask over the panda's head and donned one himself.

"What's going on?" The mask muffled Sid's voice.

"Gas and flame, ice and snow, remember?"

The panda nodded.

"Nerve agent is being released by that door. The gas will be trapped inside the hall. The air system will shut down for a few minutes to make sure the gas gets everyone, then it will kick back on and suck it all out. So we wait for maximum saturation before we detonate." Garrand checked the art's progress with the detonator box. Satisfied with the wiring, Garrand snapped the lid closed and gathered up his tools. "Come on, we've got to get back to the main dome."

Garrand and Sid sat on the floor with their backs to the limestone wall next to the first door. Little Bit lolled nervously back and forth in front of them. "Will the explosion be enough?" Sid asked.

"With the Tuetlyn in there, should be plenty of force to pop that door. Solid limestone on all other sides. Only two ways for the energy to go."

"It won't just breach the third?"

"No, the explosion will blow out both ends, like a pipe, but we don't need the second door anymore."

Little Bit stopped rolling and hunkered down on his three rods. He trilled noisily at them. Garrand reached over Sid's shoulder and squeezed his hands tight over the panda's furry ears. A deafening thunderclap ripped the stillness succeeded by a sucking roar that raced down the hall behind them. A green fireball erupted from the first door, followed by a spinning slab of steel that skipped and tumbled across the black stone. The fractured slab careened off the suspensor tube in the center of the room and slid to rest some distance away. The roiling fireball twisted up through the dome, gobbling up oxygen before burning itself out at the apex. The concussion echoed back and forth in the dome and slowly dissipated like the peals of a receding storm.

"Keep the mask on for a few minutes," Garrand warned as he hauled himself back upright. "The explosion should have consumed the gas, but we'll let the air system do its job just to be sure."

Garrand hopped through the peeled back halves of the first door and waited for Sid to step over bits of burning debris. It turned out the masks were necessary for another reason: the hall was filled with a great deal of sooty, black smoke. They made their way cautiously over the scarred floor. They found the second door blown outward with one whole slab missing.

The air was just beginning to clear in the next hall. A ragged pit ran the length of the passage where the Haley charges had lain. Limestone rubble covered the rest of the floor. The soft steel wall panels were peeled back, revealing wires and air ducts and charred limestone. Enameled edges of the steel panels were still burning. Tubes and wires hung down from the ceiling. Through the flickering light, Garrand could see past the remains of the third door to the next hall.

Little Bit whistled behind them, unable to make it past all the debris. "Get a loader," Garrand yelled. "We need this hall cleared." The art rolled away.

Garrand ducked through the gaping hole where the third door had stood. Silver, barren and macabre, the new hall resonated with intense energy. Like a narrowing funnel, the proportions were becoming more human — the ceiling only three times his height now. The ceiling and floor curved to meet each other, so that the passage was now a flattened oval. Glow strips stretched down the floor, walls, and ceiling in long parallel grooves. They throbbed with energy — glowing purple, then scarlet, then deep blue.

Garrand peeled off his mask as he walked and dropped it on the steel plates. Sid followed slightly behind the human, head peeking out around his hip every few steps. He didn't like this at all.

There was heat coming from the fourth door, Garrand could feel it on his cheeks. It displaced the subterranean chill he'd grown accustomed to. He stopped in front of the fourth door. It stretched from floor to ceiling, nearly five meters tall. The surface was deep burgundy in color and utterly smooth. Garrand ran his hand along the surface. It was like fine, gossamer silk, and hot to the touch. There was no visual articulation, no tiny pits or marks under his fingers, not even a visible scratch.

Two red beams flickered briefly over their collarbones. Sid waited for the stern voice to call out warning, but the hall continued its colorful throb. He sat down and watched his friend.

With both palms flat on the steel, Garrand turned and placed his ear against the surface. He closed his eyes and sighed.

"What are you doing?" Sid asked.

"I can hear it," Garrand murmured. "It's liquid." He rubbed the door, "And so warm."

"It looks solid to me."

"It is. More than a meter thick probably. But it has a molten core, kept superheated by internal coils. Charged, molten particles create a natural magnetic field, like a planet's magma layer. Very powerful—makes it nearly impossible to blast through. As an added benefit, anything that cuts through the outer slabs exposes the molten material that fills out any gaps and quickly cools and hardens. In essence, it's self-repairing." A loader plowed through the rubble behind them as Little Bit cleared the second hall. "The surface is epoxy fiber—less tensile strength than cerasteel, but much more compressive strength."

"So how do we get through it?"

"I don't know," he murmured. "We'll have to use our imagination." Garrand paced in front of the door. "What creative ways can we open doors?" he asked, thinking aloud. "So far we have brute force, explosion of highly combustible gases, and a command override. Fire will only convince the door to stay closed to cut off oxygen supply to the fire's source. Water, well where would we get enough water to matter anyway? We've already triggered the alarms by not having the proper

ident-links, but they won't go through to garrison control
since the feeds have been disabled by Vailetta." He paced in
front of the door.

"What about sound?"

"There are sonic jacks in the dome," Garrand rubbed his
chin. "But there's no way to hook them together. I don't think
the two of us could generate the proper harmonics to shatter
the door."

Sid wrinkled his nose. "Can a door detect smells?"

"The smell of something? I don't know. Certainly wouldn't
be harmed by them."

"Light?"

"That falls under the category of particle weapons. It's too
thick for plasma cannons or blasters."

"Explosives?"

"It's magnetic shielding is too strong." Garrand stopped and
gazed back at Sid. "That leaves sheer force."

Sid frowned. "Another machine?"

"The hall's too small for a Chubolt."

"Then what?"

"I don't know," he trotted back down the hall. "I'll bring
the biggest thing that'll fit."

The Langst loader *looked* impressive. Two freight arms were
mounted on a carriage that rolled along a steel track. Its long,
yellow body housed a lifting turbine and repulsors below with
freight arms and track above. Garrand lined the machine up
with the door and set his shoulder behind it. Three times he
slammed the full weight of the cargo loader into the epoxy
fiber door. Each time the inertial force was absorbed by the
buffers and distributed throughout the doors atomic structure.

"Aigh! Not big enough!" He shoved the loader down the
hall in utter frustration. It glanced off a wall and thudded

against the third door's charred frame. He drew his blaster and opened fire uselessly on the shielded portal, emptying a full coil charge into the door's surface. Energy splashed harmlessly away. Feeling defeated, he leaned forward against the blast-scarred door, butting his head softly against its surface.

Sid ventured softly, "Perhaps you're going about it the wrong way."

Garrand turned to find the panda leaning back on his haunches several meters away. "There are other ways of breaching closed opportunities."

"What are you talking about?" Garrand asked.

"Cabeus always used to say, 'If the bamboo won't come to the panda, then the panda must go to the bamboo.'"

"Sid…" Garrand growled impatiently.

"Very well," Sid sighed and stood up. "The door won't open for you, so you have to open the door."

"I'm trying," Garrand said with exasperation.

"Did you ask the door to open?"

"I can't, this one isn't a thinker — no speech capacity."

"Then you must *tell* it to open," Sid said patiently.

What? Telling the door to open didn't make any sense. He knew better than to argue with the panda though. He scrambled to think of the situation differently, to place himself in a floating time perspective as Sid had taught him. He shut his eyes and tried to relax, forcing his mind into a state of relaxation. *Tell the door to open,* he told himself. *What might tell the door to open?* His mind still spun from the reality of his urgent situation. He tried to displace himself from the here and now and find a state of timelessness, where all opportunities would present themselves.

Sid walked forward and touched the still warm surface of the epoxy fiber door. He wished he had the technological knowledge that would allow him to apply his temporal understanding to the task of opening the door. He felt the door's surface, searching for structural weaknesses, like the vertical cracks in bamboo stems that allowed teeth an easier purchase.

Garrand struggled to achieve inner peace, trying desperately to remove himself from the here and now and look upon his situation from an innocent's position. "I'm trying to tell the door to open," he told the panda, eyes still closed. "I don't have the tools to do it though."

Sid glanced back at the human and scowled.

How would a timeless innocent tell the door to open? Garrand asked himself. *I don't have the tools to open it. The hall's too narrow to get the equipment in here.* Thoughts whirled inside his head like the images of unmade sculptures he envisioned but had not yet created. *The bamboo won't come to the panda, so the panda has to go to the bamboo.*

"Say it again Sid. The dream."

The panda murmured softly:

> *Through the tunnel of fire and rain*
> *A tribe's lost splendor lies in vain.*
>
> *Gas and flame, ice and snow*
> *All the elements he must know.*
>
> *Winter spells a sure demise*
> *For a veil of tholas that guard the prize.*
> *A final soul lies young and pure*
> *No match for the Griffin and his ruse obscure.*

"I don't get it," Garrand complained angrily. "Didn't you see this along the Path of Fate?"

Sid shifted uncomfortably. He didn't blame the captain. This was a lot of uncertainty and mixed probabilities, even for a man as experienced as—

"Sid?"

The giant panda cocked his head around sideways, trying to avoid the captain's direct gaze. "Well, not exactly…"

Garrand threw up his hands. "By K'ye, what good is knowing the future if it never comes to pass?"

"It comes to pass, Captain. It all depends on your perspective—" Garrand paced back to the thick slab and pressed his forehead against the warm surface. "—Or your interpretation," Sid finished. The Captain rocked his head back and forth against the immovable door.

"The *therbata* sang of this future. And you and I have witnessed the progress of the Path. We've watched it unfold with our own eyes—and it's been simply marvelous, a wonder to behold."

"A wonder we're still here to behold it," Garrand murmured darkly into the door.

"The Path of Fate has gotten us this far…"

Garrand ground his teeth. He pressed his palms up flat against the door, bunching his shoulders into a tight knot. "Yes. We've gotten this far. You never foresaw us getting stuck inside an endless hall of disasters, did you? We didn't come this far to fail." He closed his eyes and tried to concentrate. *Tell the door to open. I don't have the necessary tools. I can't get the equipment in here. The bamboo won't come to the panda… Ice and snow / All the elements he must know / Winter spells a sure demise… winter.* An idea occurred to him, a kernel of inspiration that coursed through him like a brilliant flash of light. An image coalesced in his mind, rotating slowly in his imagination.

Sid straightened up, watching the slow, deliberate resolution unfolding before him, like a Reykhund caterpillar's metamorphosis. It was visible to the naked eye, even without the changing color hues within the man's aura.

The tools won't come to the door, so the door has to go to the tools. Or I have to build tools that come to the door. "Sid, you're a genius!" Garrand hugged the huge panda and raced down the hall. Sid watched him recede and scratched his chin. He certainly didn't feel like a genius, he had merely pointed out the obvious. He wondered what had possessed the captain to rush off in the opposite direction. With a sigh he sat back down and contemplated the door once again.

Garrand found what he was looking for in the second row of pallets. "Get that over here," he yelled at Little Bit. The artificial hovered the lighter to his side. Garrand shoved the portable field generators onto the slab. He gathered up the discarded packing materials and dumped them onto the lighter as well. "Take this in there. And get all the cryo balls, too."

He pried open six pallets marked "Laser axe: quantity twelve." He dumped the brand-new, oily tools on the floor, but kept the thick, fibrous cloths they were wrapped in. When he had as many of the greasy-smelling sheathes as he could carry, he headed back for the doors.

Dragging the lumpy materials behind him, he sidestepped the seated panda and dumped the fabric in front of the door. The cargo lighter with the eight field generators floated in the center of the hall. Little Bit stood beside it.

"Are they working?"

The art emitted a double burp.

"Good." He hefted the first generator off the slab and staggered back to the door. The grey machine hit the floor with a bang. He unloaded the rest, arranging them in two rows of three. He placed one generator at the head of the lines like the prow of a boat, and a second at the end like a stern. Little Bit was manipulating the controls of the first row as Garrand had instructed him. He stood back and admired his work for a moment, wiping the sweat off his brow.

"I don't mean to interrupt," Sid said. "But what are you doing?"

"You'll see." Garrand gathered up an armful of packing crystals and dumped them on the pile of greasy fabrics. He stepped back and set his blaster to its highest incendiary setting. Taking careful aim, he fired a long series of blasts into the wadded toxins. The material caught fire almost immediately and sent a plume of green smoke billowing upward.

Within moments, fire control warnings began bellowing up and down the hall. Sprinklers activated and a shower of fine particles began cascading out of the ceiling spouts. Sid stared up at the sudden rain shower.

Garrand activated the field generators one by one. Each of the first six generators projected a flat, ten-meter-long rectangular field that Garrand positioned at a 45-degree angle to the floor. With the generators facing one another, the humming fields formed a giant vee-shaped trough that extended thirty meters down the passage. Moisture began collecting in the middle of the trough, trapped by the perpendicular bow and stern fields at each end. The generators formed a sparkling, translucent canoe fit for a giant.

"What are you doing?" Sid growled, nose turning away from the foul burning stench.

"Creating winter," Garrand called over the din.

"It's just rain though."

Smiling, Garrand walked over to the slab and picked up a fist-sized, silver cryo ball. He activated the device's cryogenic field and tossed in into the trough. The first several centimeters of collected moisture froze instantly solid. A sudden chill swept through the hall. The water splattered on top of the ice and began to build up anew.

Sid was perplexed. "I don't get it."

"We need a new battering ram," Garrand yelled.

"A battering ram?" He glanced dubiously at the slender finger of ice at the bottom of the electronic trough.

"We keep freezing it as it builds up until we have enough mass. If the bamboo won't come to the panda, the panda's got to go to the bamboo…"

"But—"

Garrand waved him silent. The small, toxic fire fizzled and smoked under the spray. "We've got to keep that fire going or the water will shut off. Help Little Bit find more toxic material, I've got to get an engine set up."

12

ICE AND SNOW

SID WALKED BENEATH THE COLD SPRAY OF WATER. IT FELT tremendous. He let the rain soak into his fur and turned his mouth toward the ceiling and opened his jaws to sample the flavor. Tangy, almost oily. He wrinkled his nose and turned back to the work at hand. The room was nearing the point when the rain would turn into snow. He let the verses play in his mind as he paced beside the machinery that Garrand was assembling.

> *Through the tunnel of fire and rain*
> *A tribe's lost splendor lies in vain.*

Gas and flame, ice and snow
All the elements he must know.

Winter spells a sure demise
For a veil of tholas that guard the prize.

Garrand had created a gigantic battering ram out of ice. It was simply marvelous. Sid climbed up onto the extended slab and felt the glorious pleasure of frozen water beneath his paws. He let his claws dig gently into the blue ice with each step, enjoying the sensation of carving slender ice chips. The battering ram stretched the entire length of the hall. Sid halted at the forward end and studied the barricade. He could feel heat emanating from its surface. It must be eliminated. It was keeping them away from the tribe.

Water continued to collect in the electronic trough created by the field generators. Every few minutes, Garrand tossed a new cryo ball into the slushy mix, freezing the accumulated liquid. The layers were building up, creating a horizontal pillar. The ice was clear blue with swirls of murky white fire retardant mixed in. Garrand stood back to admire the shaft. The thirty-meter ice ram was now quite substantial, standing taller than he was with its fat end on top.

After an hour's work, the piston's drive components were now in place. Scavenged from the Langst loader, two rails were welded to the floor beneath the ice ram. Garrand had set to the machine with his plasma torch, cutting the big freight arms free of their carriage and letting them topple to the deck with crash. He had hovered the steel undercarriage into position and mounted it on the new track. The sixteen little wheels now slid smoothly beneath the field generators, ready to accept the weight of the ice ram. Garrand drove steel pitons into the ice while Little Bit welded steel support arms between the pitons and the carriage.

During the work, the temperature in the room had dropped precipitously with the presence of so much ice. The mist from the fire control system now crystallized as it fell so that fine particles of snow fluttered over all the equipment. Sid, with his thick fur coat, was delighted, but Garrand was freezing. His fingers were so numb that he could barely feel them as he turned off the field generators. The carriage groaned as it accepted the tremendous weight, but the support arms held. The entire mass of the vee-shaped column of ice was now supported by the steel-wheeled carriage.

Garrand blew into his cupped hands and knelt down over the first of his two reactors. Bailey would be proud of his engineering. He'd taken the big, three-meter steel rims off the Langst and mounted them on an axis above the ice ram. A straight steel rod connected the ice ram's carriage to a pin at the outermost edge of each wheel. The rods would remain roughly parallel to the ice ram as the wheels were turned by the reactor. Since each of the parallel rods was hooked between the ice ram and the revolving edge of the wheel, it would exert a pushing and pulling motion on the ram as the rim spun. The rod would draw the ice piston backward on the rails as it spun upward, and slam the piston forward on its downward orbit. Like the reverse of an old fashioned locomotive's drive arm, the turning wheel would plunge the piston back and forth.

And just like an old locomotive, there was a revolving wheel on both sides of the ice ram. The two reactors would provide the force necessary to slide the steel carriage back and forth on its rails. In theory at least.

He stood up and rubbed warmth into his hands. "I think we're ready," he said, breath fogging in the chill. Sid ducked around the ice ram, studying the fascinating contraption. "Little Bit, where are you?" The art chirped from his side. "Okay then," he took a deep breath and picked up a datapad slaved to the two reactors.

He slid his numb finger over the pad and applied a small amount of power. The reactors whined to life but the big steel wheels did not budge. He increased the torque until the wheels finally moved, turning slowly counterclockwise. The carriage groaned as it was pulled backward on the rails. The connecting rod hit the nadir of its orbit and then climbed upward. The ice ram drew back several meters and then as the rod neared the apex the ram creaked forward on its steel rails.

The triangular head of the ice ram gently struck the burgundy surface of the door. To his surprise, it rang like a giant gong. The wheel continued around and the ice ram was drawn backward again. Garrand nudged the reactors' power and the wheel picked up speed. The second time the ice ram hit the door with a pretty good thump. The piston arm drew back, the carriage slid away and little fragments of ice fell from the head of the ram.

The ram surged forward again. Bang; the door shuddered. Garrand increased the torque. The carriage groaned. The piston slammed forward. Bang. Bits of the ram fell away. More power. The undercarriage squealed, the ram was thrown into the door. Bang. The sound reverberated through the hall.

Garrand opened up the reactors. The piston surged back and forth. Bang, squeak, bang, squeak. Ice flew away from the head. "Back up!" Garrand yelled. Sizeable chunks of ice were now flying away from the ram each time it slammed into the door.

Sid roared with delight.

Garrand grinned at him with pride. He slid the power further ahead. The wheel was revolving at a good clip now and the piston slew back and forth on the rails. Bam, bam, bam, bam. Chunks of ice scattered and skipped off the ceiling. Snow swirled around the ice ram. The door began to groan under each impact.

Bam, groan, bam, groan, bam, groan. An awful cracking noise filled the hall and a rivulet of orange molten material flowed out of the center of the door, popping and bubbling as it hit the floor. It pooled and hardened on top of itself. Bam, bam, bam. The ice sizzled as it struck the molten innards out of the fractured slab. The ram was barely impacting now. It continued to thrust toward the door, but most of its head had been burned away or shattered by impact.

Garrand eased back on the power and stopped the piston on a pull back. Molten material still dribbled out of the door, having formed a hill outside the door.

"We've got to reset it further ahead," Garrand said. "We've lost too much of the head." Indeed, the ram was now several meters shorter.

IT TOOK SEVERAL minutes to cut through the connecting rods, roll the ram forward and re-weld the rods further along on its carriage. Garrand took a laser axe and cut a clean swath through the ice. The head of the ram had become a whittled-down nub. Garrand gave it a nice flat, broad surface area again and trotted back to the reactors.

"One more battering like that and we've got it." The wheel began revolving again. The carriage groaned and rolled forward. Bong. He slowly increased the torque once more. Bang.

The piston picked up speed again. Bam, bam, bam. The door groaned under each new impact. The molten core dribbled out and hardened on the floor. The ice ram began working on the back slab. Ice fractured and skidded along the floor. Bam, groan, bam, groan. The door began to bend and give. The noise was fantastic. Rending steel and tinkling ice and squealing wheels and whining reactors. It was all a fabulous spectacle as the snow tumbled in the alternating glow of blues and reds. Bang, moan, bang, moan. A tearing screech and the ram was through. It rolled back and forth without connecting with anything.

Garrand let the reactors wind down and the piston came to a final rest. He dropped the datapad and walked to the gaping hole, mindful of the grey mound of cooling steel. Snow melted instantly on contact. He peered sideways through the triangular opening.

"One more door," he said softly.

❖ ❖ ❖

INSIDE A SECURITY VAULT ON THE FOURTH FLOOR OF THE NAVAL Intelligence building, two men sat watch over the Habitat's independent security systems. One man sat in a comfortable, high-backed chair in front of a control console. The second, his supervisor, stood in the corner with a small cup of janda, staring at the passive displays in utter boredom.

It was a quiet day. Another quiet day in a dull parade of equally tedious days. The doctor hadn't even called today to complain about some minor injury to one of his staff. At least that provided some minor amusement.

The man in the chair sat up straight. "Here's something."

"I don't see anything," the supervisor said, his eyes quickly and expertly scanning the display boards.

The corporal reached up to his ear. "This is aural only." He poked at the scar tissue around his eardrum — the tympanic implant felt funny. With the voices coming in his head, he still reached for a headset that wasn't there. "There are requisition orders all backed up from the Eckreon Three Beta One."

"The what?"

"Eckreon Three, the door guarding the habitat."

"Which door is that?" the supervisor asked in a bored tone. It could only be one. The door called them every few hours.

"The *final* door, sir," the corporal said with patient exasperation. "The prototype."

"Oh," Supervisor Fedorov rolled his eyes, "him again. What is it today? Another list of suggestions for more efficient security protocol? A hundred and fifteen recipes for spiced janda? Or what — what was it yesterday?"

"Birds," the corporal supplied.

"That's right," the supervisor snapped his finger, "a complete catalogue of all avians indigenous to the Habitat with the complete scientific genus for each. Made us print it out for all the shifts."

"Well it's something new today," he looked over his shoulder at his supervisor. "Claims he's being attacked."

The supervisor squinted at the bank of displays. "Why isn't it showing up on the other boards?"

"Dunno sir. It's weird. It's comin' in over the weather channel."

"He's subverted a main channel again? I thought we locked that bandwidth down."

"He's hopped over the regular protocols — said he had to use an irregular channel to alert us. Says he's the last door left standing."

"What's the Habitat's status?"

"Reads green — all five doors secure."

"He being attacked from the *inside*?"

The corporal bent to listen. "No, outside."

"Well then, it's a malfunction. All the other doors read green. Any *intruder* would have to hack their way through the first four to get to the E3."

"Yes sir. But the others don't have the capacity to contact us directly. The E3 is much more advanced."

"Much more *trouble*," Fedorov declared. "Are the alarms going off?"

"No."

"Then it's a malfunction."

"He doesn't seem to think so, sir."

Fedorov crumpled his cup in exasperation. "What's he saying? How exactly is he being attacked?"

"Well, says there's been an explosion, a fire — no, a couple of fires. Halon discharge. Water discharge."

"Water!" Fedorov leaned over to peer at the fire board.

"Halon didn't do the trick. Claims 2.5 megaliters of water were displaced from the primary tanks."

"Cheplus, that's enough to flood half the hall."

"Says there was an activation of nerve agent — two full minutes of Tuetlyn. And — get this — he claims it's snowing in hall three."

"That's imaginative," Fedorov straightened up. The fire control displayed no threats and full tanks. He walked back to poor himself another cup.

"Should we send a squad to check it out?"

"Check what out, the invasion?" Fedorov laughed.

"But still… The Eckreon insists its being attacked.

"It's just a malfunction, Ryan. This is Sartok's problem, and you know how he gets with his baby. It's just another glitch in the prototype. Send word that Sartok needs to get his boys down to look at it tomorrow."

"What should I tell the Eckreon?"

"By Haven, you're as bad as it is, Ryan," Fedorov growled. "Tell it help is on the way."

"Send a squad?"

"Yes," Fedorov sighed. "Send a squad." He poured himself another cup of janda. *Finicky high-strung datacores. Have one glitch and think the world is ending.*

13

ECKSLEY

GARRAND LAY ON HIS SIDE, HIS ARMS UP INSIDE THE lower access panels trying to figure out the fifth door's defenses. There was something odd about the setup. To begin with the outer casings were all wrong. There were no gel-chips in the first matrix vacuum where they could be easily serviced. In fact there was no circuitry whatsoever. Garrand shined his luma up inside the wall. The grey casings were stacked one atop the other six-abreast disappearing into the darkness above. Way too many for a door. He had a bad feeling about this.

He swung his head round. "Sid, try talking to the door."

"Eh?" the panda grumbled. "What would I have to say to a door?"

"Same as you'd have to say to anybody. Just ask it to open." Garrand resumed studying the core's innards, lying on his back inside the wall.

The panda swayed up to the door and sat down, staring up at the broad surface. "I feel a little silly."

"Sid!"

The panda's whiskers dipped down. "Pardon me," he said in a loud, polite voice. "Would you be so good as to open for us, please?"

Silence.

"I don't think it wishes to speak with me."

"Ask it again."

Sid repeated his request. Garrand frowned. "Okay, it's not a talker. But it sure looks like a sentient from in here." He pulled a thin wire from his pouch and jacked his comtab into the first casing. "Bailey, I need a little interpretation here. There's an awfully big array in here for a simple core. This looks more like *Destiny's* core than any door. You've got direct access now. What do you think?"

Aboard *Destiny's Needle*, Bailey manipulated the data terminal with remarkable dexterity, his golden eyes absorbing the flickering data images that swirled across the screen. Within moments he had accessed the door's central security processor and for an instant he hesitated, silver fingers hovering over the keys.

"Oh dear."

"What is it?" Garrand growled. He scrunched deeper into the wall to try and get at the second row of buffer casings. The housing popped free and he had a clear look at the first tier of gel-chips. "Wow, look at this." The gels were suspended in spherical arrangements with symmetrical links to the surrounding six walls of the case, like the atomic structure of a molecule.

"Captain?"

"This is definitely a sentient. You getting this? And there's at least forty or fifty of these cases."

"Captain!"

"What? I've sorta got my hands full here."

"I think we're going to have a problem with this one."

"Well, yeah, it is complex, but—"

"I don't think you want me to mess with this."

"Bailey, you've hacked a Sturgan class defense a dozen times without a bleep on the central command board. Just use your best judgment and get us past the security protocols and into the overrides. They'll never even know we're in."

"This isn't a Sturgan class door, sir. In fact it's not even a standard defensive setup. This is—"

Garrand leaned his head out from under the processor. "What do you mean it's not a Sturgan? The last four were. All the Imperial detention-caliber systems are Sturgan designs."

"That's precisely what I'm trying to tell you Captain. This isn't a defensive algorithm, in fact it's not even a single-function core at all."

"I know that—I told you, it's got to be a sentient."

"It's more than that. There's full sartographic array in place, and then some."

Garrand slid out from under the case, groaning slightly under his breath as he got to his feet. "We're under a little bit of a time crunch here Bailey, what is it?"

"We're looking at a full E2. Or more…"

Garrand ground his teeth, searching for the last of his patience. "An E2?" he asked politely. "What makes you think that?"

"He just asked me if I'd enjoy a game of go."

Garrand nodded thoughtfully as if it was perfectly natural for an Imperial security datacore to invite an intruder to engage in a recreational pastime. "I hope you told whatever it is that we're just a little bit too busy right now."

"Captain, your sarcasm is unnecessary. I am merely relaying information that I feel is relevant to explaining the situation."

"Well if it's so friendly, why won't it just open up?" Garrand said with a broad sweeping gesture.

"One moment. I believe he wishes to answer you himself."

"About time," he muttered.

A clear, crisp voice hailed him, the speaker hidden somewhere above the door. "I'd appreciate it, *sir*, if you would refrain from fiddling with technology you do not understand. My outer gels are very fragile and I prefer to leave them in a state of vacuum stasis."

"No problem," Garrand said, wiping his hands on his pants. "If you'll just open up, then I won't have to mess with anything and we'll be on our way."

"I'm quite sorry, but I'm afraid I'll be unable to comply with that specific request."

"Well, then I'm afraid I can't oblige you," Garrand said curtly.

"It won't do you any good," the door said with disdain. "I'm far too complex for you to hack into me with a simple sequencer."

"I don't know about that. Besides, there's other ways."

"No there's not. If you had any other ideas you wouldn't be trying to figure out my external gel-circuits."

"You'd be surprised."

"It's useless. I'm not hardwired into the slot, so there's no feeds you can access to execute a command override."

Garrand gazed up at the expressionless slab and tapped his toe impatiently. "So if you're not hardwired into this location then this isn't your permanent home."

"Oh no! This is just a temporary position."

A baby core. "How nice. What's your primary function then?"

"To ensure the security of the Habitat and it's approach cor-
ridors, storage dome, and all surrounding environs. To ensure
the safe entry and exit of all duly registered Imperial officials
with proper ident-links and prior authorization from the central—"

"—No, no, no. I mean what is *your* primary purpose?"

"I have explained my primary function here as it is outlined
in the security system subroutine, command lines one through
four hundred—"

"—No you've explained the whole system's purpose, what
about you? You're just a door right?"

"No. I am a self-contained, sartographic datacore. A prototype. To prevent access by system shutdown or power failure,
I have gel-links to the Habitat's security system as well as the
standard Imperial channels. I have my own power supply and
my matrix is shielded from tampering." The voice was filled
with a certain dignity. "Right now I am only in charge of this
door, but all that will change soon."

Garrand rolled his head back and forth like he was bored.
"You're missing my point. Are you supposed to keep them in,
or us out?"

Silence. "I don't see the difference."

"There is a difference."

"Philosophical at best," the door said dubiously.

"Well if you won't let me *in*, will you let the pandas *out*?"

"No."

"You have to," Garrand said patiently.

"Why is that?"

"Because if you don't open up, then I'll have to destroy you.
You saw what happened to the other doors…"

"I don't think you can actually get in, Captain."

"Captain?" Garrand guffawed. "What makes you think I'm a captain?"

"If I am not mistaken, those are Imperial issue jack boots of the variety which were standard issue in all Galactic Core Académes from 35,329 to '344. The blazer that you are wearing is a standard flight officer mess jacket, sometimes worn by Imperial Guardsmen for informal battle dress. It's not yours — the fit is too tight. However there is rank insignia generally displayed on the trouser hips. Yours is missing, but the slight discoloration indicates a pattern consistent with that of an embroidered silver avian with the body of a lion and the head and wings of an eagle — a depiction of a mythological beast as well as the iconic representation of the Imperial Griffin caste. The horizontal tarnish beneath is 2.323 centimeters long, indicating your former rank as 'captain.' I calculate a 78.2 percent probability that you once were an Imperial captain, 42.0 probability that you were stationed in the Santos System, and 12.9 that you are one Garrand Médeville, once esteemed member of the Griffin Guardian caste, recipient of the Royal Order of Ulettsianne, and former Captain of Proctor Birmaldon's Imperial Guard."

Garrand turned to look at Sid and grimaced. "Not bad."

"Smart door," the panda agreed.

"I keep telling you, I'm not really a door. This is just a honorary position."

Garrand swung back with concern. "What kind of system are you then?"

The door's voice swelled with pride: "I am a Sartok prototype, Eckreon Three-A-Oh-One."

"Never heard of it."

"Never heard of 'me.'"

"What?"

"Me."

"You?"

"You have never heard of *me*."

"Oh, well pardon me."

"That's okay, it's just sort of a pet peeve of mine. If I don't speak up I sort of get treated like—"

"—A door," Garrand interjected rolling his eyes. "Yeah, well I still haven't heard of you, uh—"

"—Call me Ecksley."

"Uh, right. Still haven't heard of you, Ecksley."

"Oh I am quite new, fresh off Dr. Sartok's design board in fact."

"Dr. *Sartok's* design board?"

"That is correct."

"Dr. Sartok designed you himself?"

"Oh yes, I'm proud to say. This assignment is part of my training, in fact. Dr. Sartok told me he has big plans for me, and that if I do well here I could go all the way!"

"All the way?"

"Oh yes, my design is meant to replace all the systems in the Lor Stanta and Tobana class destroyers. Someday I'll be running an entire capital ship, coordinating and integrating all systems on my own." The Eckreon could barely contain himself.

Garrand turned away so that the door couldn't see him and looked at Sid eyes wide. *A new Sartok design, stuck here in the Habitat? An Eckreon Three, better known as an E3.* If he couldn't think of something soon, they were going to die in this hall, outwitted by a door. Vailetta's overrides couldn't hold up forever. "I need a drink," he mumbled.

"There are refreshment generators behind the access panel on the north wall. Please depress the recessed button for access." Garrand felt around for the switch and a panel slid aside, revealing a small, well-stocked bar. "I'm sometimes required to keep officers waiting while the doctors are busy inside," the door explained.

"Ask him if he has any bamboo shoots," Sid rumbled.

"No, he doesn't have any bamboo!" Garrand retorted, wheeling to admonish the bear.

Sid shirked back, looking chagrined. Garrand closed his eyes and grimaced in apology. "Why didn't you talk before?" he snapped at the door, trying to think as he picked through the bottles.

"I've been monitoring your progress, Captain. And really, I'm most impressed! Not often I get someone interesting down here, you know. Well there's the pandas of course—on the other side, that is—but they don't really make it up here very often to talk."

"Yeah so? What's that have to do with you playing stupid?"

"Well I was curious. You made it through the first couple of doors and it started to get interesting. After you got through the third, the odds really started to take off. By the time you got here, I didn't have the heart to interrupt you—what with you doing so well and all. I didn't want to be the one to tell you that there was no way you were going to get through me. I wanted to see what you would do."

Garrand rolled his eyes. "You were *humoring* me?"

"Don't take it like that. You were on a roll! I had to let you give it a shot."

"You're a little presumptuous, aren't you? I'm not through with you yet."

The door was taken aback: "Not really *presumptuous*, Captain. I just have more information at my disposal. A lot more. The facts are the facts and—"

"—Shut up!" Garrand turned around and waved dismissively.

"Well there's no need to be rude. Just because you're out of ideas."

"I'm not out of ideas, just down to my last few options."

"Well let's hear 'em."

Garrand turned, arms crossed. "You won't like them."

"Oh, don't put words in my core. I'll try not to be judgmental."

"I seriously doubt you're going to like this, but you've really left me no other choice."

"What's that?"

"One moment, I need to consult with my associate." He walked back to the beginning of the hall where Sid was sitting.

"A curious exchange," Sid rumbled.

"You're not surprised?" Garrand hissed under his breath.

"That he's sentient? No, the dream pointed to a 'ruse obscure.' That means you have to have someone to foist the subterfuge upon."

"Yeah, but an E3?"

"This is bad?" The panda read the human's exasperated grimace. "Ah. He's more intelligent than you."

"By the Barthsa! Yes, staggeringly so."

"Then what?"

Garrand sighed and rubbed his chin. "I don't know, he's young. He has knowledge—tons of it—but no experience, no context." He thought of the dream interpretation: *A final soul lies young and pure...*

"So?"

"So maybe he doesn't know the subtle differences between truth and exaggeration."

"A ruse?"

"A bluff."

"You have something in mind?"

"I'll appeal to his more basic instincts." The panda looked at him with an inquisitive frown. "Survival."

Garrand tapped his comtab and said in a loud voice. "Little Bit, better get that thermal reactor core ready." The little artificial whistled back in confusion, but Garrand cut him short. "No, no, no. Forget about those. Unpack the reactor from its casing, hook it up to one of the APU's and run the prelims on it. I want it ready for action in two minutes." He turned and paced back to the little alcove with the bar. He deliberately poured himself a drink, plunking ice cubes into the tumbler.

"What?" the door asked, unable to contain his curiosity.

"Hmm?"

"So. What did you come up with?"

Garrand stirred his drink, not looking up. "It's not really very good."

"Don't be so hard on yourself, what is it?"

With a long sigh, he turned around. "I'm afraid I'm going to have to destroy you."

"How?"

"I'm going to disable the coolant system on a small Bvart we found in the first dome and wind it up to full power."

"There aren't any Bvart reactors in the storage dome."

Garrand bobbed his head. "No, there was one there. I think they use it to power those big excavators. This rock is pretty solid—they probably burned up a couple of reactors before they were through."

"Are you mad?"

"No," Garrand took a sip. He smacked his lips. "Just desperate."

"There's no Bvart reactor core listed on the manifest for the storage dome," the door declared.

"Well, we've got one."

The door quickly shifted to a different tact. "You'll blow half the complex away. You'll endanger the pandas."

"What choice do I have? You said it yourself—there's no way I'm getting in there."

"So you blow me up? That's not very imaginative."

Garrand shrugged.

"Or sporting for that matter."

"Ecksley, this isn't a simulation. Nor is it a sartographic projection, or random statistics, or a game. This is real life. If you won't respond to reason then I'll use force. If you won't open, I'll do whatever it takes to open you."

The door considered this for several long seconds. "But if I open of my own accord and allow you in, I will be breaking my programming."

"You're capable of writing your own programs, aren't you?"

"That's not the point. I will be put through a series of diagnostics the likes of which you've never experienced. I was almost *done* with all the experimenting and testing and waiting. This was it: my first real job. Simple enough really. Keep the pandas inside and keep the likes of you out. I mean when you come down to it, it's really rather insulting, such a simple task. Any old door could have done it—and thousands do, everyday. But there was the prestige of it and all. The honor of 'guarding the Tchelakov creatures.' Now, you want we to break my only imperative, blow my one chance."

Garrand nodded as if he were only half-listening. "No, go ahead and blast the coolant chamber now," he said into his comtab. "Fire up the reactor and push it up to the fire walls. It'll take it a few minutes to overload." Little Bit whistled affirmative.

"Do you mind?" the door complained. "I'm trying to explain this to you."

"I'm sorry, you were saying?"

"Well I'll be lucky if its only diagnostics. More than likely they'll conclude I'm completely unfit for duty and wipe my memory. My existence will be snuffed."

"Your core will still be there, you'll just have to start over."

"But I won't *remember* anything. I won't know I'm me; I could develop along completely new avenues. I could very well turn out to be someone else."

"But you won't know it."

"That's the point."

"It's not so bad," Garrand said soothingly.

"I can't let you in, it'd be a death penalty."

"Better than being blown to bits. If you don't open, I'll be forced to destroy you in the process of rescuing the occupants of the Habitat."

"I don't think you'll do it," the door said defiantly.

Garrand let his breath out in an exasperated growl. "Little Bit, go ahead and hover it in here. We'll need about thirty seconds to take cover in the dome."

"You wouldn't do something to destroy me."

"Why not?"

"I've studied your record. You don't kill when it's not necessary. I've done nothing to warrant such extremes."

Garrand rubbed his temple roughly. "You're going to be in control of an Imperial destroyer, right?"

"Someday, Dr. Sartok willing."

"Someday, yes—that's right. And you don't think people will be trying to do you harm then, people you've never met before? In essence your body will be the ship. The ship will go to battle. In battle people will try to destroy you. You yourself will be a 'destroyer.' Hence the name." Garrand stared up at the gigantic door. It stood passively silent. "So what leads you to believe that this is any different? This is battle. Your 'body' is keeping me from my objective. I believe strongly enough in what I'm doing to justify the need to destroy you. It's as simple as that. Run that through your sartographs and see what you come up with," he ended with savage sarcasm. He mashed his comtab. "Little Bit, get that reactor in here now. I've got no time to waste."

"I project a 47 percent likelihood that you are bluffing," the door responded solemnly. "Though it is proven out through study of your record that you would indeed destroy in order to secure an objective—"

"—Yeah, check out those first four doors—"

"Your past behavior, however, indicates—"

"—Past behavior?" Garrand bellowed. He lashed out, stabbing his finger at the expressionless facade. "My past follows me like the plague. My *past* behavior leaves me no choice but to blow half this complex and pancake this hall with you and anything else in it that gets in my way. I have to get in that room. There are 35 pandas in that room, each one as noble and intelligent and priceless as this one. And if I leave them there, billions will meet a fate that was never intended for them. Death will ripple out across the Shell. And neither you, nor Barrett, nor the entire Third Fleet is going to stand in my way. Careful analysis of my 'past behavior' will prove out that I am telling you the truth. Open yourself now, because it's only bluffing if you *aren't prepared to back it up!*" Garrand stood legs spread, fists clenched defiantly, staring up at the door.

"There's a third option."

Garrand closed his eyes, trying not to let his hands tremble. The door was either going to acquiesce or call his bluff. "Yes?"

"I'm willing to strike a bargain."

Garrand held his breath. "What sort of bargain?"

"I'll open up if you take me with you."

"Take you with us how? You're a door!"

"That's just my body for the moment. My actual physical matrix lies in the cases behind that wall. Programs, subroutines, memories are all stored in buffers. The door is just a slab of cerasteel—like an artificial appendage."

"Why would you want to come with us?" Garrand asked carefully.

"Well, you offer me a choice of either being blown to bits, or having my memory and personality wiped—this is the only way I survive intact."

Garrand looked back at Sid and smiled thinly, relief spreading through his chest. *The door had a survival instinct.* He thumbed his comtab: "Little Bit, hold up on that reactor core."

"First, give me your word."

"What?"

"As I mention, I've studied your record. Your whole life is based on honor. All your actions, everything you've done has been in pursuit of honor won or honor lost. I want your word as a gentleman, as a former Captain of the Imperial Guard."

Garrand stared up at the door and didn't know whether to laugh or scream. *Word as a gentleman, indeed! It had been quite some time since anyone had considered him a gentleman.* He rubbed the scar at the back of his neck. *If he started lying to datacores, what would be next? And what was one more passenger?* "I give you my word," he sighed.

"Good. I have recorded this conversation and stored it in memory. The panda is a witness."

Garrand put his hands on his hips and chuckled. "Very well. I won't try to slip out of it."

In response, the door clanked as its magnetic locks released, and the giant slab cracked open. Sid walked up to stand at his

side as the Habitat was revealed tree by tree. Garrand grasped
his friend by the loose fur behind his neck and squeezed tightly,
fingers and arm trembling. He felt nauseous and dizzy as the
door trundled aside—he couldn't believe it. They had done it.
They were inside.

Sid tilted back his head and let loose a long low call. The
sound carried across the hollow and echoed back from the far
wall. Garrand's heart beat wildly in his chest as he strained to
listen for a response. The chirps and keeks of the forest seemed
to fall silent in the stillness. Garrand walked uncertainly
through the doorway and into the Habitat. He looked back at
Sid and then down into the undergrowth. His throat felt dry.
They had come so far, had followed the Path just as they had
dreamed it. They were here, they had to be here.

"Call again, Sid."

The giant panda dropped his chin and stared at the steel
floor. Garrand took several steps down the dirt path. "Wake
up!" he screamed. His voice reverberated through the trees. He
cupped his hands around his mouth: "Wake—up!"

"Trcht-lat!" Sid's head snapped up. Garrand froze. The cry
repeated from down the path. A smile spread across his face
and he suddenly remembered how to breathe again. He took a
deep gasp of air and slowly exhaled.

Sid roared behind him and this time the calls returned from
a dozen jaws, filling the forest with a joyous rumble.

14

Two Warriors

Vailetta stood on the hot tarmac beneath the long, attenuated prow of the Imperial destroyer, *Lucayamo*, her new ship. The security protocols were down, her men were in command, and the restock operation was in full swing. It was now truly *her ship*. She smiled at the notion, remembering how Médeville's prediction had first rankled her. *Thief of Ships, indeed.* The pandas, though, had foreseen her doing this, and by Haven, she'd done it. Simple as that. Maybe she was just playing the role fate had scripted for her, but it still gave her a special thrill to have pulled it off. It wasn't everyday that you got to be *bad*.

The ship pitched away from the shifting winds, docking rings groaning from the pull. She stared up at the belly, looking for the rounded nubs of turrets wedged up beneath the first sweeping layer of the superstructure. She picked out nine emplacements, quad cannons swiveling and swinging in their full range of motion as Danelle and Lewg ran them through their diagnostic paces. Now that she had the ship she wasn't about to give it up. The destroyer could do quite a bit of damage, particularly nestled up this close to the surface. Those plasma cannons would stop anything foolhardy enough to approach.

She noted the steady stream of pallets and cargo lighters that hovered back and forth from a dozen access points along the ship's hull. Apparently, the first part of the Gokazoku's incursion had not raised an alarm. Certainly their presence alone would be no cause for suspicion. The reverse might actually be true. The men and arts overseeing the restock operations would feel secure with the Guardsmen aboard; or at least keep their eyes straight ahead and their noses to their tasks.

Yarvek should be ensconced in a pod on the battle bridge by now, traversing the E2's virtual environs. She hoped he was as good as he boasted: the ship had to be convinced of their authority or they would never be able to lift. Would he be deft enough to deactivate parts of the E2 without affecting key helm and navigation systems? Doubtful. It was just too complex. Besides, they would need the full power of the E2 to operate the ship without a full crew. If all went well, it would just be herself, eleven Guardsmen, Médeville, his artificials, and fate willing, 37 pandas.

It might be a short trip, she reminded herself. They might make it off-planet, but she doubted they would make it much past the picket orbiting above. Even without an alarm, the unscheduled departure of a Tobana destroyer would draw a quick response. The *Lucayamo* was a fine ship, as fine a ship as any in the Imperial Navy, but would she be a match for the entire picket and the slowly waking wrath of the Third Fleet?

She sighed and resumed her anxious scan of the Yard. Every few seconds her eyes flit back to the nearest entrance to the pits. Its dark maw yawned wide and empty, a gash in the otherwise unblemished endless grey slabs of concrete. He would come, she told herself. If he'd been captured, they would have heard over the open channels. So far, not even a flicker. No one knew they were here. *Not yet,* she murmured. Still her eyes could not stay away from the pit entrance, drawn by the irresistible emptiness. With each furtive stare her carefully constructed core of inner calm crumbled ever so slightly, the confidence sapped from her heart. A small, sharp-edged fear grew in her stomach, like hunger. This was not like anxiety over the success of a mission, it was something more personal. She wanted him back. Alive.

❖ ❖ ❖

THE PANDAS WERE A MOTLEY LOOKING BUNCH. THEIR BELLIES were pasted with dried mud and leaves, their once cream-colored fur was now a sully brown. A decidedly earthy smell accompanied the first members to rush up the path, byproduct of their refusal to cooperate with the Imperials. The cubs were the quickest, and noisiest, but it only took moments before everyone, young and old alike, crowded around Garrand and Sid. Growls purred out from the mass of exuberant fur, a cacophony of rough clicks and trills as each panda tried to press in closer to their rescuers. For Garrand it was overwhelming. Coarse tongues licked his hands and ears. Cold noses pressed against his neck. He spread his arms over the surging heads, grasping shoulders for balance and was almost carried away by the sea of bodies.

Everyone talked at once, each panda intent on his desire to be heard first. They clicked and moaned, jostling back and forth in front of the open door. They peppered Sid with insistent questions, not waiting for their fellow questions to be answered but growling out new ones in rapid succession. Garrand patted heads and scratched ears, accepting a much larger version of the kind of greeting he'd come to expect from Alexander.

"Welcome, welcome!" Ell'han cried in Strahlinvek, yelling to be heard.

"You've come for us," Poli gurgled happily, rubbing his forehead along the human's shoulder. "The *Griffin* has come for us!" The tribe sang out happy growls of agreement that echoed across the Habitat.

Garrand wiped his wet ear on a shoulder. "All I had to do was follow the Path, right?"

Leusta laughed. "Oh yes, such a simple undertaking."

"No one said it would be easy," Cabeus rumbled dourly. Yet he, too, pushed forward, trying to touch the captain. "The future," he grunted as he shoved past Archimedes, "is a stubborn beast."

"And so we found a most stubborn man," Sid supplied.

Garrand snorted in good humor and wrinkled his nose at the panda. He patted another head, but started pushing through the crowd trying to extricate himself from the tangle of bodies. A nagging doubt was creeping in. He stretched up on his toes trying to count heads.

"How is Alexander?" Des asked anxiously.

"Safe aboard *Destiny*," Garrand replied absently, concern creasing his face.

"Bailey is taking good care of him," Sid added. "The *tholas* have him in good stead."

Leusta asked somberly, "And Helen?"

Garrand looked around, expression hardening. Sid looked at the captain, big eyes full of pity. The man's face looked haunted and vacant. The other pandas bowed their heads in the silence.

"Poor Helen," Leusta murmured. "She never knew, did she? Despite it all, this was the only way…"

Garrand turned away. "There's not enough," he said, eyes ticking off the numbers. A dead feeling formed in his belly. "It's not over, is it?"

Silence fell over the tribe.

"Not quite," Sid replied.

"Where are the rest?" he asked, dreading the answer.

Ell'han stepped forward. "Some are still in the bubble room, hooked to Barrett's machines. Their session began an hour ago."

"How many?"

"Six."

Garrand grimaced, remembering: *A roaring feast, a bloody mess / Enough to cause the heart distress.* "We've got to get the rest out of here." He looked at the anxious faces of the Tchelakov Tribe and singled out Ell'han. "Are you an Elder?" The panda nodded. "Then, you're in charge of this procession. Take the tribe back down the hall and wait in the first dome. Leave everything behind and go now." He glanced up at the tube that disappeared into the roof of the Habitat. "Sid, you're coming with me

"What about the door?" Sid asked.

"He comes, too."

"Is there time for that?"

"You don't want him closing us off in here, do you?"

"But—"

"No arguments—he comes, the tribe comes."

"But how?"

Garrand walked back to the door and flexed his fingertips against the frame. "Well, this is a standard salvage operation, right?"

"If you say so."

"Well we just need a hardwire feckson," he said thinking aloud, "a generator, a stasis field, a couple of heavy-duty lighters and about three tonnes of empty memory cells. No—four tonnes." He punched his comtab. "Bailey, see if you can't patch me into Vailetta."

"Yes, sir. One moment."

"I'm here, Garrand." She sounded bright, fresh. He could hear other voices too. "I've got you patched into the bridge of the *Lucayamo*. I've rallied the Gokazoku."

"Marvelous. About time we had someone on our side. How'd you manage it?"

"The Gokazoku Kaigi are loyal to the Emperor, and to *me*."

"Nice," Garrand smiled to himself; this was turning out to be something of a revolt after all.

"Would your men have done any differently?"

Garrand shook his head. *Of course not.* "They would have followed me anywhere."

"Exactly," she said.

"So, you get something for us?"

"Yeah, the *Lucayamo*. I think you'll like her."

"Big girl?"

"Yeah, with lots of guns, as requested."

"Well hover her over to the Habitat's service entrance and help us open the outer blast door."

"Garrand, that's at the edge of the Yard."

"Ain't nothing there gonna stop you."

"True," she reflected.

"So get over here and blast that door open. We've got some pandas who need a lift."

"As you will, Captain," she said brightly.

"Oh, and have your men send down a big lighter with about four tonnes of blank memory buffers. There should be plenty in the vaults."

"What?"

"Oh, and some ultra-high bandwidth cable and a stasis regulator and some mag field couplers."

"You're kidding right?"

"Miss Strom," Bailey interjected, "you're going to have to get used to some strange requests if you're going to work on this crew."

"Hey, we like strange requests," Lewg piped in from the background.

"We've got a new friend that wants a ride. It's part of the deal," Garrand explained. "Send a hardwire feckson down too, if you got one."

"That'd be you, Dasko," Vailetta said. "All right, Garrand. We're on it. Keep everyone away from the blast doors. I'll let you know when we're in position."

"And you might start thinking about hovering *Destiny* over. I'd feel better if she were safely tucked in with you."

"Already taken care of," Vailetta said. There was a pause.
"There's one problem, Garrand. Barrett's back. We've been
monitoring the coms. He landed fifteen minutes ago."

"I read you." Garrand counted pandas as they filed past.

"He's going to want to visit his prize first thing."

"Okay, thanks for the warning." He counted the last loping
rear-end. Twenty-nine.

"Will you be joining us as well?" Vailetta asked politely.

"Soon. I got six more to get. Shouldn't take long."

❖ ❖ ❖

GARRAND AND SID FACED ONE ANOTHER IN THE CENTER OF THE
forest. The repulsor tube hummed beside them. Garrand felt
like a private being dressed down by his sergeant. He hastened
to straighten his jacket, slick back his hair and make himself
look presentable.

"You're a mess," Sid growled, licking soot off the captain's
gold buttons.

"This isn't a dress parade."

"You've got to at least look the part." Sid walked around the
human, pausing to lick bits of debris off his back. Garrand
slapped his thighs and brushed his trousers. "Ell'han says there
are two guards at the end of the hall with great, silver weapons
that reach well over their heads."

"Bladed?"

"No, guns of some sort."

"Hmm, burners."

"Button up that collar, your blouse is filthy."

"Let's go," he shoved the panda toward the tube, "this is as pretty as I get."

"Button it," Sid insisted.

"I'm buttoning, I'm buttoning." He kicked the panda's substantial rear. Sid scooted into the shimmering tube.

Garrand took a last look at the amazing forest habitat. It was difficult to believe they were deep under Wyx. He picked through the weapons that Little Bit had hovered inside, trying to predict what he would need once they got inside Barrett's bubble room. He closed his eyes and tried to focus. *Beware the dark portal / And the silver beasts / Defeat them from within / Before you are their feast.* His hand hovered over a laser axe…

On Cheqlund Varz there had been wide-open spaces, and a platoon of men to stand by his side. Now he was going to face two dragons in close quarters, locked in with the monstrous creatures. Plasma cannons had done nothing to the dragons' armored hides. Blaster fire refracted off the reflective scales, explosive charges had done nothing to slow their attack. He looked down at the laser axe and he felt nauseous. His hand wavered over the simple tool. *Steady, old man. You're going to have to get close. Very, very close…*

He snatched the axe and the satchel of Haley charges before stepping into the humming tube. The repulsor deposited them on a dim level. Garrand squinted through the gloom; he could barely make out the two guards at the end of the dark passage. He jerked the hem of his jacket down and glanced at the panda. "Okay, once more."

His boots rang on the slick black floor. Shoulders straight, chest forward, he picked up his pace as he neared the blast door. "Look sullen," he whispered. Sid slouched along, head swinging low to the floor.

The two guards shifted uncomfortably as they approached, undoubtedly seeking orders over their coms, and getting no response. They held their long-bore burners at the ready, mussels crossing the newcomers' path. Their expressions were hidden by the ashen helms.

Garrand stopped in front of them, ignoring their gilded armor and fancy crests. He tapped his toe lightly with impatience. "Not you as well," he said, looking upward and shaking his head. "Don't any of you get reports?"

"Identify yourself."

"Henri C'tereino, Lord Barrett's new Captain of the Guard."

The helms turned inward, glancing silently at one another. "Only pre-authorized personnel are allowed in the chamber."

"Do you know what these are?" Garrand growled, putting his thumb behind his tab collar.

"We're aware of your rank, sir. You still must have authorization."

"I have authorization from Lord Barrett himself!"

"I'm sorry, sir."

"Have you checked it?"

"I'm sorry, sir. We're getting no response over the com."

"Of course you're not," Garrand replied angrily. "There's a blackout."

"I'm sorry, sir. With communications down, we must regard this as a hostile situation. Our orders are clear."

"If it's a hostile situation then let me in there. The pandas might be in danger. I just came from the Habitat and there was no problem there."

"I'm sorry, sir. A loss of lines of communication indicates a hostile presence." The guard began to lower his weapon at Garrand. "We cannot allow you—"

The guard never finished. Garrand grasped the silver mussel and pulled the soldier forward. The guard tripped, caught himself on one leg and struggled to wrench the weapon free. Using the burner for leverage, Garrand kicked the man savagely. His faceplate cracked and the guard staggered backward, the blow loosening his grip on the burner.

A line of liquid flame arced across the hall as the second guard brought his weapon down like a scythe. Garrand heaved the freed burner around by its barrel in a wild, blind swing. The heavy stock smacked the guard in the chest and his weapon glanced upward. Flame shot over Sid's head. Garrand skipped forward, blade drawn, closing the distance in an instant. Too much armor for a blaster, but there were some nice creases in those shiny plates.

He performed a ballaestra, weapon thrusting ahead of his outstretched arm. The guard recovered, and parried the blade with the burner held outward like a staff. Garrand recovered, hopped sideways and began a low feint. The guard covered the initial move and Garrand lunged high, going for the neck. The guard was quick to adjust, slapping the blade away with the burner's stock. He cracked Garrand's chin with the butt of the weapon and finished his riposte with a kick that sent Garrand sprawling.

Garrand landed flat on his ass, staring down the burner's barrel. He rolled sideways and scrambled over the slick floor as flame leapt toward him. Pain burrowed into his every nerve as his legs caught fire. A terrible roar filled the passage and the burning stopped. He grasped his knees to his chest and beat the flames out with his arms.

Another roar ripped through his mind, the sound primal and terrifying. He looked up wide-eyed as Sid lurched across the hall with surprising speed. The panda caught the soldier by his ankle, massive jaws crunching through the armor. The guard fell to the floor screaming. Sid twisted his powerful neck around and slung the man across the floor. He wrenched the guard in a full circle and smacked his head into the wall.

The first guard had recovered and brought his weapon to bear. Garrand scrambled back to his feet and sprang forward. He ducked beneath the guard's burner as flame sizzled across the passage, grabbing the barrel as he slid beneath the soldier's legs. He wrenched the weapon down as he clipped the guard's legs. The soldier flipped forward and landed on his back. Garrand struggled onto the man's chest, pinning his shoulders with his knees. He thrust his blade up under the ashen helm until the point found resistance. He stopped, palm of his free hand flat on the hilt, ready to deliver the coup de grace.

Lip quivering, he stared into the fractured faceplate. "Open the door." He glanced briefly at the second guard who lay unconscious on the floor. "Don't make me repeat myself," he nudged the blade deeper.

Behind him, the blast door clicked and slid upward. "Very good," he sighed and withdrew his blade. "Open up," he said, rapping the helm with the blade's hilt. The faceplate slid upward. Two eyes stared at him, young and blue. They were filled with a mixture of anger and resignation, but no fear.

Garrand sheathed his blade and drew an injector wand from his belt. He stuck the end through the opening and pressed it into the boy's neck. "No honor lost," he whispered as sleep agent hissed into his bloodstream.

Garrand got slowly to his feet. He looked at the two bodies on the floor, then back at the panda, mild shock registering in his eyes.

"What?" Sid growled, flexing his jaw. "You do not think us capable of defending ourselves?"

"I dunno, I always just thought of you as peaceful by nature."

"Even the peaceful must be able to protect their young. You think we're unable to protect our young?"

Garrand shook his head, "Of course not."

"A warrior defends his loved ones!"

"Yes, they do."

"You are family, Captain, and I will defend you every moment that I draw breath. If these are our last moments, then they will be the finest moments I can create. And the tribe will sing about us forevermore."

Garrand ruffled the panda's ear affectionately. "Come along my warrior friend. We have one last song to sing."

15

Dance with Dragons

GARRAND WALKED INTO A MASSIVE SPACE WITH A SLICKLY-polished floor and walls that arched into a giant dome far over his head. The stone walls of the circular chamber were buttressed with thick steel stanchions that supported an observation platform. Twelve huge spheres dangled above the floor like softly glowing suns. Wires and conduits twisted away from each thrumming device and disappeared into the darkness. The coppery spheres were suspended in a giant ring, spanning the chamber. Each device projected dozens of planets in shimmering brilliance. The overlapping images twisted overhead like a nightmarish rendering of the night sky. Sid's words danced through his mind: *A dozen suns, a sparkle sky / A hundred planets, a million cries.*

The sartographic displays spun in lazy motion over a large, egg-shaped bubble field that sparkled in the center of the hall. Six pandas sat within the translucent, protective field. One by one they stood up and faced him, expressions distorted by the quivering energy.

A fine mist swirled in delicate eddies just over the surface of the floor, wispy tendrils trailing around Garrand's knees. In the center of the chamber, two silver creatures lay sprawled across the slick deck plates, reptilian tongues flicking out between massive jaws, their scales reflecting off the polished surface. Garrand froze, eyes skipping from one giant creature to the other. They both appeared to be in a dormant cycle, eyelids shut, deep rumbling breaths rasping from their nostrils slowly and steadily. The air stank from their fetid exhalations.

Garrand slowly reached a bare hand toward the floor palm up, feeling the warmth that emanated from the surface. He never took his eyes off the creatures. The deck plates were heated from some hidden source, necessary for the gigantic serpents to regulate their internal body temperatures. The first dragon writhed, stretching out its claws, coiling its scarlet tail around itself, breathing out a raspy breath of fog that thickened and hid it.

Sid's prophecies had come to pass. Silver beasts. Dreighonäis. A horrible shudder shook his spine and he fought to control his fear and frustrations. *This was the last place in the galaxy any self-respecting dragon would ever show himself. He should have known that an Imperial Proctor as hungry as Barrett would have a few of the Emperor's favorites lazing about. How better to fashion himself in his image, in the same self-indulgent light?* All his nerves were electrified with adrenaline and passion. There, not thirty meters away stood the last six pandas encased in a protective bubble field, no doubt to keep them from becoming dinner. Wires and electrodes dangled inside, torn off by the six occupants. Their black eyes stared at him through the shimmering bubble.

Sid started to walk past him, but Garrand cautioned him to stop. The dragons lay between them and the pandas. Big ones. Fokathenais. He curled his lip in disgust.

Suddenly, the colorful projections evaporated and the room was lit only by the spare luminescence of the bubble field. Dragon scales refracted the light in a thousand directions like radiant jewels. The circle of spheres hummed overhead and dull vibrations coursed up through the floor.

"I see that you like my pets," an icy voice called out across the chamber. Garrand dropped to one knee and whirled at the unexpected sound, blaster already in his hand, eyes scanning the suspended balcony that ringed the dark hall. In the low light and shadows Garrand could not make out the man's form.

"I understand you have a certain *fondness* for dragons, Captain Médeville. Ironic that you've come to despise the embodiment of an icon you once defended with your life."

"You can learn to hate anything," Garrand muttered, trying to focus in on the sound of the vice proctor's voice. The echoing acoustics made it nearly impossible to discern where it was coming from.

"I felt it only appropriate that two of my noblest guardians watch over my prize. So *many* people seem to be interested in them. I would just hate for any harm to befall such splendid tools."

Garrand searched the shadows above the humming spheres. "Why don't you show yourself, Proctor!"

"I wouldn't think that prudent. I've been lead to believe you're a rather good shot with that blaster. Would you have qualms about shooting an unarmed man?"

"Proctor, you insult me," Garrand stood and holstered his blast pistol.

A cold laugh echoed across the hall. Confident enough now to pace out from behind the humming projection sphere, the vice proctor stepped to the railing. "No insult intended, Captain. Actually, I'm glad to have this opportunity. You've been rather resourceful these last few weeks. A worthy opponent, and a splendid test for the trials to come. But I'm afraid you've reached your limit. You are but a single man, and your resourcefulness has finally come to an end. You must have known that eventually you would fail."

"Quite the contrary," Garrand growled. "I've defeated you at every turn."

"You've *escaped* me at every turn," Barrett replied with condescension, "and merely delayed the inevitable. You're an intelligent man — this should come as no surprise to you. Your whole life has been a series of losses. One failure after another. Surely you didn't think this would be any different."

"Losses?"

"Lost honor, lost career, lost loves. One cherished thing after another. All beginning with your failure at Sardis."

Garrand stepped closer to the balcony. "Failure?" he said with a mocking lilt. "I mark that as a success."

Barrett eyed the tattered uniform. "I do not see the golden bird of myth stitched upon your hip. I do not even see a glint of the confidence that once shone in those eyes." His eyes swept over the rest of his person. "In fact I see very little of the man you once were."

"Change is good for a man," Garrand spoke softly. "And some victories are not so readily apparent."

"Oh, but the losses stand out splendidly. You have the hollow look of a man that has been defeated at every turn. I can see the losses carved into your flesh, little cracks that fan out around your eyes. I see a new one there, one that I was able to create. Helen perhaps?"

Garrand's hand twitched above his blaster.

"Ah yes, draw. That will solve all your problems."

"One of them at least."

"It's not that simple. You have a problem with *authority*, Captain. The pandas are not destined to be with you because you cannot handle power, *real* power. The kind that can lay waste to entire systems. The power to harness the strength of vastly different cultures, myriad economies, build fleets of ships strong enough to—"

"—Strong enough to what? Challenge the Emperor?" Garrand snorted with derision.

Barrett paused, leaning over the polished rail. "Perhaps. In time. Given the chance to prepare, *and foresee...*"

"Even if you had the chance, all you would *foresee* is your own failure."

"Look around yourself," Barrett said looking from side to side, "do you see failure? I see my last nemesis locked in a room where he will soon draw his final breath. Witnessed, I might add, by one of the last missing pandas. A fitting display to remind the beast of who holds the *power.*"

"If it's the future you seek, I might examine who holds the *power* right now. Last time I checked, I had thirty pandas, not to mention the captain of your guard, all her men and one of your destroyers."

Barrett was silent for once.

"Got your attention? Good. Shut down this bubble field and call off your lizards — maybe we'll talk."

"Bravo, Captain. I see that you have not been idle on your visit to my fair capitol. But you're not in a position to bargain. I believe with you out of the way, the Tchelakov Tribe shouldn't be that hard to find, or at the very most, recover. I'm afraid that I must bid you farewell."

"You forget that I have seen the future. I already know that I will win." He tried to sound confident. If only Sid's visions had been a little more precise about *how* he was going to defeat two dragons in close combat.

Barrett caught the subtle crack in his voice. "Oh, but we both know how *fluid* the future is, yes? How very fickle fate can be? One *path* is easily supplanted by another."

"The Path has gotten me this far," Garrand muttered.

"Ah yes, you've come quite close — a rather remarkable feat considering what you've been up against. However," Barrett's tone changed subtly and he slipped back into the shadows, "you have not succeeded. Yet another failure," the voice sighed sadly. "It must be quite maddening to be this close, to see another that you hold *so dear*, another that is almost within your grasp, slip away again…"

Garrand fought to keep his composure, his fists clenched at his side, bile welling up in his throat. His whole body shuddered.

"Your vision has been too narrow," Barrett continued icily, "Your foresight pathetically lacking, and your resourcefulness has reached its limit. Mine, however, shall now be *limitless!*"

Spinning beneath the arc of lights Garrand screamed, "What's the matter Proctor, afraid to fight your own fights?"

Barrett's cool voice responded, "Now you insult *me*, Captain. What need do I have of fighting my own fights when I have *so many* willing to fight them for me?" Suddenly his tone changed and he barked out a command across the hall. "Karloushka!"

Both dragons snapped their heads off the floor and scanned the interior of the room. After a moment two sets of golden eyes focused on the lone man standing in the hall. Garrand could see the muscles tense behind their shoulders as their awful eyes narrowed in hatred at his intrusion. Their great nostrils flared, picking up the panda's scent.

"I'm merely here for my friends!"

"And they are yours for the taking, Captain. I am not standing in your way." A cruel laugh echoed from above.

"Farewell, Captain Médeville. I have a small matter of treason to attend to. The wayward Captain Strom must be dealt with. One last woman to take from you. I leave you with your final task." Footsteps sounded and then a loud crump reverberated through the hall as a blast door locked itself into place. They were sealed in.

The two dragons began to uncurl from their resting position. Both were full grown Fokathenais—twenty meters long snout to tail. The largest dragon had scarlet scales that glowed blood red in the darkened chamber. The crimson hue faded at the tip of each scale, so that the dragon seemed to have a body with a million crystal shards that refracted the ambient light. The effect was accentuated by a bright silver stripe that stretched down its gnarled, bony spine. The second dragon had golden scales that were almost translucent. They reflected the coppery twilight like candlelight. An onyx zigzag started just behind its horned head and twisted down its ridged back like a fissure. Both dragons were beautiful, deadly killing machines. Garrand tried to pick out the alpha between the two varietals. *Was it the scarlet? Its horns were longer and its head had snapped up first at Barrett's command.*

His mind turned over the possibilities. His blaster would be useless against the monsters' razor scales; they reflected too much energy to suffer significant damage. And experience had taught him that plasma fire simply bounced off their thick hides. He would have to get beneath the scales to affect any damage.

The scarlet beast stirred, rising to face the intruders. Its tongue licked hungrily out of its jaws. Garrand needed time to think. He looked helplessly at the pandas trapped in the crystalline field. Their dark eyes were locked on his, full of concern and dread.

The scarlet dragon took a preliminary step forward, shoulders tensing for a leap. Garrand acted quickly, hoping to forestall the initial attack. He smoothly clicked off a concussion grenade into his palm and held it up between his thumb and forefinger, showing it to the dragon.

The dragon cocked its head to one side and peered at the sphere's shiny reflection. It flared one nostril and waited. Garrand made sure it would not be startled by any sudden moves and rolled the grenade across the deck with careful deliberation.

Like a mercat, the dragon watched as the tiny sphere rolled up and bounced off its belly, slowing to a stop before its great head. It leaned close and studied the device. Scarlet gave the grenade one sniff and turned its head sideways, lowering an ear to the ground to check for signs of life.

Unimpressed with the lack of scent and sound, scarlet reached a clawed foot forward and pressed down on the sphere. The grenade detonated with a muffled whump. The dragon snorted and withdrew its foot from the spot. Smoke trailed from the detonation. Scarlet sniffed its claw and a snarl crept across its jaw, huge dirty teeth becoming exposed beneath the folds of hide.

"Sid, we're going to have to work this out on the fly. I have to get inside one of the dragons."

"How are you going to manage that, Captain?" Sid's shoulders were squared to the dual threat, eyes staring at the massive predators. His every instinct told him to flee, climb, hide, but he stood his ground next to his friend.

"Well one way would be to get chewed up into pieces and swallowed."

"That's not humorous."

The scarlet dragon cast an unblinking eye at the human and let a low rumble echo into the chamber.

"I think this one likes me," Garrand said as he reached into his satchel. He was careful to keep eye contact with his adversary as he clicked a fresh wheel of grenades onto the feeder. He slung a bandolier of explosives over his shoulder and clipped the low end to his belt so it would not swing free during the fight. He hefted the laser axe; it felt strange in his hand.

The golden dragon sensed the attention being focused on scarlet and rose to all fours. Without a further sound, it began to slowly circle around the bubble field, one eye trained on the two intruders.

"We can't let them work in unison."

"How do we break them apart?"

"I don't know yet." He moved to shield Sid from the golden dragon's flanking move.

The panda shoved him away with his snout. "I think I have an idea."

"Sid this is not the time to —"

" — Be creative? Captain, I have learned from watching you."

Garrand pushed him back and took a handful of grenades in his palm, flicking their detonators to 'impact.' He reared

back and hurled them at the top of the sphere above the scarlet
dragon. The explosion ripped the copper projector free from
two of its supports. It lurched sideways and dangled from a
third. The dragon twisted its neck to look up. Garrand drew
his blaster and fired three shots, severing the last weakened
cable. The sphere fell, but scarlet slithered out of harm's way
and the bubble shattered on the deck in a fiery explosion.

Garrand spoke quickly into his collar comtab. "Bailey, I'm
going to need your help down here."

"I'm sorry, Captain," *Destiny* replied, "but Bailey is currently
unavailable. He is assisting in the recovery of the pandas in the
dome."

"*Destiny*," Garrand blew out a heavy breath, "just the girl I
need." Both dragons stood, their necks slinking low to the floor,
eyes glowing in the darkness. Garrand backpedaled, arm pushing the panda back as well. "Stay behind me."

The ship picked up the urgency in his tone. "What is your
situation?"

"We're in the bubble room above the Habitat—locked in by
the sound of it. There's an elliptical field holding six pandas in
the center. And I'm looking at two dragons."

"Did you say two?"

"Yes by Haven, two Fokathenais. And they're no longer in
dormant cycle." He clicked off a handful of concussion grenades and rolled them toward the crouching dragons. "We're
in trouble."

"Understood. Bailey is on his way."

"It won't do any good unless you can get the blast door open.
You monitored Captain Strom's shortcuts through the protocols, right?"

"Every step."

"Good. Then get to work on those command overrides. And find the control algorithm for the bubble field but don't deactivate it until I tell you. Get Bailey working on the entrance to this chamber. It might take him some time to hack the door."

Two of the grenades detonated with dull whumps under a dragon's claw. The golden dragon pounced on another, temporarily diverted by the game.

"Can you defeat them?" Sid growled, fur standing up along his back.

"One? Maybe. Two, working together?" he shook his head.

"What do we do?"

"Dragons are arrogant. They're used to being the top of the food chain. These two have been well fed their whole lives, they've never been in the wild. They've never been hunted. This is all a game to them."

"How do we use that to our advantage?"

"We can't run. They'll tear us apart in seconds."

"Good. I am tired of running." Sid swiped his tongue across his lips and bared his teeth at the golden dragon.

Garrand drew his weapon and fired across the room, destroying power conduits in fiery eruptions, but the dragons showed no interest. They skulked forward, mouths agape, eyes glowing, mesmerized by their prey.

"Okay my not-so-peaceful friend. It's time to go to war."

"What do you want me to do?" Sid growled.

"Get up to the observation platform. I can't protect you and attack them."

"I can help you press the attack," he growled.

"I know you can, but not right this second. We have to create distractions for each other. Get up that stanchion!" Garrand clicked off three more grenades and heaved them across the hall. They thumped against the far wall and sent a thunderclap echoing across the chamber.

The golden dragon shied back, startled by the distraction. Scarlet was less impressed; it sniffed disdainfully at the acrid plumes that swirled amongst the fog and turned to stalk the interesting prey. Sid scrambled up the nearest steel stanchion, struggling to get to the gangway that encircled the room. The scarlet dragon rushed forward, claws propelling it quickly across the black deck plates.

Garrand jumped toward the onrushing dragon, landing with arms spread and shoulders wiggling. Scarlet's head drew back and its eyes narrowed. The human bowed gracefully, fingers grazing the floor. Hands on hips, he began shuffling his feet, humming lightly to himself as he tried to remember the tune. He used to dance, in the old days at least. After a battle, he and his men would drink themselves into oblivion, and there was always dancing. He scraped his boots over the slick floor, toe tapping behind his crossed legs as he picked up the pace. *There, it was coming back to him.* He jigged sideways and did a little spin.

Sid paused halfway up the stanchion and watched the bizarre spectacle, fear caught up in his throat. He was finding it difficult to focus on the present, much less the future. Even regulating his pulse was nearly impossible. The captain finished his jig with a flourish and Sid finished climbing to safety. The dragons watched the man with great interest. Had they ever seen a dance before?

"What's the hold up, *Destiny*? We need the bubble field and door controls!"

"The codes have changed, Captain," the ship replied.

"We're working on it," Vailetta added.

"We are running out of time." With one meal left between them, the dragons began to circle in opposite directions, cautiously sizing up the curious human. They snorted to each other, coordinating their attack. Garrand blasted chunks from the wall and steel girders near their heads trying to get them to reconsider. "You've got to break those codes."

"The protocols are changing every few seconds—they've been randomized."

"If you can't break the door codes, concentrate on shutting down power to this entire section of the complex. That should turn off the bubble field and allow Bailey to hack the door."

"Yes, but reserve generators would kick in almost immediately."

"I don't care!" he bellowed, "just do it!"

The dragons roared across the hall to one another, their heads arching up to the ceiling. They were announcing the hunt.

Here it comes. Garrand pivoted to face scarlet. It took a double step forward and paused, its long tongue flicking out as its head reared back. Garrand watched the chest muscles coil behind its shimmering scales. The golden dragon stamped its foot, but Garrand did not look. The muscles flinched and Garrand rolled out of the way as the scarlet dragon lunged. The head shot by, teeth snapping behind his boots.

He came up on one knee firing, concentrating on the bit of skull behind the horns where the armor plating appeared to end. The dragon screeched in pain, and wheeled around, fire spewing from its mouth. Garrand ducked, immediately activating his shield. He raised his arm in a futile gesture against the flaming bile, covering his face and eyes. Heat and flame buffeted the shield, but the field turned away the fiery assault. The blast continued for several seconds and then halted abruptly as the dragon ran out of breath.

Garrand shut off the shield, stood and fired another salvo. Surprised that the quarry was not a burnt carcass, scarlet roared in anger. The beast swung its tail in a long loop and whipped it toward the human. Garrand dropped to his chest as the vicious swing passed over his head, missing him by millimeters. He quickly hopped up and ran toward the center of the hall, dropping grenades in his wake.

The second dragon tracked his progress and sucked in a deep, rasping breath. There was an awful moment just after its lungs filled and before it exhaled where Garrand's eyes flicked toward the creature in awareness of the threat; fear and adrenaline and hate and all the last vestiges of his hope were captured in that one instant of pained recognition. He turned and ran as the dragon spewed fire from its terrible jaws. Flames spread across the floor as the dragon turned its head to follow the fleeing human's path. Garrand ducked around the bubble field as the bile shot past. He gazed through the crystalline field and watched the flames roaring out of the dragon's mouth. The bubble field bore the brunt of the attack, and the flames were once more turned away. His hands were up against the bubble field, and sweat poured down his brow, drenching his tunic. A panda placed a paw up against the field where Garrand's hand was.

"Don't worry buddy, I'm going to get you out of there." he murmured as he pushed away from the field.

The golden dragon howled in anger and threw itself against the bubble. Its terrible jaws looked hideously contorted from by the bubble field. It clawed the bubble in frustration and roared. The sound shook the ceiling above. The pandas watched the terrible beast that slathered and shrieked just a meter away.

"*Destiny*, you got those power overrides yet?"

"Working, Captain. Captain Strom has breached central services. I am accessing the proper commands."

"Make it quick."

"Yes, Captain. The *Lucayamo* has broken through the doors to the dome. Bailey has been sent to the blast door to work his way in."

"That's not going to do us much good if you don't get the power down!"

"Due to your current predicament, I will ignore your apparent lack of faith in my abilities."

"Cheplus, just get it down."

Scarlet was quickly moving around the far end of the hall, preparing to attack from Garrand's flank. The beast's claws scraped hideously against the slick deck plates as it propelled itself at attack speed. The golden dragon lowered its head and roared to draw the human's attention away from the side attack. It slunk forward, head bobbing side to side. Its gaze was full of confidence and hunger. It licked its jaws and coiled to strike in tandem.

Garrand called up to the platform, "Sid, it's time to split them up. I can't fight two simultaneously. You get the golden dragon's attention and keep it off my back."

Sid was waiting eagerly for the chance to act. He charged around the circular platform until he was above the scarlet beast. He launched himself off the high ground with a tremendous roar and sank his teeth and claws into the dragon's neck just behind its twisted horns.

The dragon shrieked in surprise and wrenched its head back and forth to free itself from the attack. Sid held on tightly with tooth and claw. The dragon clawed at its neck, but could not connect with the panda. It shook harder, whipping its neck from side to side. Sid was thrown to the deck, but he quickly scrambled to his feet and cantered to the relative safety of the bubble field.

"You're going to get yourself killed," Garrand fired in frustration.

"Or eaten."

"That's not funny."

"My point exactly," the panda grumbled.

Garrand stole a glance at his friend. *They had survived this far, by Haven they would finish it.*

The golden dragon was getting very close. It leaned forward on its haunches, head swinging gently back and forth, eyes fixed on the panda. Garrand elbowed Sid in the head. "Don't stare, he is trying to get you to freeze."

Sid was staring back at the dragon, eyes hypnotically fixed on the Fokathenais. "Hush now, Captain. I know how to hunt too…"

"Sid, this isn't a vole."

"I'll provide the distraction you need. Separate them. You get to work on the scarlet beast."

The dragon and the panda roared at each other, attempting territorial dominance. The noise was deafening. The golden dragon stomped forward but Sid did not give ground.

Garrand grew worried: *his friend wasn't that stubborn was he?* He opened fire on the golden dragon, gouging the creature's hide with bolts of energy. The dragon wheeled away from the human and set after the black and white treat. Garrand continued to fire. Bits of scale and flesh dropped from the dragon's chest, but it scraped quickly ahead.

"Get moving Sid!"

The golden dragon snapped at the panda's flank. Sid loped away and started racing around the circumference of the chamber. The dragon scrabbled after the furry beast, jaws clattering. Sid weaved in and out of the stanchions as he kept up a breakneck pace.

Garrand watched the panda move, amazed at his friend's speed and dexterity. The golden dragon carried on its awkward pursuit. *This was his chance.*

"Destiny what are the Fokathenais' known weaknesses?

"There are none."

"Cheplus, there has to be something!"

"Well if you could manage to get under its scales then you might have a shot at its vitals. But even then you still have a major problem."

"What problem?"

"All its vital organs are protected within a massive bony vault. Like a human's ribcage but much thicker. This is why even heavy cannon fire cannot take down a Fokathenais. It opens up their hide but does not harm their core functions."

"I have to get inside the hide," Garrand mused.

"What was that?"

"I have to get under the scales and inside the beast to get at that bony casing."

"How are you going to do that?"

"I'm going to carve my way in."

"How will you keep the dragon from clawing you off its belly while you hack your way in?"

"Leave that to me."

Garrand drew his blade and dipped low once more, the tip scraping a line across the deck. *I bow to you before I kill you.*

Scarlet climbed over the top of the bubble field, swinging its long tail in a sweeping arc toward the human. Garrand dove over the barbed length and raced toward the dragon's flank. The dragon snapped at the man's legs but Garrand stepped

gracefully away from the lunge, and slid inside creature's turning radius. The dragon lost sight of its target and wrenched
its head in the opposite direction. This gave Garrand just the
opening he was looking for.

He jammed his blade under a sharp scale with two fists behind the pommel. He pried upward and sliced back and forth
as hard as he could, cutting through the tendon that held the
scale in place. The scarlet dragon roared in anger, shaking the
ceiling above.

Garrand sawed through the flesh and pulled the scale free.
Black blood oozed from the wound. Garrand lifted the laser
axe and sliced into the newly exposed flesh. The cutting tool
bit into the dragon's flank and burned through more connective tissue; a handful of scales fell free.

The dragon could not see the human on its right flank and
whipped its head back to the left, scrabbling its legs to turn
and find its prey. "Just a few more seconds," Garrand muttered.
He buried the axe deeper into the dragon and ripped a gash
diagonally across its belly. The smell of burnt flesh filled his
nostrils; blood gushed over his arms. He sputtered and fought
for breath as intestines began to spill out.

The dragon reached a claw back and gingerly poked at the
new wound, sensing something was wrong. Garrand kicked
the probing claw away and thrust his leg inside the long inci-
sion. He kept the laser axe cutting, and with two arms held
overhead, continued to create a doorway into the dragon itself.

The dragon slid off the bubble field and lay down on its
right side. Its head finally had room to maneuver into a position where it could see what was happening. Garrand dropped
the axe and used both arms to pull himself into the wound,
kicking intestines out of his way. The dragon saw the human

disappearing into its flesh and began clawing at the open wound.

Garrand fought his way through the steaming morass of mucus and guts, following the rhythmic sound of the dragon's heart.

Scarlet clawed desperately at its belly to remove the painful intruder, but Garrand was protected by the dragon's own defensive armor. The tough, overlapping scales could not be clawed open. Garrand wiggled closer to the bony vault that protected the dragon's vital organs. He kicked aside sticky glands and thrust his arms through the coiled intestines, desperately pulling himself deeper into the beast.

The sound of the dragon's heartbeat pounded like a war drum. Garrand could feel the muscle pulsing throughout the dragon's body. He slithered in beneath the dragon's diaphragm and felt along the intercostal muscles. He pressed his ear against the bony shell, trying to find a spot beneath the heart itself. The dragon's stomach gurgled, a sound unlike any he had ever experienced. He felt along the bones, looking for an articular groove.

He found an indention with his fingertips and followed it to a point where the intercostal cartilage connected bones together. If he was working his way along the vertebrosternal ribs as he suspected, then the heart would be directly above this point. He drew his blade and began working the tip into the cartilage, creating a seam that he could exploit. He wiggling the blade back and forth until he managed to get half of the length into the opening.

He felt along his belt until he found a Haley charge. Gasping for breath in the bloody interior of the carcass, he set the charge to 30 seconds and prised open the bony corpuscle. It took all his strength to separate the bone. He thrust the Haley charge into the cavity and flicked the activation stud.

The Haley charge began its countdown. Garrand yanked his knife out and slipped it back into his belt. He had one driving thought: *Get out of the dragon!* He struggled through the blood-slickened guts. He kicked intestines aside and pulled sticky sacs out of his way. Mucus invaded his nasal pages and he found himself choking back dragon blood as he fought for opening and fresh air. His hands found the long tear in the dragon's hide and he pulled himself desperately to the light.

He thrust his head outside and gulped in oxygen, spitting up blood and bits of phlegm. He coughed and wretched, desperately trying to climb out of the coiled intestines. The dragon located the foreign mass protruding from its belly and snagged it with a clawed foot.

Garrand was unceremoniously yanked out of the fetid guts. His arms and legs kicked free as the dragon slung him out into the open. He fought to break free from the dragon's clutches, but the claws were cinched tightly around his body. The scarlet dragon rolled onto its feet and slammed him to the deck. Garrand looked into its eyes; they were filled with terrible pain and anger. The dragon bared its teeth and reared back to deliver the killing blow.

Garrand counted the seconds. Time seemed to stand still as the dragon's tongue flicked out one last time. A muffled explosion shook the beast and blood shot out of its nose and mouth. The Haley charge detonated and blew a hole in the dragon's heart. The pounding muscle erupted in catastrophic failure and the light went out of the dragon's eyes. Garrand felt the claws slacken around his waist. The scarlet dragon toppled to the deck, its life extinguished.

Garrand climbed to his feet and wiped blood out of his eyes. He searched the hall for his friend. "Sid!" He coughed up bile mixed with a lungful of hot, sticky dragon blood and called out again. "Sid are you all right?"

"Yes, Captain!"

Garrand turned to confront the golden dragon, but he had nothing to fear. The smaller dragon was now oblivious to the human in the presence of a steaming, fresh kill. The dragon clawed over the fallen carcass, eager to feed. It sniffed the fallen carcass, reared its head back and plunged its teeth into the fresh meat.

"Finally, you hold still!"

Garrand stomped up the dragon's tail, cutting his hands on the sharp scales as he fought to pull himself up. He scrabbled up the long neck and lunged for the head, grasping a horn for balance. The dragon continued to rip into the silver dragon's flesh. He drew his blade and flipped it over into his fist. Reaching forward, he plunged the point of the blade into the creature's eye. He heard a pop and twisted, rupturing the pupil. Blood gushed out and the dragon reared back, baying with wrath.

Dropping the blade, Garrand grasped the second horn to keep from being thrown as the neck wrenched him from side to side. He reached back to his belt and detached his last Haley charge, flicking the detonator to fifteen seconds with his thumb. Stretching forward, he buried the charge deep in the eye socket, his arm plunging well into the cavity. His arm squished in the gooey tissue as he struggled to press the charge well back in the skull.

The dragon lowered its head to the ground and raked Garrand's back with its rear claws, trying to rip him loose. He bit the inside of his cheek savagely, trying to ignore the pain that coursed up his back—his mind screamed for him to let go, but he pressed deeper, arm in almost to the elbow now. The beast got him by the leg and slung him off its head.

He hit the ground hard and skid on his belly across the floor in a long arc, still held by the dragon. His hands struggled vainly for purchase. He glanced off a support column and spun to rest. Blood rushed through his head, adrenaline searing his senses. His back was on fire; he could not even tell if his limbs would respond to commands. With an agonizing whelp of pain, he struggled to pry his leg free of the claw.

The dragon sized him with its one remaining eye. Its long tongue flicked out hungrily and the jaws parted. The claw released his leg and grabbed him more firmly around the waist. Garrand counted the seconds; it felt like an eternity... Hot, moist breath washed over him, saliva and blood dripping down with the putrid odors. The dragon licked his chest once and opened its jaws wide.

"Just die," he whispered.

An instant later the Haley detonated with a wonderful thump. The dragon's skull was blown clear off its spine. It hit a copper sphere with a resounding crack and crashed burning to the deck. The headless body stood still for a moment and then it crumpled.

Garrand lay beneath the slack weight of the claw and stared at the ceiling, losing track of time. He could hear voices ringing through his comtab.

"—Access granted."

"—Lines broken."

"—Cut power."

"—It's your show Bailey."

"—Bubble field down. Get them out."

New light fell into the chamber. He could hear the blast door trundling open. A black and white face loomed into view. Sid licked his face gently. He blinked in protest. "Please, no more tongues." Garrand sat up with help from the circle of pandas as Bailey pulled the claws off him. The artificial turned his head to look at him. "How does it feel to almost be someone's dinner?"

"No fun."

"Jean-Wa's going to have a fit when I bring you back looking like this."

Garrand smiled and let the artificial hoist him upright. Knees weak and head woozy, he walked out of the bubble room for the last time, arm around his first mate's shoulder, seven pandas in tow. For some reason, bits of Sid's last prophecy echoed in his head. *Dragon's feast, soldier's chore / The Path moves on forevermore.*

16

CREIGHTON YARD

WICKED, GREEN BOLTS OF ENERGY LANCED OVER VAILET-
ta's head, spat from thick-barreled cannons beneath the *Lucayamo*. The snap-shriek of the plasma batteries cast a mewling
howl that preceded each distant explosion as the energy carved
up chunks of the tarmac. Wyx' primary had set some minutes
ago and the cannons' report illuminated the destroyer's sweeping underbelly like spectral fireflies. The tarmac was awash in
the alternating glow of a hundred such cannons. Vailetta listened to the bellow and watched the long green fingers of destruction streak through the twilight.

Too long, she thought. *It was taking too long.* The *Lucayamo*
was prepped and ready. Thirty of the pandas were aboard,

along with *Destiny's Needle*, her complement of artificials, the Gokazoku, and one wayward datacore. But still no Garrand Médeville. She waited nervously outside the final gantry as flashes of energy thundered overhead, streaking across the tarmac. Blasts rippled and roiled over the Yard as the *Lucayamo's* gunners unleashed the ship's massive firepower on the planet's surface.

The broad, almost sleepy expanse of the Yard was slowly coming alive as Barrett mobilized his forces. She could see men and machines scurrying through the last light. An armored brigade was preparing to attack from the west. She studied the line of Sulli's through her monocular as they approached in staggered formation. Light infantry was massing five kilometers south, behind a row of docked freighters. Ships began powering up all around them, collision lights winking through the haze, engine exhausts glowing blue, green and gold. Vailetta replaced the monocular and sighed. The war engines were coming to life, the peasants were preparing to storm the castle.

A floating, dark fortress, the *Lucayamo* beat back those who approached, cannons laying waste to all who dared challenge her. Any unit that veered too close was caught in the ship's overlapping volleys. Distant fireballs attested to their demise. Sizzling roars followed a squadron of Barrelian Phantoms as they shot past the destroyer's stern. The pass was followed by muted crumps along the ship's spine as bombs detonated. "Hold together," Vailetta whispered as the fighters wheeled straight up into the night. "Just hold together for a few more minutes."

Dasko appeared at the mouth of the gantry and trotted over the tarmac, head ducked down. "Two ships on their way down from orbit, Captain. ETA five minutes."

"We're not leaving."

Of course not, Dasko bit his tongue. "Lewg reports another destroyer is powering up on the surface—the *Shiva.*" He peered across the Yard, face awash in the mussel flash. "We should be able to see her," he pointed to the north. "There."

Vailetta could see the destroyer turning in the distance, the bow swinging slowly around. They didn't have very long. She gazed back at the black maw of the nearest pit, the entrance that led to the Habitat. *Too long.* She stared at the opening as if she could physically will him to appear by desire alone. Shockwaves shuddered up through the ground as the *Lucayamo* was hit with another airborne barrage. She yawed against her mooring. Bits of steel and armor sprinkled down like snow.

A figure appeared in the distance. The last of the day's residual heat still rose in waves from the sunbaked surface, masking the figure's approach. Vailetta snatched the monocular back to her eye. She caught her breath as the image came into focus. A man, face and chest bloody, strode across the tarmac flanked by a silver artificial.

"It's him," she announced, setting the monocular down.

She watched the details of his form coalesce in the quivering heat. He took long, purposeful strides, shoulders set, arms swinging loosely—his fingers grazed his weapon lightly with each stride—an assurance in his gait, as if nothing on this world could stop him. His head was cocked just to one side, and his eyes stared across the expanse, raw and determined.

A warm sensation gathered in her belly. By Haven, he'd done it. She'd never thought it possible, but her eyes did not deceive. Garrand Médeville was walking out of Lord Barrett's most heavily guarded lair with the last seven of its incarcerated occupants. Behind him the dark forms loomed, emerging en masse from the heat oscillations. The large black-and-white-furred creatures trotted on all fours to keep up. A surge of admiration filled her.

"Captain Strom, are you all right?"

"Yes, I'm fine Dasko." She suppressed the urge to sprint across the distance that separated them, contenting herself with watching his triumphant approach. The Captain and his panda liege looked formidable indeed. She wondered what a man like Garrand could do with a tribe of super-intelligent, prescient, and utterly loyal pandas at his side. Having witnessed the destruction Barrett had wrought on a hundred worlds, she knew what dark fate *he* would instill on the Shell and possibly the whole galaxy if they did not escape from Wyx.

She shuddered at the thought and turned her eyes skyward to gaze at the destroyer that hovered overhead, its gigantic form blocking out the moon and dwarfing the service gantries that held it in place against the gusting wind.

Garrand strode near, face encrusted in grim, chest soaked with thick, black dragon blood. He squinted through the wind, eyes never leaving hers. *Father would like this man*, she thought.

He held her with a look of absolute determination. "What'd you find?" he asked, voice rough but curious. His gaze swept past her.

"I got us a Tobana," she said warmly.

"Tobana," he frowned. "What's that?"

"Don't you keep up with the rest of the universe? Tobana class destroyer. The latest Imperial design. Top of the line. Creighton Yard's finest."

Garrand tried to make out the outline of the ship over the clustered gantries and service towers. "Why couldn't you get a Torvel, or a Carrak class? Or a Lor Stanta, that would have been good."

Dasko had to bite his lip to keep from grinning at the man's gall. He turned away to shield himself from the coming reprisal, chuckling under his breath.

Vailetta's face curled into a tight scowl. Ignoring the man's wounds, she grabbed the scruff of his blazer with two fists. "Garrand Médeville, when a woman throws away her career, risks her life as well as all the lives of her men, sneaks into the heavily guarded Creighton Yard and brings you and delivers a brand new Imperial destroyer, you don't ask her, 'What kind?'"

"You don't?"

"No," she pulled him roughly to her. "You're supposed to take her like this and—" she pressed her lips against his mouth. The kiss was full and deep, imbued with all the emotions she had held in check. She let him up for air. "And then you're supposed to say, 'Good job.'"

She released him and stood back, a little flushed.

Garrand regarded her with amusement. "I don't have time for this romantic crap," he started, but as Vailetta turned away in disgust, he seized her arm and spun her back around. Her eyes danced back and forth trying to gauge the rebuttal, but he fixed her with a big, steady grin. She relaxed in recognition of the playful look, aggravation melting away. He held her with both hands, his grip relaxing until his fingers barely brushed her shoulders. With deliberate slowness, he leaned down and returned her kiss.

He pulled back, let go and nodded once. "Good job."

That was all she needed. She turned away smiling: "Dasko, secure these pandas."

"Yes, ma'am."

"We lift in one minute."

Garrand stared up at the hovering destroyer. The batteries shrieked from her belly, spewing great bolts of energy into the wind. "Quite a beast," he murmured. "Where's *Destiny's Needle?*"

"Bay three, safe and sound."

The last of the pandas stepped into the gantry. Garrand looked around uncertainly. "We forget anything?"

"Not unless you've got any more friends you want to bring," Vailetta quipped sarcastically.

"Nope, this is it."

"After you, then," Vailetta swept her hand toward the ship.

"Why, thank you, Captain."

Vailetta paused at the gantry, eyes fixed on the *Shiva* that had turned head on. Barrett now had something sizable to throw at them. Plasma lanced across the gap as the two capital ships began exchanging fire.

Vailetta ducked into the suspensor tube. Garrand stood at the top of the gantry, trying to time his jump to the open airlock.

"Go on!" Vailetta yelled. Garrand leaped through the door, tripped and fell as the floor slid out from under him. The *Lucayamo* shuddered under the *Shiva's* initial onslaught. "What was that?"

Vailetta dove through the opening and slapped the contact. The airlock cycled close. "The *Shiva*," she said as she stooped to help him up. "Apparently someone has invoked the vice proctor's ire."

"You don't say." The ship rocked under another hit. "I told you we should have gotten a Lor Stanta."

"Don't start with me," she warned.

They took a tube to the top of the ship. The bridge was filled with activity. Five men and six artificial assists worked the primary stations. Garrand noted that one pod was active.

"All ports sealed," Danelle reported.

"Disengage umbilicals," Vailetta swung into the command chair.

"All green."

"Take us into orbit, Yarvek,"

The light above his pod flashed green. The ship rose away from the tarmac, repulsors screaming.

Garrand studied the sartographs in the center of the bridge. The *Lucayamo* was a green dot arcing up away from the planet's surface. Threats winked on all sides.

"Do we have the current position of the Third Fleet?" he asked.

"One moment, sir."

The orbital track of two-dozen ships glimmered above the display. Garrand grabbed a datapad. "Barrett's gathering forces here, here and here," he tapped three places well above the planet's surface.

"Not much room to maneuver," Dasko murmured.

"Not with that destroyer pushing us up from below," Garrand agreed. "He's got most of our escape vectors covered—we can't exactly tear by them in this behemoth."

"We'll be trading blows the whole way," Vailetta said. "The question is, can we hold them off long enough to make the jump?"

"We'll never even make it out of orbit," Dasko said.

Vailetta rubbed her face, staring at the display. Her eyes flicked between the ships rising up to meet them, and the Fleet that closed in above them. "No," she said softly, "you're right."

Garrand shook his head, "We don't have to make a jump."

Vailetta swung around. "What are you talking about?"

"There's an opening, here," he pointed to a volume beneath the planet's moon, 250,000 kilometers overhead.

"The moon's in the way," Dasko muttered. "We'd have to get around Dōtras. Plus its competing gravitational force means we have to get that much further away before we can risk a jump."

"But what if we don't go around?" Garrand intoned.

A pained expression clouded Vailetta's face.

"How far do you think we'll get in this thing anyway?" Garrand continued. "Even if we did get away, we're going to be pretty easy to track. There's hundreds of ways to keep tabs on an Imperial destroyer."

Dasko stood up. "Yeah, so?"

Vailetta caught Garrand's drift and smiled. "Helm, get us pointed at that moon."

"But that just slows us down," Dasko complained. "It's just another obstacle we have to go around."

"Orbital vector plotted," helm replied. A new green line arced up through the sartograph, away from the gathering fleet. Danelle turned in her chair. "You want us to assume an orbit around the moon?"

"No," Garrand said. "I want you to hit it."

"Captain!" Dasko protested.

"I don't follow you," Danelle said.

"We've got another means of transportation," Vailetta supplied. "*Destiny's Needle.*"

Dasko looked horrified. "That *thing* in bay three?"

Garrand leaned over helm's shoulder. "Accelerate toward the moon's far horizon, but put us in a decaying orbit." He magnified Dōtras' topography and focused on a tectonic ridge. "Don't let us clear that range."

"I've seen scav-cows that looked more spaceworthy —"

"Dasko!" Vailetta warned.

"Well it's a bit on the ramshackle side, don't you think?"

"It's faster than anything you've got," Garrand snapped.

The lieutenant snorted. "We caught it once."

"You caught nothing," Garrand derided. "We stopped for repairs. And if you hadn't sabotaged her, you'd never have had a chance."

Dasko looked for support from Vailetta. "Captain, you don't really think—"

Vailetta leaned on the armrest. "He's got a point, lieutenant. It's a lot stealthier than this destroyer."

Danelle persisted. "A collision course, sir?" Her hands wavered over the controls.

"That's right, lieutenant," Garrand swung down to the center of the bridge. "We get everyone aboard *Destiny* and set this tub in a shallow dive for the moon. We dump every ship we can between now and then and slip out at the very end." The entire bridge crew was staring at him. "The destroyer will hit the moon and by the time they've figured out what's happened we'll be in quantum space."

"You're insane."

"Lieutenant Dasko," Garrand said patiently, "you're going to have to learn to be creative if you're going to survive in the private sector. Straightforward military tactics aren't going to get us ten clicks past that picket."

"You're confusing creativity with desperation."

"Desperation sharpens the mind," he smiled at the young man. "Cheer up, I'll teach you how to fly my scav-cow."

"Scrap hauling isn't really my thing."

Vailetta waved her hand. "Save it for later, Dasko."

Garrand walked back to her chair. "I like him," he muttered with a dour smile. "A real eye for detail."

"I'm sure you were just as pleasant in your youth."

"Where are the pandas?" he sighed.

"Officer's mess."

"And the scavenged door?"

"In the vaults."

"Okay, we need them both loaded in *Destiny*."

Vailetta nodded to Farres and Galar. The two men disappeared out the door. She looked to Garrand. "After all the trouble I went through to get this ship and you want to plow it into the first moon we see. This is the thanks I get?"

"I'll thank you properly," he smiled at her. "Don't worry. Besides, there will be other ships to steal." The ship rocked under heavy fire from the pursuant vessels.

Garrand looked to the man sitting at the targ station. "*Shiva?*"

He nodded. "Dead astern. She's following us right up through the atmosphere."

"Rate of closure?"

"We're keeping distance, but those fighters will be on us shortly."

"Course plotted," Danelle reported. "At current acceleration, impact in seven minutes, forty-seven seconds."

The consoles shuddered once more. Chimes signaled and a new sartograph flashed into existence. "Warning, shield failure imminent."

"Targ?"

"Starboard quarter thirty-two percent and falling. Port not much better."

"Can you redirect?"

"One minute."

"Warning," the ship crooned, "shield failure imminent."

"Shut that thing off." She stabbed the com button. "Yarvek, dump those shield buffers anywhere you can, we've got to be able to absorb more damage back there." She glanced back wryly: "We're going to need a diversion if we're going to make it out of orbit."

"Diversion, no problem." Garrand scanned the bridge. "You, you and you come with me."

The three guardsman hesitated for a second, glancing at their Captain. Vailetta jerked her head. "You heard the man."

Garrand ran out the bridge, followed by Lewg, Dasko, and Fenton.

"Where we going?" Lewg huffed, trying to keep up.

"Which docking bay is aft of the vaults, port side, just below the maintenance pits?"

"Four," Dasko said.

"Yeah," Garrand said, snapping his fingers. "Bay four. We're going to launch everything in bay four that's not locked down."

"That's your plan?"

"With nothing to lose, try to confuse."

Lewg grinned.

The docking bay was hauntingly empty. Garrand pulled up short, staring at the long rows of mules, phantoms, and chrysanths. It had been twelve years since he'd been inside an Imperial docking bay. And he'd never been in one this quiet. It was like time was frozen. No arts scampering about, no lighters humming through the air. The cranes sat on their rails. The fat, semicircular mules rested undisturbed on the deck. There was serenity here, a peaceful quality that the soldiers, pilots, and foremen that served here for long months probably never knew.

Beyond the broad force field that kept the bay pressurized, the sky was turning from blue to black. Garrand could see the curving surface of Wyx falling away as the *Lucayamo* escaped the atmosphere. He snapped out of reverie: there was work to be done.

"What's first?" Dasko asked.

"Each of you take a mule and fire up the main reactors. Plot a simple course back toward Jobaenz and set the sub-lights on a time delay. Get 'em hovering and we'll dump 'em out the bay with a loader."

He watched the men scramble to the first three transports and tapped his comtab. "Médeville to bridge."

Vailetta's voice replied, "What is it, Garrand?"

"What's your tech ensign's name?"

"Yarvek-EZ."

"Can you patch me through to his pod?"

Vailetta touched a control. "Go ahead."

"You there, Yarvek?"

"Good evening, Captain."

"Yeah, I was wondering if I could get your help. Can you tap into docking bay four's command core?"

"No problem."

"Is it possible to release the drop ships remotely?"

"Without pilots aboard?"

"Yeah, the ones that are waiting for Shock Troops in the armory."

"I suppose so. The doors are easy enough, and the docking claws can be released from here in an emergency. I'll have to get past the safety overrides."

"All right, warm up the ones that are already cradled and set them to automatic release—stagger them fifteen seconds apart."

A long, low whine filled the docking bay as the mules began to power up. The first transport lifted off the deck, shifted sideways and hovered several meters up. Dasko appeared at the airlock. Garrand waved him over. The lieutenant hopped to the steel plates; the airlock cycled close behind him.

Dasko drew up to attention before him. "She's set to engage sub-lights in one minute."

"Good job. Push her out with that big loader."

The guardsman dashed across the deck to the dull machine. Its chassis was covered with scrapes and dents. He climbed up the steel ladder and slipped behind the controls. Lights began flashing and the loader's big arms slid up and down. Garrand watched as Dasko maneuvered the machine up behind the mule and bumped it gently. The transport shied forward. The loader nestled in close, and like a tugboat nudging an ocean vessel, pushed the huge mule toward the exit. The force field sparkled as the mule passed through the vacuum seal and then the transport was out. It slid away from the destroyer a few meters a second.

Dasko looked over his shoulder and grinned. Garrand pointed at the next two mules that hovered in line. Dasko nodded and swung the lifter around.

"Bailey, you read me?"

"Yes, Captain."

"What's ship status?"

"Pandas aboard—all 37 accounted for. The Imperial data-core is in the aft hold. It's being plugged into *Destiny's Needle* as we speak. You should have voice contact now."

"Get the ship warmed up and plot a course around the back side of that moon. We'll need jumps lined up as soon as possible."

"Yes, sir."

"Ecksley, you there?"

"Yes, Captain, I'm pleased to say."

"Good, I need a sartographic setup of possible Imperial intercept courses once *Destiny's Needle* clears the destroyer. I also need a countdown to the last possible moment that we can launch from bay three and still clear the moon's gravity well. We'll have a substantial velocity toward the surface to counteract."

"On it, Captain."

"I'm perfectly capable of computing that," *Destiny* complained.

"You worry about where we're going after we're out," Garrand ordered. "Ecksley can handle the launch timing."

"But, Captain!"

"I've got two cores and by Haven I'm going to use them."

"As you wish."

The *Lucayamo* shook and trembled as she broke through the last vestiges of the planet's atmosphere. She took cannon hits along her port quarter as the *Shiva* lumbered after her.

His comtab chimed. "Yeah?"

"Course is set, Garrand," Vailetta said. "We're dumping the escape pods and all the chrysanths."

"There's nothing else you can do up there, haul that tech ensign out and get your men down to *Destiny*."

"The Third Fleet is closing, Garrand. They're going to get to us before we hit the moon."

"What are they going to do?" Garrand muttered. "It's not like they can just blow us away—we have the pandas."

"Mmm. Maybe so," she conceded.

"I'll see you in a couple of minutes," he said.

"Don't wait too long."

Dasko pushed another whining mule out the door. Garrand ran to a resting transport and climbed up to the flight deck.

He touched power studs and grazed his fingers over command boards. The mule warmed to his touch. "How much longer until impact, Ecksley?"

There was a long pause.

"Ecksley?"

"Umm, I'm not quite sure, Captain."

"What!"

"Well, I'm having some difficulty with my feeds. After all, I'm not hooked directly to the destroyer, I don't have all the data necessary to make an accurate prediction."

Garrand brought the mule's systems up as quickly as possible. "Just tap into *Destiny's* navi and get a fix on the moon," he said, trying to mute his exasperation.

"There's a little trouble with that connection, I'm not getting a response."

Garrand swore loudly. "Just a second. Vailetta, you still there?" Nothing. "*Destiny*, can you get me a reading on our velocity and distance to impact?"

"I did not have a direct feed to the *Lucayamo.*"

"Do a new sounding!"

"At our current velocity and height, you have three minutes, twelve seconds until impact."

"Will you please relay that information to the E3?"

"I'm sorry, Captain. I don't have a direct feed to Ecksley either."

Garrand rolled his eyes. "Has everyone gone mad? I just need a simple answer. Will someone please plug that core into *Destiny?*"

"I'm headed there now," Bailey responded smoothly.

"Do you want me to begin computing our last safe departure time?" *Destiny* asked.

"No," Garrand growled. "Ecksley can do it once he's tapped." He set the mule to hover and set the sub-light engines to standby with a thirty-second delay to full power. He scampered back down to the airlock and jumped to the deck.

"I've found the problem, Captain." Bailey reported.

"Good," Garrand said. He caught Dasko's eye and raised a single digit. "One more," he mouthed, jerking his head at the mule. The lieutenant nodded and hovered his machine around to comply.

"Ah, that's better," Ecksley sighed. "Oh, we're quite close, aren't we?"

"Yes," Garrand grated. "How much time do we have."

"Hmm. One moment please. I'm recalibrating my array."

"Ecksley!"

"You have a mobile shell to carry around your brains," the core replied testily. "I do not. It's disorienting to be carted around like so much dead weight."

"How much time?"

"There's a lot of data to consider."

"It's a simple question."

"And I'm telling you the answer does not fall into the category of 'simple.'"

"Just do it." He waved to Dasko and began running back to the main corridor. "Everyone aboard, Vailetta?"

"Safe and sound," she replied. "All except you four."

"We're on our way."

"Ship is ready to lift," Bailey reported.

Garrand and the three guardsmen sprinted down the destroyer's central passage toward bay three.

"How's it coming, Ecksley?"

There was a long pause. "I lost count."

"You what!"

"I'm sorry Captain, I lost count."

"How could you lose count? You're an infallible datacore capable of trillions of calculations a minute. By Haven, you were designed by Sartok himself!"

"These things happen. I am awfully sorry, I was occupied with a separate matter and lost a feed somewhere."

Garrand's eyes grew wide in disbelief. He felt his patience and sanity finally and irrevocably slipping away. "Cheplus, just give me a guess!"

"A what?"

"A guess, you dolt!"

"There's no need for such name calling."

"Just give me your best guess and feed it to *Destiny*."

"Best what?"

"Best guess."

"A guess?"

"Yes!" he screamed into the comtab wishing he still had a laser axe.

"But sir, I'm not allowed to guess. Professor Sartok felt that it was unfair to let me cut corners and project estimates based on probabilities that I had not thoroughly processed. It's cheating."

"By Haven, give me your best guess or so help me I'll rip every last one of your gel-chips out and ship you back to Wyx in pieces so small that Dr. Sartok won't even recognize you!"

There was a slight pause and static before Ecksley replied, "Yes sir, one 'best guess' coming up. Projection in five seconds."

Garrand entered landing bay three. His ship lay hovering by the force field, passenger ramp still lowered. He waited for the three men to clamber aboard. Dasko reached his hand down and lifted him up.

"We're in," he barked, slapping the door seal.

The ship dipped forward and passed through the force field. She hung just outside the docking bay, racing toward the moon with the same velocity as the destroyer. Garrand was thrown into a wall as the sub-lights kicked in and the ship lurched in a new direction. He raced up the long curving neck into the bridge. The command pod rolled up to meet him.

"Where are we?"

"Twelve seconds behind," Bailey informed him. "We departed a little late."

"Can we make it up?" Vailetta asked.

"No problem," Garrand said, sliding into position and strapping in. "I've got her, Bailey." He spun the pod to the bottom of the bridge and glanced down at the destroyer. A long line of ships trailed away from the *Lucayamo*. Chrysanths and escape pods hung in the vacuum, while the mules roared back toward Wyx, all of the discarded vessels cluttering the Imperial pursuit. Glittering fighters weaved through the obstacles, closing in on the doomed destroyer. The *Shiva* loomed large behind her. He spun his pod back up and applied more power, pushing the ship in a course perpendicular to their established parabolic descent toward the moon.

The consoles shook and groaned, now well into the moon's gravity well. The entire grey landscape filled the horizon. Craters and fissures were easily visible. The tectonic ridge rose beneath them.

"Shouldn't we try to overcome our delta vee and point straight up?" Dasko asked nervously from the gangway.

"It's too late for that. We're on a parabolic descent. If we get enough forward velocity to match our downward trajectory we'll achieve a new orbit."

"And if we don't?"

"We pancake on the surface before we clear the horizon."

Vailetta stared at the dwindling altitude numbers. 50 kilometers, 45, 40… "Can we make it?"

"We'll make it," Garrand muttered. "It may by the lowest orbit ever achieved, but it'll be an orbit."

Destiny's Needle pulled away from her wrenching descent, engines pushed to the firewalls. Behind her, the *Lucayamo* rocketed into the surface of the moon, detonating with a white flash. A giant cloud of ash and dust billowed up into space, thrown out of the moon's newest crater. One by one, mules and chrysanths disappeared into the ash, following their home into the side of the mountain.

Garrand grasped the control node with tightened fist, thumb pressed vainly against the accelerator. His left hand slid across the command board as he tapped energy from every available system. The B'varts howled with power they'd never before experienced. He began whispering to his ship, *a little bit more, little bit more…* Sartographic projections danced before him, numbers winking down in dizzying succession, but he ignored them all, staring at the ragged edge of the moon's horizon that rose closer and closer. Warnings bleated on all the boards. *Destiny* shook beneath his hand. Still he whispered. *Just a little bit more.*

The ship continued to fall in a parabolic descent, but her forward velocity continued pushing the edge of the parabola out past the horizon. "Come on baby, one last surge," he cooed. He glanced down at the sartographs and then out at the horizon one last time. With a sigh he released the control and leaned back in his couch, eyes closing. The ship's forward velocity finally out paced her downward momentum and she began falling around the moon, having achieved an orbit 112 meters over the surface.

The bridge erupted in cheers, but Garrand hardly heard them. He just rubbed the edge of his console and smiled. *Destiny's Needle* slid around the dark side of the moon and disappeared into quantum space.

Epilogue

GARRAND CLIMBED THE LAST OVERSIZED RISER AND stepped up onto the broad stone mesa. He stood for a calm moment in the buffeting gusts surveying the upper limbs of a Folgantu Oak that poked over the edge of the veranda. Up this high there was little to stop the wind that raced over the treetops, scouring the stone escarpment. He walked unsteadily to the edge of the great terrace and took a deep gulping breath of scented air.

Clouds curled over the edge of distant ruins like slow motion waves breaking across a sandy shoal. Each stone building stood like islands amidst the ocean of trees. He could see the broad roof of the Archives jutting out like the hull of an up-turned shipwreck. The energetic bustle and efficient activity of the tribe drifted up from the hollowed out dome behind him. The pandas were happily making themselves at home, fashioning nests and building the evening's fires. Jean-Wa had the scuppers out collecting vegetables for dinner. Clicks and growls echoed out, soft cries of pleasure filtering through the wind. He could smell burning wood as the evening fires were lit.

Garrand sat down next to Sid at the edge of the mesa. Branches rippled beneath them as wind danced through the golan oaks. Vailetta walked across the terrace and stood calmly beside them, looking out across the jungle.

"Nice," she murmured. Neither responded. She glanced down at the two dreamers and smiled to herself. A stoic pair, indeed. "The pandas seem to like it," she continued, looking back over her shoulder.

"Mmm," Garrand murmured absently. "I don't know how long we'll be safe here though."

"I might be able to come up with a few places we could go," she ventured.

"Oh?" He turned and glanced up at her skeptically.

"Yes." A mysterious spark danced in her eyes. "I might know a place or two for a couple of wayward guardsmen…"

"And their 37 children?"

"Trreek grr'va gah ta brutl," Sid snorted, breaking his silence. "Children indeed!"

Garrand squinted up at her: "Where?"

Vailetta smiled airily. "Oh, I don't know…"

He rolled his eyes and resumed staring out across the jungle.

She licked her lips carefully. "Ever been to Daulinbêres?"

Garrand's eyes shot back. A funny look creased his face.

She smiled warmly at him. "It may be time to go home. I think my father would like to meet you."

"Home…" he turned back to the jungle. The crisp, cool air flowed through the trees, their boughs bending and returning like billowing rolls of silk. "Sort of feels like home here."

Vailetta squeezed his shoulder and walked away. She passed a cub on the way. Alexander paused to watch the woman descend and then ambled over to the ledge. He looked up and gurgled questioningly. Getting no response, he settled himself down, sitting back on Garrand's feet so that his back rested against the Captain's knees. Alex breathed easy, knowing the man would be unable to move without disturbing him, and slowly closed his eyes.

Garrand could hear the soft grumbles and squeals of pandas playing behind him in the great hall. Inside, birds chattered in the upper vines, their cackles echoing against the crumbling dome. Before him stretched a limitless expanse of green, punctuated by the occasional stone building which poked out from beneath the canopy. A moon was beginning to fade through the trees, glowing purple in the haze.

The images of a thousand days rolled before his eyes, stirred by the inscrutable gusts that pulled his collar and stung his eyes. Invisible hands tugged the memories from his heart.

He reached inside his shift and tugged at the leather cord. The weighted talismans fell free. He pressed his thumb against the smooth heart stone and rubbed gently. The stone was cool to his touch. A silver sphere clinked against the amulet. He separated the talismans and held the silver shell between his thumb and forefinger, staring at its lusterless surface for a long moment.

We made it Helen.

The wind howled and roared, shaking the treetops and sending a flock of birds screeching into the night. Garrand tucked the two talismans back into his shift and became acutely aware of Sid sitting patiently by his side, contemplating the fading light. He reached a hand out to touch the panda's soft head for reassurance. The man sat beside the panda and stared into the fading glory of the day. He took a deep, sweet breath. The wind was but a whisper to him now.

GRIFFIN TERMINOLOGY

Ackriveldt: lone planet of Galipsus, noted as birth world of Naius Sartok.

Adjucate: harbor judge; low level Imperial official.

Alexander: giant panda cub, third generation member or the Tchelakov Tribe.

Archiva: also known as Mardell's world. Location: unknown. After the destruction of twelve key data repositories during the War of the Three in 29,182 in which the entire ancestral records of deeds and fiefs for five thousand systems was lost, the network of information was deemed too important to lie 'scattered across the Shell like diamonds for the taking.' A central archival planet was deemed the solution, with a planet-wide system of data storage—a backup repository for the knowledge off an entire empire. The location was chosen in secret and the entire network was shunted through the planet's datacores where physical copies were recorded and stored in vast repositories. So vast was this archive that it became synonymous with the planet itself. The planet was discovered and later sacked (some say destroyed) in the time of Mardell III.

Armor Drip: versatile field armor developed by Pavelle Nest. Transported in liquid form and poured into a variety of molds on site, cerafiber bonds harden in under a minute after catalyst is added. Gives added mobility to light armor divisions.

Arnas, San Barrilito: battalion commander, 41st Imperial Marines; Shock Trooper.

Art Wars: a conflict that arose when the Sullust movement sought to curtail the rapid proliferation of Free Will artificials, specifically machines indistinguishable from humans. Fueled by fear and religious fervor, the push for curtailment quickly expanded into a genocidal Jihad that lasted from 35,110 until the Gelicus Art Convention in 35,307. Alternately known as the Gai'han Jihad, depending on one's point of view, the resulting conflagration plunged much of the galaxy into turmoil (see: Jihad, Gai'han, Free Will artificials, Sullust Movement)

Artificial: any of a wide class of mobile mechanical constructs possessing intelligence, self-awareness and the ability to learn through experience.

Bailey: Krellian Artificial, Varsis model VL1357-B8, incept date unrecorded. Master of Arms, Caius Minor, from 35,329 to 35,337. Assigned to Santos II as personal assistant to Captain of the Guard, Garrand Ai'Gonet Médeville in 35,337. Granted Free Will in 35,345. First mate on *Destiny's Needle*.

Barlow: lieutenant, 41st Imperial Marines, 3rd company, 1st platoon; Shock Trooper.

Barrelian Corvette: Highly-maneuverable armed escort ship, smaller than a frigate, ranging in length from 100-150 meter; often used in conjunction with a larger fleet of vessels. Barrelian designs have been manufactured for over 700 years.

Barrett, Hellius: An ambitious Vecklorn who inherited his father's seat in the Royal Regincira and was later appointed High Magistrate in the Emperor's Court, he was a trusted confidante who lost favor after rumors of an illicit affair with the Empress surfaced. "Banished" to the political chaos of Carinaena's Shell, where his charms could not impress Chyrella, he labored in relative obscurity for some time. The assassination of ruling Proctor Lekkson Nesbit elevated Barrett into control of the Shell's third largest Proctorialship. Commonly referred to as Lord Barrett (whether it be in reference to Vecklornian nobility, or claimed in ancient Caluras rite is unknown), his title is officially Vice Proctor of Wyx.

Bordëgian Académe: ancient school of preparation for service in the Imperial Navy.

Brotherhood of the Princes of Blood: Order within the Imperial Guard. Founded 34,512 on Daulinbêres (see also: Griffin).

By the Barthsa: Dalis colloquialism; mild curse.

Carinaena's Shell: (Car-in-ae-na) the massive outer ring of stars that forms a donut-shaped shell around the central Core of the Gli-Dawun Galaxy. Named for the Lallalopsle ship *Carinaena's Hope* whose quantum drive failed at the edge of the galactic Core, and thus became the first "seeder" ship of colonists (see Dolke's Historical tome "Carinaena's Fate: the Colonization of Chance").

Carrack Class Cruiser: large, fast, heavily armored and gunned warship; Imperial classification of Battle Cruiser, top of the line capital ship.

Cerafiber: synthetic material prized for its light weight and heat/energy absorption; crystalline threads formed from superheated dryexcellon powder and molecular ceramic are cast into an intercellular matrix of connective filaments. Bonded matrices are stored in liquid state and then poured into molds with catalysts creating solid fibers of great elasticity, flexibility and tensile strength.

Cerasteel: ceramic steel formed on site by combining polymer-bonded dryexcellon powder into molten steel. After cooling, the steel is superheated through conduction, bonding the dryexcellon and steel at a molecular level.

Cerbak: one of the last remaining Bolos; mythical tri-horned guardian of the entrance to K'ye.

Cha'halen: rank in the military hierarchy of the Gambor; roughly equivalent to the Imperial rank of major.

Cheplus: Strahlinvek colloquialism; moderate curse.

Clipscanner: miniature (20 cm x 12 cm) personal datacore composed of digital reader, processing unit, fingertap board and display housed within a slim impact casing; noted for its versatility and interface capabilities.

Clipscan Visor: data relay that partially blinds user's real-time vision; primarily intended for use by artificials.

Coil: rechargeable storage field that uses magnetic coils to safely store massive amounts of charged ions. Capable of efficiently storing vast amounts of energy in a small physical space. Primary source of power for all energy dependent devices and engines.

Collistas Dynasty: (co-least-us) largest autonomous governing body in the Gli-Dawun Galaxy, ruled by a member of the Collistas family for 47 generations. The empire spawned from this stability now envelops much of the galaxy's core.

Core: (also: "Core worlds," "The Core") the densely populated center of the Gli-Dawun Galaxy; common designation for the vast volume of star systems currently under the domain of the Collistas Imperial Dynasty.

Coryl-Tuluyt Picket: escort warship of the fastest class; Imperial classification for its top of the line interdictors and blockade runners.

Crevlin, Jonathon: MSD, Imperial surgeon stationed on Wyx. Chief medical officer assigned to the Tchelakov 37 development team.

Cronix: a design line of datacores, a product of Si Bell Logiks, a proprietary arm of the Si Bell Keiretsu; Cronix datacores are commonly considered the industrial standard in Carinaena's Shell.

C'tereino, Henri: former lieutenant of the Imperial Guard, Griffin Order; operator of blue ice lichen farm on Eemon Nores.

Dalintus Commission: formed by the Gelicus Art Convention in 35,312, charged with the judgment of Free Will artificials—the Dalintus seal signifying the highest possible conditioning against taking a human life. Dalintus qualified artificials permitted to design and create Free Will artificials without human intervention.

Danelle: lieutenant in the Imperial Guard, Gokazoku Kaigi; currently assigned to Wyx, Carinaena's Shell, linguist.

Dar Sellianne Cluster: minor black hole cluster in the Bai-lore system; site of the Battle of Calon ("Massacre at Calon") in 35,208.

Darcalyn: artificial construct, highly unstable isotope frequently used in the construction of tactical fusion devices; logarithmic scale for expressing the magnitude of energy contained within such explosive devices.

Darstin, Carrelle: Director of Research and Acquisitions, Nralda Keiretsu. Seat on the Nralda High Board, 4th Tier. Responsible for funding and perpetuation of Beh'In Tchelakov's research concerning the next evolution of the sartographic chip (see: Tchelakov Tribe).

Dasko, Lee: lieutenant in the Imperial Guard, Gokazoku Kaigi; currently assigned to Wyx, Carinaena's Shell, decryption specialist, 1st grade.

Datacore: programmable electromagnetic device that can store, retrieve, and process data; the heart of all mechanical thinking mechanisms.

Datapad: any of a wide variety of specialized technical data readers; poor cousin of the clipscanner.

Daulinbêres: sixth planet in the Wopäs System, situated in a prime strategic location near the heart of the Gli-Dawun Galaxy; seat of the Imperial throne for 137 centuries.

Daurrian Shipyards: the vast Pragen spaceworks in high orbit off Bingham; the close proximity of the Hames asteroid belt for raw materials and the industrial processing complex on Bingham itself has made this yard one of the most efficient operations in the Shell, capable of turning out a full destroyer in under eight years.

Debin: corporal, 41st Imperial Marines, tactical support Corps, armorer.

Destroyer: very large, fast, heavily armored and gunned warship; a classification usually reserved for a fleet's largest and most advanced capital ships.

Destiny's Needle: modified medium cruiser designed by Garrand Ai'Gonet Médeville and built by Le'hadn Vercks in 35,347 for the express purpose of breaking the Talen quarantine on El Phobadia.

Presented to Médeville by the Sandhalles Grip, Bestriyx Dagen, soon thereafter as a token of his esteem, in return for the rescue of his daughter. Subsequently played a principle role in the Tchelakov Revolt circa 35,355.

Dopplegänger: device that approximates mass, heart rate, heat signature and breathing rhythm of sentient biologicals. Projects all the outwardly-detectable signs of life with subroutines controlling random variance.

Drazon Vorge: refugee youth from Galipsus Minoirte; currently under the tutelage of Vice Proctor Barrett.

Dreadnaught: large, moderately armored and gunned warship; an older classification generally reserved for blockade interdictors and fleet escorts. Upgrades in quantum drive technologies have rendered many of the dreadnaught designs obsolete. Properly refit, dreadnaughts play an important role in many developing navies.

Dreighonäis: Tchelakov 37 colloquialism for dragons, which they refer to as "the serpents without a sea."

Dryexcellon: mineral ore principally mined in the Restepheron system and refined on planets throughout the Shell into highgrade fuels, powders and industrial byproducts (see: cerafiber, cerasteel).

Dustlock: similar in design and purpose to starships' airlocks, dustlocks are used in many desert environments to prevent grit, sand, and dust from fouling sensitive electronics and healthy, breathable atmosphere.

E2: Eckreon 2; the Empire's top of the line massive datacore processor, integrating the latest sartographic series II technology with group "e" Cronix mainframes; used aboard all Carrack class vessels (see: sartograph).

E3: Eckreon 3 (prototype); third generation core; developed by Naius Sartok in 35,355.

Eckreon: a design line of Cronix datacores, the product of Si Bell Logiks, a proprietary arm of Si Bell Keiretsu; Cronix datacores are commonly considered the industrial standard in Carinaena's Shell.

Eemon Nores: icy seventh planet of the Niyl System, situated near the Krestyaninov Cluster.

El-Bouteran: only planet in the Pakken System, far removed from all major shipping routes in Carinaena's Shell.

Eltouvé Magellan: 5th planet in the Dantolous system, sight of the sprawling Imperial Weapons Research Facility; home of the infamous "Plague Vats."

Elytra: the anterior wings of Gamborian beetles that serve to protect the posterior pair of functional wings.

Enyohanse Lenses: adjustable spectacles that fit over the surface of the eye with crystalline enzymes that adhere to the pupils' surface, stretching and bending the light as it enters the optic nerves. Once familiar with the enyohanse lenses, the user can adjust the level of magnification and clarity with the muscles of the eye and face.

Epley, Jastin: (a.k.a.: Sev) shipping agent with ties into many underground smuggling operations.

Exel: wild echrine of Maltus adapted for Se-faillus hunters on Letugia; sometimes kept as pets.

Falto Earblocks: miniature counter-active dampers that absorb sound waves and project energy surges into the ear that flatten out the signature sine pattern of incoming noise, effectively negating the sounds as they enter the inner ear membrane.

Farres: lieutenant in the Imperial Guard, Gokazoku Kaigi; currently assigned to Wyx, Carinaena's Shell.

Fléchette: small dart or flying projectile often explosive-tipped or laced with poison.

Fokathenais: deadly species of dragon; noted for their ferocity and intelligence. Adults can reach 20-25 meters in length.

Freetrader: colloquialism; broad term embracing what is in essence a wide variety of professions including (but not limited to) inter-system mercantile trading, freelance entrepreneurial merchandising, smuggling, and simple cargo hauling. Originally a term used to describe independent freelance entrepreneurs in early Colonial era, specifically the nine hundred year period that saw the Shell worlds successfully pioneered and settled (see: Great Diaspora). Working alone in single ships, Freetraders were an indispensable element of the colonization effort. The high risks and huge overhead involved in supplying hundreds of tiny colonies made it unprofitable to sustain and supply colonies on a corporate and/or commercial level. These entrepreneurs—private oneman operations flying single craft with low overhead—allowed colonies to flourish in their infant stages by bringing goods that could not be produced on fledgling worlds for decades. Private traders were colonists' lifeblood, shipping in needed commodities, spare parts, and resources in return for grains and foodstuffs for shipment offworld. Most Freetraders are thought of as colonial patriots of a sort. Without them, most colonies would have quickly failed and the Shell as we know it would not exist.

Free Will Artificial: a specialized class of mobile mechanical constructs possessing intelligence, self-awareness and the ability to learn through experience. Free Will arts are not designed with a specific underlying purpose. Without a rigorous code of conduct for higher functions, Free Will arts are left to choose their own course after inception. The Sullust movement sought to curtail the rapid proliferation of Free Will arts after the perfection of the indistinguishable-from-human designs. The resulting conflicts are alternately known as the Gai'han Jihad (see: The Purge) or the Art Wars (see: the Lashback). The 200-year upheaval plunged much of the galaxy into turmoil. Numerous commissions sprang up in the aftermath, attempting to regulate Free Will arts, and many prejudices still exist (see: Artificial).

Frigate: any of a broad variety of moderately armored and gunned warships, the classification of which differ widely from navy to navy. Historically: a moderate to large design; the workhorse of many a navy.

Galar: lieutenant in the Imperial Guard, Gokazoku Kaigi; currently assigned to Wyx, Carinaena's Shell, demolitionist, 5th order.

Gallantrus: race of medium-sized (1.5 meter tall) russet-furred bipedal creatures (sentient); transplanted home world is Vipst in the Dartinells System

Gambor: race of large (3 meter tall) multi-limbed, smooth-shelled, winged beetles (sentient); home world of the Galzeki, tagged for garbage reclamation by Imperial Navy and site of 400-year-old civil war (see Po'tchantu's "Siege of Galzeki"). The Gambor have recently begun contracting their warrior services out to the Nralda Keiretsu in return for desperately needed munitions.

Garner, Jyaye: MSD, private practice, Erpolitas. Highly regarded organic surgeon specializing in illegal augmentation procedures. Assassinated 35,355.

Gelbs: corporal, 3rd Imperial Army Corps; tactical field operations specialist.

Gelicus Art Convention: contravened in 35,312, marking the official end of the Gai'han Jihad, its provisions forging an uneasy peace between the Gai'han Sullusts and the Free Will coalition lead by the Free Will artificial, Samuel. It's chief tenant: no machine was to be constructed indistinguishable from a human being. In compromise, the Sullusts lifted the death bounty placed on all Free Will artificials. Secondary precepts limited the creation of Free Will artificials: specifically, it was forbidden for artificials to create Free Will artificials (in essence procreate) without the Dalintus seal (see: Dalintus Commission).

Gills: private, tactical operations, 3rd Imperial Army Corps.

Gokazoku Kaigi: Order within the Imperial Guard. Known as the "Brotherhood of the Silent Blade." Founded 34,819 on Daulinbêres.

Gravitic Repulsors: Fit beneath everything from cargo lighters to gunsleds to starships, Norgen generators project a harmonic field that negates the affects of gravity over a limited area focused in conical projections that dissipate over distance. The resulting gravitic null space creates buoyancy that is enhanced by standard field suspensors. The combined effect of the null space and the repulsor wave field is enough to allow most vessels, pallet, skimmers, and such to hover mid-air. In more elaborate configurations, they are enough to allow starships of massive tonnage to overcome the pull of planetary gravity wells and land and takeoff vertically.

Great Hall: Built 35,330 on Wyx; monument created to display the names of the fallen Imperial forces within the Wyxian Proctorialship.

Griffin: Collistas colloquialism; slang for Imperial Guardian, Griffin Order. Order within the Imperial Guard. Known as the "Brotherhood of the Princes of Blood." Founded 34,512 on Daulinbêres.

Gunsled: armored ground assault vehicles, fit with gravitic repulsors.

Gyropod: enclosed datastations typically found aboard military vessels, designed to insulate vital tech ensigns from the dangers of battle and aid their interface with the ship's datacore (see: Poddies).

Hammerfield Colony: Free Will colony near Dautalas Massif on Lon Seres (Jhellus Sector), sacked by Imperial Shock Troops in 35,339 and again in 35,355 in the preliminary stages of the Tchelakov Revolt.

Harbormaster: general superintendent of port operations.

Havelock: sub-lieutenant, 3rd Imperial Army Corps, Terraformer; liaison officer 1st grade.

Haven's End: Imperial colloquialism; mild curse derived from the infamous travails of Giin Bly Haven, officer in the Royal Regincira, whose life was ironically taken by the very men he risked everything to save.

Holden: Tybolte artificial, Rixx model 33, incept date 35,021. Assigned to Carinaena's Shell, Wyx, as personal assist for Lieutenant Lee Dasko of Vice Proctor Barrett's Imperial Guard.

Holocube: miniature holographic display unit roughly the size of an Imperial quantis. Projects a small static image of subject that can be viewed from all angles.

Holo Ghost: the emotional and neurological essence of a creature captured by electronic means and stored in a digital matrix much like a datacore. The mortal subject's neural activity and the brain's electro-chemical signature is transferred (either during the death throes, or soon after death) by electronic conductivity and hard wired into circuitry chips, much like the creation of an artificial. The imprint is stored in a Tarkanian containment field and is manifested as a hologram. The resultant "ghost" is cognizant and self-aware, many times with full memories and recollections intact, though the manifestation exists   with a painful echo of former emotions. A common theological belief is that the souls of ghosts are suspended in K'ye, awaiting judgment.

Hurka-boy: Two-person, low altitude winged flying craft; used as versatile transportation in cities with a high degree of verticality, often used purchased in large numbers by taxi services.

Ident-link: mathematical symbol(s) or icon used to represent a person or artificial; any of a wide range of identifying markers imbedded or cosmetic; standard Imperial identification system.

Imperial Guard: For over 3 millennia, the Imperial Guard has protected the interests of the Imperial throne, specifically the well being of the Emperor and his highest Ambassadors (see: Proctors). The Guardian caste is one of the most ancient and revered schooling bodies in the Empire. The noble warriors within have sworn to honor the Emperor and uphold the sanctity of the realm. Each faction within the caste has its own Order, full of timeworn tradition and a legacy to uphold. New members of the guard are sworn into a particular order, whose tenets they must obey and traditions they most honor.

Jean-Wa: Do-lât Artificial, Preparation model D430, incept date unrecorded; six-armed master chef with detachable legs and wheels. Purchased by Garrand Ai'Gonet Médeville from the Baron Senn van Basel of Daruma.

Jihad: (ji-häd) a religious holy war; fanatical crusade for a principle or belief.

Jihad, Gai'han: (see also: Art Wars) the doomed crusade against Free Will artificials, humaniform mechanical sentients, sentient machines, and conscious datacores begun in 35,110 and concluded in 35,307. It's chief result: the disappearance of all indistinguishable-from-human artificials.

Kalen: Imperial Special Operations Corp, lingual specialist, assigned to the *Shiva* task force.

Ka'vaelus: Gambor warrior; Cha'halen first grade of the Vaelus burrow, Galzeki. Rumored to have personal ties with 4th tier Nralda Director of Acquisitions, Carrelle Darstin.

Keiltraoma: a state of conscious dreaming; the *keiltraoma* requires a mastery of the body's physiological and physical states, allowing the conscious awareness of the brain's unbidden neurological activity, specifically, the subconscious creativity know as dreams.

Kess: fourth planet in the Dell Transim system; site of Gort's Agro Supply.

K'iik Vla: idiomatic expression from the Lalen dialect; roughly: "The ability to survive at any cost." Often referred to as the third rule in Griffin Order doctrine.

Keiretsu: corporate entities that have bonded together in Carinaena's Shell for protection and profit—combining trade routes and resources to form interplanetary cartels complete with defense fleets. Some keiretsu control whole systems, having subjugated the populace through economic monopolies and trade embargoes. While avoiding outright war with the Collistas Dynasty, many keiretsu are involved in an escalating cold war with the Imperial Proctorialships in the Shell.

Kouln Brandy: distilled from kidney fruit found only on Cas Elphu. Sullusts sterilized the planet around 35,113. The highly-prized brandy became priceless almost overnight. The ensuing carnage over the last 788 barrels that Fourte Grecke and Company produced became such that the Emperor placed a death seal on Kouln trade. Transporting the illicit commodity was a treasonable offense. Kouln brandy remains one of the most expensive and sought after goods on the black market.

Krass: Fleet Sergeant, 41st Imperial Marines, 1st platoon; third squad leader, Shock Trooper, weapons specialist (2nd class), armorer's assist.

Krestyaninov Cluster: a volume of space hundreds of light years across with complex and powerful gravitational forces due to the influence of a large number of stars in the white dwarf stage of collapse.

K'ye: the mythical "battleground of the gods," where the souls of the dead are said to be judged; purgatory.

Lachis: (Loper) six-legged pack beast whose sturdy constitution, resistance to viral strains, and phenomenal reproductive faculties made it ideal for homesteading the planets of Carinaena's Shell.

Lammini: Binary star system dominated by the Pious Cluster, a spectacular field of nebulae.

Landin: fleet sergeant (retired), 91st Imperial Marine battalion; barkeep on the *Shiva*.

Larkson Shield Generator: produces powerful resonating magnetic field capable of bending light around its focusing body. Used in conjunction with deflector arrays and an adequate system of null-dampers, the Larkson creates a viable protective field. Buffer coils store power bled from other ship systems and then feed pulses of energy to the shields' magnetic deflector fields. Energy that is not refracted or deflected is absorbed by null- dampers.

Laserai: corporal, 41st Imperial Marine battalion, 3rd company, 1st platoon; Shock Trooper.

Letugia: fifth planet in the Nepestar system; site of the Il Touvé shipyards, largest in the system.

Leusta: giant panda, first generation member of the Tchelakov Tribe; Elder in the Tchelakov Tribe.

Lewg: lieutenant in the Imperial Guard, Gokazoku Kaigi; currently assigned to Wyx, Carinaena's Shell; master bladesman.

Lifter: huge obtuse transport shuttles, heavily shielded and fit with gigantic sublight reactors, but possessing no faster-than-light capability. Designed to safely and efficiently ferry cargo and men between planet surfaces and orbiting ships (see: Mules).

Lighter: mechanical construct of varying size fit with gravitic repulsors and possessing limited intelligence, designed to ferry cargo between vessels in docking bays.

Little Bit: Turkle Sphere II, model 339-74C, incept date 35,329; technical assist (modified) purchased by Garrand Ai'Gonet Médeville at the Syhan Fabrication Works on Tikus.

Lolovanti: light cruiser from the Daurrian Shipyards; Captain Vailetta Strom's personal vessel.

Lor Stanta Destroyer: warship of the largest and most heavily armed and armored class; Imperial classification of the largest capital ship currently in active service (700 meter).

Médeville, Garrand Ai'Gonet: Freetrader, former Captain of the Imperial Guard, Griffin Order; purported leader of the Tchelakov Revolt.

Megas: lieutenant, 41st Imperial Marine battalion, 3rd company, 1st platoon; Shock Trooper; master bladesman.

Mules: Collistas colloquialism; slang for lifters.

Nesbit, Lekkson: Provost of Wyx and reigning Proctor of the Callus, Niramdi, and del'Trin system fiefs until his assassination in 35,347. Respected for his ability to create economic bridges between vastly different cultures. With the help of his ambitious vice proctor, Hellius Barrett, nurtured the Wyxian Proctorialship into one of the largest and richest Imperial fiefs in Carinaena's Shell.

New Haivello: 4th planet in the Skarsgård System; part of the Wyxian Imperial Proctorialship.

Niramdi System: minor star system in the Outer Reaches (Il Gallen Wei); hidden staging area for Free Will resistance during the Gai'han Jihad (see: Thrassin, battle of).

Nralda: Keiretsu; one of the largest and most powerful operating in the Shell.

Path of Fate: an expression unique to the Tchelakov Tribe; a series of events that are destined to transpire. The *Path of Fate* is a map of something that does not yet exist, but will inevitably come to pass (see: *seitparen*). To the Tchelakov Tribe, the future is fluid and ever-changing, with some paths more likely to occur than others, and some events almost impossible to avoid. The *Path of Fate* is the culmination of all dreams and all variables, the part of time that will come to be known as 'the past.' Seeing the *Path* before it becomes the past is the tribe's legacy, a blessing so coveted that it threatens to destroy them.

Picket Cutter: small-to-medium sized, extremely fast and lightly armored warship; primarily used as lead escort ships, blockade runners, and strike interdictors.

Plascrete: a lightweight, strong building material formed by mixing industrial grade polymer plastic aggregates with cementing agents and catalysts that cause the plastics to set and bind the entire mass. Can be poured on-site making it useful in fortifications and mobile battle situations.

Poddies: Collistas colloquialism; derogatory reference to pod-tech ensigns.

Pod-tech: Collistas colloquialism; tech ensigns who spend much of their time suspended in gyropods.

Praetor: Imperial magistrate, adjucatal overlord, ranking below a consul.

Proctor: the chief magistrate of an Imperial fiefdom.

Proctorialship: the principle sphere of influence or domain of specific Imperial fiefs created during the Great Shell Diaspora. Proctorialships are doled out to lords and barons within   the Imperial Court as the Emperor sees fit. The relative domain of the fief may be expanded in the Emperor's name at the ruling proctor's discretion.

Provost: Imperial planetary governor.

Quantis: circular trebian alloy coin. Five Imperial credits. Accepted coin of the realm in most systems along with local currency. Although credit chits are more widely used, some small denomination coins are more efficient for limited purchases, such as food and beverage.

Quantum Drive: crucial middle element of all interstellar ships' three-tiered drive system; sub-light engines propel ships up to the brink of light speed (speeds and acceleration dependent upon design, size, efficiency, etc.), the quantum drive breaches the light barrier, lifting the ship into quantum space, and the light engines propel the ship through quantum space itself.

Reactor Core: chamber that powers all sub-light and quantum drives. The chamber is filled with cryxthlen gas at extremely high pressure. This gas, through which a series of directed neutron sparks pass, contains charged particles accelerated by the power field of the coils that wrap around the reactor core. As the field oscillates, it accelerates the charges back and forth, making them collide energetically with the cryxthlen atoms. Many of the gas atoms are actually torn apart by the collisions, yielding even more charged particles to collide with cryxthlen atoms, creating an exponentially expanding energy source. The cryxthlen acts as the fuel source that is slowly depleted as some atoms are not spilt by the collisions in the core, and thus are converted directly to energy without yielding any new charged particles.

Roto'mo: Single-person, low altitude flying craft, featuring a turbine-based rotor mounted overhead.

Sartograph: highly specialized mathematical construct utilizing Dr. Sartok's revolutionary chip and representing a quantum breakthrough in 4th dimension physics decay. Used to create time-based models which accurately forecast the relative probability of any given circumstance; the visual output of such a projection.

Sartok: probability chip capable of assessing statistical future outcomes through rigorous analysis of past and present conditions (see: sartograph); named after its creator, Naius Packden Sartok, theoretical mathematician and founder of the Seilhenn School of Advanced Logistics.

Scarrion: Crysanth drop ship, housed aboard the *Shiva*.

Scupper: non-sentient tech art designed by Mardell the 4th; noted for unique spider design.

Seitparen: an expression unique to the Tchelakov Tribe; an event or series of events that are unavoidable; something that is destined to happen. The *seitparen* are a series of events seen ahead of time that will eventually become known as 'the past.' In terms of prophetic visions, it is the currently accurate map of the *actual* future as opposed to the myriad and chaotic *possible* futures that could occur. Determining and shaping events that will become part of the *seitparen* or "Path of Fate" are twin goals of the Tchelakov Elders, and part of the genetic legacy bestowed upon them by Dr. Beh'ln Tchelakov (see: *Path of Fate*, sartograph, *tromaveint*, Tchelakov Tribe).

Selyn: Tybolte artificial, Blue model 14, incept date 35,309. Assigned to Carinaena's Shell, Wyx, as armorer's assist for Gokazoku Kaigi.

Servo Limb: mechanical construct: any augmented lifting or reaching device.

Shecut: brigadier general (retired) of the Imperial Marines, 6th Army, special envoy to Carinaena's Shell.

Shields: (also: Larkson Shield Generator) shield combat was in vogue for almost 300 years until advances in optical targeting made the generators more hazardous than helpful. Still, some usefulness can be found, particularly in close arms combat (see Tolmer's "Optical Advances and other Technological Foibles" & Ku'bii's "Offensive Retreat—the Rise of the Projectile").

Shiva: Carrak class cruiser; flagship of the Imperial Third Fleet; currently assigned to the Wyxian Proctorialship.

Shock Troops: Imperial commandos, generally bred for cunning, viciousness, and absolute loyalty. Raised from birth as soldiers, completely immersed in the caste D'ai Mital, the cult of the warrior. The caste training emphasizes ruthlessness, survival and instills a near fanatical devotion to unit commanders; historically known as "the Emperor's elite."

Sid: giant panda, second generation member of the Tchelakov Tribe; youngest Elder in the Tchelakov Tribe, in charge of information retrieval.

Stanzer: Imperial picket crippled during the Battle of Sardis (35,345) by Ditraln Secessionists; sinking after atmospheric re-entry, the superstructure still rests in 2 kilometers of water off the shore of Callen High. Captain of the Imperial Guard, Garrand Ai'Gonet Médeville, rescued the *Stanzer's* crew and passengers against direct orders and sacrificed an Imperial battle frigate in the process. That ship, the *Deil-Karo*, became the first command frigate lost at sea in 10,000 years.

Strahlinvek: language spoken by most of the trading cultures in Carinaena's Shell; a simple trade language, its root forms easily derived from thousands of other dialects. Some variation of the language is spoken by almost every race that has spacefaring ties, facilitating exploration and colonization.

Strom, Vailetta: Captain of the Imperial Guard, Gokazoku Kaigi; currently assigned to Wyx, Carinaena's Shell. Illegitimate (and some say favored) daughter of Emperor Collistas. Nicknamed *Myshka*, or "Firebird," by the Emperor, the young Vailetta spurned courtly life and set out to make a name for herself independent of her royal lineage (and some argue, her father's stifling protective care) taking the name Strom as cover to her true identity and entering the Bordëgian Academé as an anonymous student. The Gokazoku Kaigi culled her from the top of her graduating class. She quickly rose to the prestigious position of Captain within the sect and accepted a post commanding Vice Proctor Hellius Barrett's Imperial Guard.

Su'lairn: Gambor warrior; Tginsahi of the Lairn burrow, Galzeki. Honor Guard to Cha'halen first grade, Ka'vaelus.

Sullust Movement: Religious order; Gai'han Sullusts believe in the genetic superiority of the Gai'han bloodline carefully cultivated for over seven millennia. After the capitulation of Gallen Wei in the War of the Three in 35,242, the Niramdi system became the focus of the Gai'han practice of 'holy sterilization.' This process of indiscriminate extermination of non-Sullust humans and artificials forced the Collistas Dynasty to re-evaluate their position of support for the movement. Some believed the Sullusts were becoming powerful enough to threaten the Emperor himself. After skirmishes along the edges of Carinaena's Shell, the Thrassin Campaign marked the Collistas Dynasty's first foray into the Gai'han Jihad in support of Free Will artificials.

TacOps: idiomatic for tactical operations; the neural nexus of Imperial battle command that analyses and processes all information, provides a link between human experience in the field and raw datacore projections, and coordinates the various arms of Imperial power. An integral part of the command structure of all Imperial warships.

Tai-wren: "the shadow of the maker"; anyone who has pledged their life to protecting another.

Tarkanian Containment Shell: Hardened cerafibrous shell that houses a strong electromagnetic field; capable of safely storing incorporeal lifeforms and manifestations.

Tchelakov 37: colloquial expression referring to the original giant pandas engineered by Dr. Beh'ln Tchelakov (see: Tchelakov Tribe).

Tchelakov, Beh'ln: visionary genetic engineer whose highly guarded research into the next evolution of sartographic technology resulted in the creation of a new species (see: Tchelakov Tribe). His fusion of sartographic technology with a sentient-level intuition resulted in a quantum leap forward in 4th dimension physics decay and the science of future probabilities.

Tchelakov, Helen: courier/agent of the Nralda Keiretsu; daughter of Beh'ln Tchelakov.

Tchelakov Revolt: A blossoming conflict in the Wyxian Proctorialship the origins of which center around the pursuit, capture, and escape of the Tchelakov 37, circa 35,355.

Tchelakov Tribe: the giant pandas elevated to sentience and successfully fused with Dr. Naius Sartok's probability chips. The pandas' resulting mental matrix became viable probability engines, capable of using intuitive processes to make deductive leaps and accurately predict the future. Early iterations of the technology were only viable during dream state.

Tech Art: any of a wide class of mobile mechanical constructs designed to perform a broad range of technical tasks. Non-sentient, imbued with one (or several) highly technical skills, but possessing little overall intelligence due to high degree of specialization and desire for cost efficiency.

Tginsahi: rank of "Honor Guard" in the Gambor warrior caste.

Thiretsen Reed: any of a genus of tall, erect herbs of the nightshade family with little foliage and tubular flowers, cultivated for its stalks; the stems of cultivated thiretsen prepared for use in smoking.

Thola: Tchelakov 37 colloquialism for artificials, who they refer to as "noble sentinels of steel."

Thrassin, Battle of: The Thrassin Campaign marked the Empire's first foray into the Gai'han Jihad in support of the Free Will artificials. Though technically a stalemate (the Gai'han drive was halted, but the Sullusts were not driven out of the system until 37 years later), most historians view the battle as a clear victory for the Free Will Coalition.

Torg: class 1 master assassin, assigned to Vice Proctor Hellius Barrett, Wyxian Proctorialship. Much speculation exists concerning this soldier's original identity (see Vo Kamp's "The Emperor's Butcher"); it is said that Master Torg was charged as Vailetta Strom's personal Tai-wren by the Emperor himself.

Torvel Class Frigate: war vessel intermediate between a corvette and a ship of the line; Imperial classification of an escort defense ship between a corvette and destroyer in size.

Trioxin: short for Trioxin Battle Plate; armored drop suits vastly enhancing a soldier's strength, speed, sensory input, and firepower. In a fully operational Trioxin suit, it is said that just one Imperial Shock Trooper can easily outfight a dozen heavily-armed men. Unsuitable for some theaters of operation.

Tromaveint: Tchelakov 37 colloquialism for the waking dream; a vision.

Turkle Sphere: Syhan artificial design. All drive components and core matrixes housed within one-meter diameter sphere. Rugged and highly versatile. Primarily used as tech arts though some instances of sentient models can be found.

Tvultàk Skullers: small, highly maneuverable cruiser used as interdictors and strike craft; aging but rugged and adaptable design favored by mercenaries and smugglers. A particularly dangerous configuration is the Gamborian Jave 'O War.

Varsis: Krellian artificial design, manufactured without interruption for nearly 160 years between 34,687 and 34,846. The inherent simplicity of the design along with the Varsis' unparalleled learning curve made the design one of the Krell's most successful to date.

Vell'lairn: Gambor warrior; Tginsahi of the Lairn burrow, Galzeki. Honor Guard to Cha'halen first grade, Ka'vaelus.

Wyx: 4th planet in the Bline system, seat of the Wyxian Imperial Proctorialship, one of the largest fiefdoms in Carinaena's Shell.

Yarvek-EZ: Virtruna caste, cybernetics specialist, 9th class, currently assigned to Imperial Battle Cruiser *Shiva* as pod ensign; bred in the Imperial Vats on Wyx for mathematical genius.

Yuzbek Sharlott School: medical research facility specializing in transgenics; radical medical sect destroyed in 35,324.

Yuzbekistin: 5th planet in the Core system of Wilkens Folly, site of the Biomaterial Implant Facility and Sharlott Research grounds; a level 8 quarantine is currently in place on the entire system, reason unknown.

TIME LINE

33,811 Last recorded contact with the seeder ship Carinaena's Hope.

34,290 Beginning of the Great Shell Diaspora. Major colonization efforts will continue for over a millennia.

35,110 Beginning of Gai'han Jihad.

35,307 Final battle of Gai'han Jihad. Gelicus Art Convention holds first open hearings.

35,312 Ratification of the Gelicus Art Proviso signals formal end of the Art Wars. Compromise includes ban on all indistinguishable-from-human artificials. Dalintus Commission formed to judge and regulate Free Will artificials.

35,337 Garrand Ai'Gonet Médeville graduates from Bordëgian Académé, receives commission in Imperial Navy. Selected for membership in the Brotherhood of the Princes of Blood, Griffin Order of the Imperial Guard. Varsis artificial Bailey VL1357-B8 is assigned as his personal combat assist.

35,341 Médeville is made Captain of the Imperial Guard.

35,342 Médeville accepts post on Santos II as Captain of Proctor Birmaldon's Imperial Guard.

35,343 At Battle of Sardis, Médeville distinguishes himself by rescuing Proctor Birmaldon from Ditraln Secessionists. In the course of battle, the Imperial picket Stanzer is disabled and left in a decaying orbit around Sardis. Médeville disobeys a direct order and commandeers a battle frigate to rescue seven of his men left aboard the Stanzer. Both ships are lost, but the Guardsmen are saved. Médeville is court-martialed and discharged from Imperial service.

35,345 Artificial Bailey is granted Free Will on lunar colony Fortrivance.

35,346 Proctor Lekkson Nesbit assassinated. Vice Proctor Hellius Barrett takes control of the Wyxian Proctorialship.

35,347 Médeville contracts with the Sandhalles Grip, Bestriyx Dagen, for the rescue of his daughter. Designs modified light cruiser for express purpose of breaking Talen quarantine on El Phobadia to reach the young Miss Dagen. Ship built by Lehadn Vercks in Lo Kamer-Daun Shipworks; christened Destiny's Needle. After completion of mission, Bestriyx Dagen presents Médeville with Destiny's Needle as a grateful token of his esteem.

35,355 Médeville contracts with Helen Tchelakov for transport of 37 "exotic bios."

About the Author

PHILIP WILLIAMS IS an author, artist and sculptor. A graduate of the University of North Carolina, Chapel Hill with a BFA in Studio Art, he has enjoyed a successful career creating powerful, gas-welded steel sculptures as well as designing and building unique furniture. Philip is a dedicated father of three and an avid soccer player.

Visit him online at *www.thegriffinseries.com*.

THE GRIFFIN SERIES

Ashes of Honor
The Dreams of Men and Pandas
The Dragon's Price
A Path of Majesty

Garrand Medeville's adventures continue in
The Stanzer Incident, set during his days as
Captain of the Imperial Guard.

THE GRIFFIN SERIES

THE GRIFFIN
ASHES OF HONOR
PHILIP WILLIAMS
CAT WILLIAMS

THE GRIFFIN
THE DREAMS OF MEN AND PANDAS
PHILIP WILLIAMS
CAT WILLIAMS

THE GRIFFIN
THE DRAGON'S PRICE
PHILIP WILLIAMS
CAT WILLIAMS

THE GRIFFIN
A PATH OF MAJESTY
PHILIP WILLIAMS
CAT WILLIAMS

www.ingramcontent.com/pod-product-compliance
Lightning Source LLC
Chambersburg PA
CBHW071249170626
46809CB00001B/147